Secret Son
of York

Maureen Fairbank

Prelude

The life of Elizabeth of York has been well documented, for she is the only woman in history to have been a daughter, sister, wife and mother of a King of England.

There have been many novels written about her life by well known writers both in fiction and in factual histories.

The story that has not been explored is the relationship between Elizabeth and her Uncle, Richard the Third.

I have based my alternative controversial novel on the words of Sir George Buck. Buck, writing in 1619 put forward in his, 'History of King Richard the Third,' that he claims to have seen a letter written in the princess's hand in which she declared her love for Richard and cannot wait for his queen to die so that they can be together... 'Richard was her only joy maker in this world and that he was always in her thoughts and heart.' He also claims that The Duke of Norfolk was a go between and that there were many letters sent between the two.

In support of Buck is the chronicler to the Burgundian court, Jean Molinet, writing from 1474-1504. He is no doubt that Elizabeth and Richard were indeed lovers and that Richard made the princess pregnant and she had a child by him.

The Croyland Chronicle written at the time, also in support reported...'that it was said by many that the king was bent on contracting a marriage with Elizabeth whatever the cost.' The Croyland Chronicle also made reference to... 'other matters which were too shameful to speak of,' remarks that have been interpreted as Richard and Elizabeth were already engaged in a sexual relationship together.

Legend has it that a child was born and because of the political climate of the time, following the Battle of Bosworth Field, lived a secret life right up until his death. The legend also says that somehow, this Richard Plantagenet ended up at Eastwell Manor in the county of Kent, working for Sir Thomas Moyles, the lord of the manor.

The story is set during the Wars of the Roses; although fictions most of the people, places and events are based on fact. It is told by two people, Elizabeth and her secret son, a son she had with Richard.

It begins in 1545, when Sir Thomas Moyles is renovating his recently acquired manor house in Eastwell. Sir Thomas notices a well educated man among his workforce and invites the elderly bricklayer to a private talk. Bit by bit the old man, who is called Dick by his work mates, tells Sir Thomas an incredible story. He claims that Elizabeth of York was his mother and that his father was King Richard the Third. Throughout the narrative Dick relives the past. His reminisces cover the major historical events of his time.

There is a secret, passionate, but tragic love story which is told by Elizabeth (Italic chapters). I have put Elizabeth's birth as 1465 although some believe it to be a year later.

The narrative also puts forward what could have happened to Elizabeth's two brothers, 'The Princes in the Tower?'

Sir Thomas Moyles obviously believes Dick's amazing tale as he gives the old man a cottage on his estate for the remainder of his life. When Dick died he was buried in the grounds of St Mary's Church Eastwell.

The tomb still exists to this day and is said by some to be that of this lost Plantagenet Prince.

With this knowledge in mind and with extensive research I have endeavoured to tell this extraordinary secret and tragic episode of Elizabeth's life.

I must add that this is a work of fiction and although I believe that there is little evidence to prove Richard the Third murdered his nephews, I do believe that it is certainly plausible that Richard had this illicit relationship.

If you have not got an open mind about Richard this may not be the novel for you.

Secret Son of York

Sir Thomas Moyles, Lawyer, Justice of the Peace and Speaker of the House of Commons was in the midst of the building works of his great manor house at Eastwell.

Sir Thomas had spent many years in London at the court of King Henry VIII, he had been thoroughly involved in the dissolution of the monasteries, but now, at almost fifty years of age and in the autumn of his life, he had planned a quiet retirement in the English countryside.

Smiling silently, Sir Thomas congratulated himself on his achievements, but now he thought the time had come to enjoy the fruits of his labours.

His surrounding Kent estate looked beautiful in its summer bloom and Sir Thomas was eager that the luxurious refurbishments to his newly acquired manor house were completed as soon as possible.

There had been a building on the sight throughout the fifteenth century, built by the powerful Percy family, Earls of Northumberland. In 1542 Sir Thomas bought the entire estate from his old friend, Sir Christopher Hales and was now determined to put his own designs into a new style of manor house that was sweeping the continent. Peace and prosperity had reigned in England for over sixty years and gone now were the stone walled fortresses of the middle ages and in their place were renaissance buildings that were full of new age splendour. For now nobles were building not to keep the enemy out but to impress the neighbours.

On Sir Thomas's request, many tradesmen from the surrounding villages had come to work for him, helping him in his ambitious building schemes.

Carpenters, bricklayers and stonemasons had been given lodgings on the estate grounds until their work would be completed and the whole area was a hive of activity throughout the year of 1545.

Although his Lordship had employed master builders to oversee the works, every day he would endeavour to see for himself the progress made and would walk and talk amongst the workmen.

As the weeks passed Sir Thomas became acquainted with many in his employ. One bricklayer in particular came to his lordship's attention, a white haired old man who his fellow workers called Dick. As each day went by Sir Thomas became more intrigued by him, there seemed to be a mystery surrounding this man, as he was quite different to all the other tradesmen. His Lordship had noticed that on several occasions, during the rest hour, while the other workers talked, played cards or threw dice, this old man would go apart from the rest, find a quiet corner and read a book. This interested Sir Thomas because there were very few tradesmen who could read in 1545. Determined to find out more about this stranger, Sir Thomas sent out a request one morning for Dick's presence.

The old man entered, what was now the main hall of the manor house. His eyes searched the room. Sir Thomas was seated at the far end, above him hung one of six stupendously carved chandeliers, which had been carefully copied to resemble those of the French court.

Hesitantly Dick approached his lordship, for he had no idea why he had been summoned, and with cap in hand, he stood and waited to be addressed.

'Come closer Dick,' Thomas beckoned with a wave of his hand.

Giving a nod of his head the old man stepped forward and stood in front of Sir Thomas and his

Lordship studied him closely. On detailed inspection he noticed that the man must be in his early sixties was rather of a short stocky appearance with a mass of greying hair and his large dark eyes, which were set wide apart and still possessed a roguish twinkle.

Dick spoke with confidence. 'You wish to see me, Sir Thomas?'

Sir Thomas's tone was welcoming. 'Yes, do come in and sit with me for a while… what do you think of my newly built hall?'

Looking upwards Dick saw a most beautifully decorated plaster ceiling that had been painted in the style of the Italian masters. A stone fireplace occupied the adjacent wall; carved Tudor roses ran its entire width, with heraldic beasts rearing on either side of it. The far wall had been constructed to incorporate several large windows and the light rays poured in and illuminated the magnificence of the room.

Dick then found his voice. 'Why it is wonderful, it could rival any of those being built in Italy or France, my lord.'

Sir Thomas signalled to a servant discretely standing close by and, fetching a flagon from the nearby side table, he began to pour two glasses of his lordship's finest red wine. After gesturing to the old man to sit, Sir Thomas began.

'I am interested in you Dick as you are like no other tradesman I have ever known. I have noticed that you read books in both Latin and English and own some very expensive looking manuscripts.'

Sir Thomas felt strangely nervous in the old man's presence, for he had a noble bearing that Thomas had not seen in the labouring classes before. Although he felt a little awkward in his questioning, he continued because curiosity had got the better of him and now he just had to know whom this old man really was.

His Lordship went on in his questioning. 'I would like to know a little about your past… where you came from…who your parents were?'

After providing his guest with more fine wine, Sir Thomas began to gain the old man's confidence, for the more Dick drank the looser his tongue became.

Now sitting in one of his lordship's most comfortable and expensive chairs and with his body and mind most relaxed Dick began to relive his past.

Dick spoke eloquently. 'I have these past sixty years led a most secret life in fear of my true identity being found out. Even now, by telling you, my life will be at risk. I therefore need you to swear to me on your mortal soul that my story will go no further than these four walls.'

Sir Thomas nodded and added, 'I swear by almighty God.' He then dismissed the two servants who were standing discreetly about the room. By locking the large oak door, Sir Thomas had made sure that they were now absolutely alone and that there was no possibility of anyone over hearing their conversation.

Dick coughed and cleared his throat and in a worn weary voice he continued. 'I must begin my story in the year of our Lord 1464, in the midst of the civil war that raged throughout the country. These wars were really a number of battles between two sides of the same family that originated with Edward III. In that year of our Lord, the Yorkist King Edward IV, had reined in England for three years after a series of bloody battles, which ended in the deposing of the Lancasterian King Henry VI.

Edward had been successful in gaining the crown thanks mostly to the help and support of his

10

powerful cousin, Richard Neville, The Earl of Warwick; know at the time as, The King Maker.'

Sir Thomas was silently thinking: It was sometimes now being referred to as the, Wars of the Roses because each side had taken a rose as their emblem, the white rose for York and the red for Lancaster.

Dick looked at his Lordship, holding what was now an empty glass and Sir Thomas began to motion to a servant, but realising that he was alone, went and fetched the flagon of wine himself from the nearby table and refilled Dick's glass. Dick nodded as a signal of thanks and took several deep swallows.

Sir Thomas could see that Dick was nervous about telling his story after so many years, fondling his beard and pondering his thoughts Thomas patiently continued to listen, to what he hoped would develop into a most revealing tale.

Sitting forward in his chair, Dick fixed his watery old eyes on his lordship, there was a weary painful look beginning to radiate from them as he continued to speak. 'It was in 1464 that the young King went against the mighty Warwick's wishes and secretly married the beautiful widow of the Lancasterian knight Sir John Grey. The lady already had two young sons. Her name was Elizabeth Woodville Grey, daughter of a lowly knight, Sir Richard Woodville and his wife Jacquetta of Luxemburg.'

Momentarily Dick stopped, sipped his wine and considered his thoughts before going on. 'At the tender age of seventeen, Jaquetta had come from Luxembourg and become the wife of Henry VI's Uncle, John of Bedford, a man then in his mid forties, with affairs of state weighing heavily upon him. The hundred years war was still raging… it was he who was in overall charge at the trial of Joan of Arc and was still in Rouen at the time of his death. When Bedford died, the widowed eighteen year old, Jacquetta was escorted back to England by a guard of English knights under the command of Sir Richard Woodville.'

Dick paused and looked into Thomas's eyes for a reaction, there wasn't any. His Lordship sat motionless as he continued to listen to Dick's reminiscences.

After crossing his body as a sign of respect for the blessed Joan, Dick went on. 'Now it happened that Woodville was considered the most handsome man in England. During the long, arduous journey, the couple fell in love and the vivacious Jacquetta married the twenty four-year-old knight, but the fact was concealed for five years.

When Parliament found out it was very angry with the union as Woodville was thought of as too lowly a match for the foreign Princess and furthermore the couple had not been given the king's permission to wed. The Duchess dowry was confiscated, King Henry refused to see them and the pair were ostracised from the court.

But over time Henry was mollified by the payment of a large fine, the Duchess's land was restored and Jacquetta and her young knight took up residence at Grafton Hall.

The Woodville couple went on to produce thirteen children, each and every one of them handsome or beautiful and the most beautiful of all was their eldest daughter Elizabeth.'

The old man paused and looked at his Lordship for some reaction, but there was still none. Uncomplainingly and silent Sir Thomas sat, hoping that the old man's story would soon become relevant.

With a long sigh Dick continued. 'The Duchess Jacquetta was a schemer, some even suspected her of witchcraft, as legend had it that she could trace her lineage back to the Water Goddess Melusina. Her Luxembourg ancestor, Siegfried, claimed to have married Melusina even though she was thought to be half human and half fish.

With the help of her mother's sorcery, where Jacquetta used poppets, two little doll like figures bound together to represent her daughter and the king, the newly widowed Elizabeth, who was still very beautiful, devised a plan to meet the young handsome king.

She waited in a forest clearing when Edward was out hunting in the same forest at Whittlebury, near Grafton. Sitting most prettily, with her two infant sons about her, Elizabeth remained for most of the morning until the king came to pass. Edward could not help but stop and inquire who this gorgeous creature was and why she sat so.

Although the king was more ardent in the pursuit of fair ladies than deer in the royal forest, he had never seen one to compare with the slender, stunningly beautiful woman in front of him. He remained in the saddle in a state of breathless wonder.

Her hair was the colour of gilt and her eyes were large and of the deepest of blue, her features were delicate and moulded. Certainly she played chaos with the beating heart under the sumptuous velvet riding jacket of Edward's. Almost immediately Edward became enraptured by Elizabeth and wanted her for his mistress.

The wily Elizabeth refused, even when Edward held a knife to her throat. My liege, she is reported to have said; full well I know I am not good enough to become your queen, but, dear lord, I am far too good to become your mistress. So Edward, full of desire, felt that he had no option but to marry her, even though she was five years his senior, widowed, and was the mother of two small sons.

The wedding took place in a most secret manner, in her father's house, upon the first day of May. Only after several months did Edward confess his marriage.'

Sir Thomas gave Dick a quizzical look, and narrowed his eyes and thought silently. Did this old man really have some intimate knowledge of the revered King Edward?

Although he felt that he should question his story, Thomas said nothing and allowed Dick to carry on with his rendition. 'It was at a council meeting that Warwick had proudly reported that negotiations were proceeding well for Edward's marriage to the sister in law of the King of France, Louis XI. The earl had been in negotiation with Louis for Edward to marry his wife's own sister, the French Princess, Bona of Savoy. The earl wanted a permanent peace with the French and thought that this marriage would be a step in the right direction. He was on the point of going to France to see the fair Bona and to discuss terms with King Louis when Edward's revelations disrupted his plans for; Edward suddenly announced that he already had a wife.

Could you imagine Warwick's reaction? Warwick was extremely angry, for not only was Edward's marriage to the Woodville lady considered most unsuitable, he would be made to look a fool in the eyes of the French nobility. The council was shocked at Edward's actions and when the news reached the people they also were disapproving.

Edward however, had his own ideas about the French King. He though Louis to be devious, a man who could not be trusted and the young Edward had other plans about making an alliance with France. He had already made a treaty with France's archenemy, Burgundy, as there was much to gain in trade.

Warwick was furious that his authority was being eroded and from that time on an uneasy peace prevailed.'

Dick paused to catch his breath and looked at the face staring back at him. Sir Thomas appeared bewildered as he waited for the old man's story to enlighten him. He conceded that the old man was articulate and told an interesting tale but could not see where it was leading.

Inhaling deeply, Dick went on. 'Soon after her marriage Elizabeth displayed a very shallow understanding in the workings of the court and together with her meddlesome ways made many enemies. She had over one hundred servants and with the exception of the king's mother and sisters none of the ladies in her presence were allowed to rise from their knees until her permission was granted and sometimes after three hours many were in acute discomfort.

Revelling in power, ignorant of the growing hostility, she quickly advanced her relatives, of which there were many, to high estate and most of her siblings, to the dismay of many, were married to the old royalty of the realm. The entire court was shocked when it was announced that Katherine, Duchess of Norfolk, a sixty eight year old grandmother and sister of the king's own mother, was to be married to John Woodville, Elizabeth's twenty-year-old brother.'

Sir Thomas blinked and sat sprawled back into his chair and gave a deep sigh. The old man's ramblings were becoming a little tedious to him, but still he listened with new patience.

'On the eleventh day of February 1465, just nine months to the wedding day, Edward consolidated his marriage with the birth of his first child.

It was true; the king had hoped for a boy and was indeed promised a boy by all the wise men and astrologers. The court astrologer, Master Dominici, told Edward, a short time before the child's birth, that there was not doubt that a prince would soon be in this world. The following week a princess was born. Hearing the child cry, the astrologer called to one of the queen's ladies, asking what her grace had had. The next day Dominic was seen slinking away from the palace with his charts under his arm.

Edward had indeed hoped for a son and heir, but he was ecstatic with the arrival of his beautiful, healthy daughter and immediately arrangements were made for the child's christening.'

Dick gave a rye smile as he pictured the scene, but there was not a response from his lordship and Dick swallowed hard and went on. 'Dressed in a tiny robe of white and gold she was carried beneath a canopy decorated with fine embroideries and precious jewels. She was brought to Westminster Abbey from Greenwich at a few days old and in the glimmer of a thousand candles she was baptized in a magnificent spectacle. They named the child Elizabeth, for her mother, but before long she earned the name Bessy.

Edward asked Warwick to be the child's godfather, to which he agreed and the king's haughty mother Duchess Cecily, became, for the time being, conciliated with Elizabeth Woodville and her mother.

There was a lavish banquet after the ceremony where the wine flowed freely. The king was proud of his firstborn and carried her into court to display her to

16

his subjects. He doted on the beautiful little Bessy who possessed golden curls and the face of a cherub.'

Sir Thomas's stamina was getting a little weary, for he had sat almost an hour with Dick and had learnt nothing new in his renditions, for his lordship already knew most of what he had been told and could not understand why this old man deemed it fit to give him such a lesson, although he was impressed with his knowledge of the period.

Thomas leant towards the old man and laughed out loud. 'Come now Dick, your tale is tedious as I am aware of what you tell me. Why do you talk so of things that are of no relevance to you?'

Old Dick's expression changed immediately to one of distain. 'My lord, you bring me here today to hear my account as you are most curious to know in what circumstances I was taught to read and write.'

Dick sipped his wine and gave Thomas a wry smile and continued. 'You see this information is important, as Bessy, later known as Elizabeth of York and The Queen of England was my mother!'

Swallowing hard and nearly choking on his wine, Sir Thomas stared deeply into old Dick's eyes. Although a little bleary they seemed sincere in what they had just said.

'Go on… don't stop,' for now Thomas was indeed interested in what the old man was about to say.

Dick sat back and stared unto the heavens. A single tear rolled down his wrinkled cheek as he continued, what for him, was to become a most painful rendition. 'My mother was born a royal princess, the daughter of a king. But throughout her short life she suffered unbelievable heartache and was but a pawn in the political game that was being played at that time.'

Sir Thomas blinked and digested what he had just heard.   He now sat silently in keen anticipation as he could see that Dick was determined to tell him the whole fascinating story.

******

The bullion window was crowded with servants who attended us little Princesses. Only moments before the nursery had been a hive of animation, but all had stopped their work and were waiting patiently.

Peg Adams bent down to my level. 'Come quickly Bessy, or you will miss everything!'

I was so excited for today my Aunt Margaret, my father's sister, was leaving England to go to Burgundy. She had been married, several years earlier, to Duke Charles by proxy and now, at the age of twenty two, was saying goodbye to both her family and the populace before leaving England to become his Duchess.

Although my younger sisters and I were not allowed to attend the prayers at St Paul's Cathedral, where a special mass was said, our old nurse, Anne of Caux, who had been both nurse to my father and my Aunt Margaret, had promised me that I could see the royal procession as it passed by the Palace.

I was now four and a half years old and because my sister Mary was only two and my sister Cecily was just a baby of a few months they were deemed too young to understand what was going on. They were both sleeping in their cribs in a quieter corner of the nursery behind a lavishly decorated screen.

I knew of my aunt's journey as my magnificent royal uncles, who were regular visitors to the nursery, had told me of the news. They would often visit, and with me in excitement and delight sat upon their knee they would retell tales of battles and tournaments.

Running to Mistress Adams, who had agreed to hold me close to the window to see my aunt's magnificent convoy go past, I was lifted into her arms. I was thankful for the old glass had only recently been replaced with lighter, clearer glass. The thick muddy brow glass which had been on the south side of the nursery would have made it almost impossible to have seen anything.

After a few moments of being hoisted very close to the large oval window, I shrieked, 'I can see many people in the streets.' Wide eyed I started to take in the most amazing extravagant happening I had so far witnessed in my young life.

Held safely and securely in the young woman's arms, I took in every detail of the unfolding scene and in wonderment I waited for my aunt to appear. The London streets were decked with banners and pendants all fluttering in the gentle breeze and they were full of happy citizens, both rich and poor, waiting patiently to behold the royal parade; all were holding candles waiting to wish the young Margaret of York a peaceful and happy future.

Focusing my eyes, I whooped and wailed with delight.

'There she is...there is Margaret!' Anne of Caux excitedly exclaimed while pointing out the fact to me.

Slowly the royal party came into view. At the head of the parade was my father, The King, my mother, The Queen. Both were magnificently dressed in jewelled covered cloaks, flashing with colour. Directly behind rode my uncles; on my father's side and the youngest at sixteen, Richard, Duke of Gloucester, who everyone in the family called Dickon. Next to him and three years older rode his brother George, Duke of Clarence.

Behind them and on my mother's side rode the dashing twenty six year old Anthony Woodville, Lord Scales.

There followed many important people that I did not recognise, all flamboyantly dressed in golds, purples and reds, with jewels and chains hanging about their person, all were escorting the young bride who was sat in a wonderfully decorated open wagon. Four magnificent white horses with plaited ribbons in their mains pulled it through the streets. The two lead horses were being led by grooms who glittered in magnificence to match the horses.

Margaret looked breathtaking as she sat smiling and waving to the thousands who had gathered to wish her well. She was dressed in a magnificent gown of rich red velvet trimmed with gold cloth and her whole body was adorned with glittering precious jewels. Her light brown hair hung free to her waist and was adorned with a tiny golden crown studded with pearls.

The whole procession passed all too quickly and with deep sighs from all who watched, I was carefully put down to the rush strewn nursery floor.

I had eagerly overheard Anne of Caux talking to the servants and had learnt that after a day of pageants and jousts and an evening of lavish celebration in London, the whole noble party was to leave the city and to ride on to Canterbury to the shrine of Saint Thomas a Becket where more prayers would be said and then finally on to Margate to board, The New Ellen, a ship bound for Sluys. At Sluys Margaret would no doubt say many tearful goodbyes before going to go to live with a man, much older than her, that she hardly knew.

Several months later, on his return from the Burgundian court, my Uncle, Anthony Woodville, who was in overall charge of delivering the young Duchess safely to the Duke, paid a visit to the nursery.

Everyone sat in awe on the day of his visit. He was full of stories of the Burgundian court's extravagancies. The court had become famous as one of the most opulent and cultured courts of the day.

Settling back with my younger sisters and me sat comfortably in his ample lap he began to describe to us in great detail his time spent there.

He told of the lavish wedding celebrations, which were held. The festivities there included, 'The Tournament of the Golden Tree,' that was arranged around an elaborately detailed allegory, designed to honour the bride.

During the festivities Margaret wore a magnificent crown adorned with pearls and with enamelled white roses for the House of York set between red, green and white enamelled letters of her name, with gold C's and M's entwined with lovers knots.

He went on to tell of the splendid parades, with streets lined with tapestry hung from houses; there was much feasting, together with masques and allegorical entertainments.

The splendour did impressed, not only Rivers, but also all observers. It was deemed as the marriage of the century.

******

In marrying Charles, Margaret had become a political pawn in the ambitions of her brother. The trade with the Low Countries, especially in cloth, was far too important to Edward to let any of his female family members choose anyone but his preference of husband for them.

It was the fate of princesses to leave their home and country for the sake of foreign alliances. All too

21

soon the kings' daughters would be used to make political marriages, none more so that his eldest.

The people of England loved their young charismatic King more than any other monarch before and during this time there were many royal progresses taking him to all parts of his kingdom.

The king revelled in the adulation of the populace and would often travel with the whole family. The court made an impressive spectacle as it went around the country. The sight of the royal caravan, with hundreds of wagons, carts, litters and well bred horses, together with over three hundred courtiers travelling through the countryside was a picture to behold and both the peasants and the towns' folk would gather to greet it with waves and cheers.

Edward loved meeting his subjects and frequently journeyed between his most esteemed residences. His family would often travel from Greenwich to Windsor, Shene, Mortlake, Hampton and the Tower.

Bessy loved the Palace at Westminster the best of all, for it was where she was born and it was at the heart of the capital it had a buzz of excitement all of its own for the Great Hall was used as the King's Parliament where her father would sit in council or in judgement.

Although life at this time, cocooned inside the royal palaces, for Bessy and her sisters was crammed full of affection and attention, life outside was becoming a political minefield. During this period there was much tension at court as Warwick felt his power slipping further and further away.

The over mighty subject could not reconcile himself to the loss of his political control and be content to take up the position Edward would have assigned to him. Things had gone from bad to worse as Edward, time and time again would go against his wishes.

The earl was angered beyond belief when Margaret married Charles as this was at complete odds with his political beliefs and it was not what he wanted.

The young King had been willing, during the first years of his reign, to let his mighty cousin take the burden of government from him, while he enjoyed more pleasurable pastimes, feasting, hunting and the bedding of beautiful women, but now he was determined to lead and not be led.

For more than four years The Earl of Warwick withdrew largely from active co-operation with Edward. The earl was enraged at the way his power had been taken from him and he blamed Edward's queen's side of the family, the Woodvilles for his downfall.

All that were close to him began to see that Warwick's character had noticeably changed, as did his appearance. His face no longer wore its customary smile and in its place was a suspicious scowl.

His head was full of schemes, which he kept strictly to himself. He began to meditate treason and as the months went by Warwick was gaining continuous support from various quarters and a plan was hatched to oust the king, his upstart queen and her relatives.

From the summer of 1468 to the spring of 1469 an uneasy truce prevailed as Warwick's plans matured. All the while he plotted to replace Edward with another who would be more conducive with his wishes. There was the deposed Henry who was still alive and languishing in the Tower or perhaps Edward's younger brother, George, The Duke of Clarence?

The meeting with George took place in private. Every servant had been dismissed.

Pacing the room Warwick scratched his head and studied his cousin George. The earl had known the young man all his life.

But Richard Neville was much older, in fact twenty years older than the immature Duke of Clarence. The forty one year old Warwick was still in fine physical shape, although his hair had begun to grey and his face was now lined and redden, the earl made a dazzling impression on the young Clarence; it was Warwick who had been George's father, The Duke of York's, staunchest ally during his fight against Henry VI, which culminated in The Duke's death at the battle of Wakefield 1460.

On a cold wintery December, Richard Duke of York, had gone from his castle at Sandal with a limited army and engaged in battle with Henry's forces led by his, formidable Queen, Margaret of Anjou. To this day Warwick could not understand why the Duke did not wait for the reinforcements that were only a day's ride away.

Margaret showed no mercy, she had the Duke, his brother-in-law, the Earl of Salisbury, and his sixteen year old son Edmund beheaded and their heads adorned with straw crowns and placed on spikes over Micklegate Bar, the southern entrance to the city of York.

With young Edward only seventeen and his brothers George and Richard eleven and eight respectively Warwick had become a father figure to all three of the Duke's remaining sons.

However, now only George remained on speaking terms with his powerful cousin. Edward had long ago decided to keep the earl at a distance and Warwick felt betrayed by the young King. The earl had become increasingly angered by Edward's actions, the alliance with Charles the Rash of Burgundy was in complete contradiction to Warwick' plans and it now dawned on him that Edward was no longer his protégé. Edward's preference to Burgundy over France was the final straw for Warwick.

The youngest brother, Richard, although he had grown up as Warwick's ward and lived at his castle at Middleham for a number of years, idolised his eldest brother and was undoubtedly now the king's man.

Turning his head Warwick now faced the Duke of Clarence. George was handsome, tall and fair with a certain amount of royal bearing. But he was also vein, ambitious and extremely selfish. The earl also knew him to be slow witted, to lack mental ingenuity and that he was more given to posing than to making policy, a perfect candidate for a king who would leave governing to him.

Warwick fed the young man's ambitions and had arranged a private meeting with him this day at his most mighty of strongholds, Warwick Castle, to gauge whether he had an ally in him or not.

Edward had betrayed his trust but his brother George may be more easily led. With George as king he would rule once more and one of his first acts would be to severe the alliance with Burguandy.

'George sit you down,' Warwick began, pouring the young man some of his finest Malmsey wine. His voice was strong and steady. 'You must know that the situation between your brother Edward and me is now irretrievable.'

Nodding vigorously in agreement George began to listen with great interest.

Warwick paced the room as he went on. 'Well, I believe your brother Edward to be most ungrateful, for if not for me he would not be king. Did I not take him under my wing and support his claims to the throne and did I not with every fibre of my being fight for this? Now he favours the queen's kin over his own and I did not fight for this!'

Pausing for a moment he then slumped down into a fine oak chair closely by and began to study the young man sitting opposite him, trying to gauge his reaction.

Sipping his wine the young man did not answer and gave Warwick a bemused look.

Clearing his head and taking a deep breath he finally turned to the Duke. 'Well…what do you think?' Warwick finally concluded, looking straight at George for an answer.

Arching his eyebrows, his fine features creased in thought and lifting his head in bearing, George fixed his eyes firmly on the earl. 'My brother is indeed an unthankful king, for you only do what is best for our family, and he has gone against you and his entire Neville kin in marrying that wretched woman Elizabeth Woodville.'

Warwick sat easier into his chair, it was what he wanted to hear and he now felt confident in putting his plan forward to his young cousin.

Standing up and rubbing his chin in thought and with his body swaying gently the earl spoke with emotion, his voice resonated with authority there was a fiery passion in his eyes as he did so. 'I could make any one of you king, for my wealth and power are unassailable they outstrips every noble in the land. I have thousands of men who wear my livery of the Ragged Staff, why I have over six hundred men alone garrisoned at my London residence and I have over two thousand in my employ here at Warwick Castle. What with my many other strongholds I have throughout the country, I have a personal army bigger than any king could muster.'

George continued to nod and to drink. Then he reiterated his cousin. 'Yes I remember the magnificent banquet you gave when your brother became Arch Bishop of Canterbury. People still talk of the splendour of the food which was prepared by over six hundred cooks.'

Warwick took a long look at the young man, and then decided to speak openly to him and to put forward his intentions. Moving closer to the young Duke, Warwick's voice softened. 'I think that your brother has abused his position and I also think that it is time he was taught a lesson on who really holds the power in this land.'

Moving even closer the earl looked deep into the young man's eyes to give credence to his next statement. 'George, I intend to depose Edward and to make you the next King of England!'

George stood up and puffed out his chest as he spoke. 'My mother swore, the day before my brother's marriage, that he was not the issue of our father and that he was in fact the son of a French archer.' A puzzled look came over George's face as he went on. 'Edward mixes with lowborn men. It is said that he has the common touch and it is rumoured that he takes the lowliest of women to his bed.' After a thoughtful pause George continued, 'maybe it is his low base blood that makes him do these things?'

Warwick thought on what the young man had said had said. For years it had been rumoured that the Duchess Cecily had a dalliance with the handsome archer when her husband was away fighting at Potiois. Cecily herself confessed as much when her son announced that he had married the Lady Elizabeth Woodville, but within weeks she had recanted the confession.

27

Tightening his jaw as he spoke a determination could be heard in George's tone. 'I believe that I would make a better king than Edward and am willing to go along with anything you suggest to place me in his stead.'

Smiling broadly Warwick slapped George heartily on his back for he was overjoyed with this development and inwardly congratulated himself on the result of the meeting with his young cousin.

The earl's thoughts went into overdrive; he did not want anything to go awry with his plan to put George on the throne in his brother's place. He knew that he had to bind himself to George in a way he had not done with Edward.

Warwick gave a broad smile and clapped an arm around George's shoulder. 'To show that there is a common purpose and to bond our plan I propose that you marry my eldest daughter, Isobel.'

George knew Isobel very well and had a great fondness for her, she was pretty and kind in nature and the thought of marring her was most agreeable to him.

George beamed his reply. 'I believe that our marriage would be a wonderful idea as I have much fondness for Isobel.'

Lowering his head in thought George hesitantly continued. Unfortunately I feel that my brother Edward would never give his permission for such a union, for the match would be too politically strong for him to contemplate.'

The earl stood up and walked towards the window and beckoned George to join him. Looking out over his vast estate the earl concluded. 'Let me worry about your brother. You just go and woo Isobel for I intend the two of you to marry no matter what Edward's wishes are.'

When the young Duke had left his presence, the earl was deep in contemplation for he knew that George was right; Edward was no fool and knew the implications of such a union and would never allow a match between these two.

A few weeks later, because he could see no way in which he could execute his plans in England, Warwick decided to make haste for Calais, a port across the channel that still belonged to England. He had been in overall charge there for almost twenty years and the people of the garrison would not dare to ask awkward questions.

Although Isobel had a fondness for George her feelings would not be taken into account. She too, like all royal women, was just a pawn in the political game being played and she had no choice but to obey her powerful father.

And so in defiance of Edward, George and Isobel were married quietly in the Church of Our Lady, across the channel, in a very private ceremony without the pomp and circumstance befitting people of their rank.

Warwick was euphoric with the developments and had complete belief in his own ability to ride the future with a firm rein, come what may.

To compound his plans he had courted the assistance of Louis XI of France. The French King delighted in the possibility of greater influence in England.

Louis's policy had been to keep the English fighting amongst themselves because only in that way could he prevent them from swarming over into France to fight for the French throne.

Warwick promised Louis that he would join England with France in an anti Burgundian alliance.

Louis offered men and supplies if Warwick led an invasion to place Clarence on the English throne.

In England, busy with the office of Kingship, Edward remained unaware of the unions between his brother George, Warwick and King Louis. He was oblivious to the plots and alliances that were taking place across the channel.

It was many months after Warwick's departure that news reached him of the earl's and his brother's deceitful actions in Calais.

When their betrayal became clear beyond all doubt, Edward was stunned and unable to accept it and was utterly at a loss on how to react.

While still in Calais the Earl and the Duke inspired a series of rebellions in England. Uprisings were occurring throughout the country led by the Neville fraction of the family. Sir John Conyers, who was one of Warwick's retainers, move north to Nottingham. Here he waited for William Herbert and Humphrey Stafford to bring their retainers from Wales and the West Country. Meanwhile Warwick and Clarence landed in Kent.

Edward was finally forced to realise that a confrontation was now imminent as a war between the Nevilles and the Woodvilles took hold.

******

I could sense that something was terribly wrong, for my mother was clutching me close and weeping uncontrollably.

'Why do you cry so mother?' I asked calmly, as I knew my mother could be easily agitated and upset.

My mother tried to calm herself for the sake of us children. Taking a deep breath she struggled to explain her actions. 'Your father and his mighty cousin have become the greatest of enemies and I do fear for all our lives.'

When she spoke I could see the tension in her eyes; it was almost impossible for her to contain her grief or her anger as she clutched at her rosary hung about her waist.

There had recently been a battle at Edgecoat Moor. She had received news after the battle that her father, Sir Richard Woodville and her brother, Sir John had been taken prisoner at Chepstow. Then a few days later she had got further news that, after a hasty trial, both had been executed on the orders of Warwick.

This news had left my mother completely distraught and ever since it reached her she would sit for hours gazing at the space in front of her, no doubt, reflecting on the series of events that had brought her to this point.

She was probably trying to come to terms with the actions that had put her into this predicament and had brought her to this place.

It seemed an eternity had passed since the beginning of the conflict, since Warwick had roused his supporters in England to rebel against their king and then to return from Calais himself and join forces with Robin of Reedsdale.

My father, through overconfidence had been captured at that fateful battle and was taken to one of Warwick's strongholds, Middleham Castle, as his prisoner. Warwick's brother, George Neville, Lord Montague was in overall charge of my father whilst in captivity.

I began to feel uneasy as I remembered my grandmother, Jacquetta's broken heart when she learnt of the beheading of her beloved husband and dear son and of her fears when news reached her of my father's

31

capture. I remembered Jaquatta's voice trembling one night as she sat and spoke with my mother, as my younger sisters and I played about their feet.

Jacquetta's voice was almost a whisper as she spoke. 'I have heard that Warwick and his brother Montague are talking to Edward in a derogatory manner about me.'

My grandmother was aged and had already bore so much grief. Trying to be reassuring with her words my mother took hold of my grandmother's hand; she did not want to upset the elderly lady anymore than she had been already.

My mother's tone was soothing, as she answered her. 'They try to insight hatred into my husband against you mother, but Edward knows that you are a dear sweet woman who has no dislike for any man.'

Breathing a deep sigh my grandmother continued to vent her fears. 'They have tried to prove that I am a sorceress and have practices, several times, in witchcraft. Warwick has even tried me, accusing me of making poppets of you and the king, but he could prove nothing.'

Putting her arm about my grandmother, my mother spoke reassuringly. 'Edward would never believe such a thing. Do not worry no one is going to take you away from me again and put you on trial for crimes you did not commit. Warwick knows that you are a kinswoman of Queen Margarite and that you became close friends with her when she first came to England as a fourteen year old when you were her chief lady in waiting...come we must rouse the people of London not to support Clarence as their king.'

Jaquatta nodded in agreement and gave my mother a brave smile and the two women hugged one *another for they had to cling together and believe that they could win support for their cause.*

In the days that followed my mother worked frantically to gain support for my father and her hard work bore fruit when the eminent citizens began to make their unease heard. They did not want Henry or George ruling over them. The people of London were not accepting any other king but Edward and demanded their sovereign back for my father was beloved by all his people whether high or lowborn. To see him dressed in his gold armour astride his white charger made every English man want to support him.

Warwick realised that he must have the recognition of the people of London. That city, because of its trade links and its vast riches, had to give its support to any monarch.

Knowing that the job of replacing my father was going to be near impossible he decided to oblige the Londoners in the expectation that my father would now do as he was told.

He hoped that my father now realised that he, Warwick, still had the power and control to make any one he chose king. In fact, it was at this point that the people began to call him, 'The King Maker'.

To the unbound joy of the citizens of London, my father returned to the city. Vast crowds greeted him with cheers and shout of delight. The metropolis was perfectly devoted to him. To every ones relief my father had returned to his family, he was king once more.

But there was now a difference in him that everyone noticed. He had matured. He was no longer the naive eighteen year old who first ascended the throne. Publicly my father declared that he was once again reconciled with Warwick, privately he prepared to reduce the earl's powers.

33

I was puzzled for although my father was now living within the same palace, his time was spent shut away for hours at a time with those loyal to him.

My mother explained the best she could as to why my father was spending so little time with me. In fact, I began to understand that my father was plotting how to break free from his cousin's hold, as he needed desperately to be his own man.

I knew that there was no one more loyal to my father than my Uncle Dickon. I knew that he adored his eldest brother and would do whatever my father commanded. He had been at his brother's side since his return to the capitol.

As time went by I guessed that days spent in the halls of Westminster were becoming tedious for the teenage Dickon, with incessant talk of state affairs, he found it increasingly a relief from the daily politics to come and visit us children in the nursery.

He would first appear serious and solemn, but within minutes of our company he was full of laughter and joyous talk.

He loved to sit and play with my sisters and my self, talk of heroic deeds and play fun games of blind man's bluff and hunt the thimble, while the older statesmen talked affairs of state.

All in the nursery could not help but notice that when Dickon came to be with us his manner was much less serious, full of wit and mischief.

I always looked forward to his visits and would shriek with delight when I saw Dickon's head appear from around the nursery door.

My eyes widened to the size of saucers on particular dreary afternoon. 'Uncle Dickon!' we children screeched as the nursery door flung open.

Dickon chuckled at the sight of us children. 'I've come to spend some time with my favourite nieces.'

Mary, Celia and me made our way towards him and in a chorus of lively voices would chime. 'Can we play some games?'

Dickon looked toward Anne of Caux and on her nod of approval shouted... 'yes!'

We spent hours that day playing blind man's bluff and hunt the thimble. As the afternoon passed into early evening, we girls gathered to hear Dickon talk about his time at Middleham, for he told detailed accounts of how he had to learn to become a knight, in readiness to serve my father. He had indeed taken as his motto, 'Loyalty Binds Me.'

We loved to hear his renditions and we would command him to tell and retell the same thing over and over again.

As night began to fall and us girls began to tire. Anne of Caux quietly signalled to Dickon and he gathered us about him.

'I am afraid I have to leave you now,' Dickon told us.

Cecily yawned, 'Oh do you have to go?'

Mistress Caux Looked at us and sighed. 'You all look exhausted. Now let your uncle leave without protest.'

Dickon then lifted each of us in turn and kiss each on the cheek. 'Now be good until I am able to come again.'

We all nodded and with a wink to Mistress Caux, Dickon was gone.

******

Edward and his supporters had spent months in the planning. The earl had seriously under estimated his young cousin who was now a man who would not be governed and when he got the chance he left Warwick in no doubt who was king.

The battle of Losecote was so called because the army of Warwick was in such a hurry to escape the victorious Yorkists, led by a very determined Edward, that they discarded their coats in order for them to make a quicker retreat.

Warwick was defeated and with only a few hours to collect his family fled, with those few nobles who were still loyal to him, back across the channel to Louis of France.

Whilst still on the boat, unable to land in Calais, as the garrison now declared for Edward, Isobel who was heavily pregnant with her first child went into premature labour and gave birth to a stillborn baby and nearly died herself.

After days of uncertainty and some hardship aboard their ship, the party finally landed a littler further along the coast and made for Louis court at Amboise, on the Loire.

The French King gave Warwick and his party a magnificent reception and wooed him with lavish banquets and magnificent gifts.

A single-minded Louis was still resolute to help Warwick in his ambitions and suggested that the feeble Henry be re-instated as king.

With some resolution, Warwick thought this a good idea and decided, to his subsequent mistake, to sideline George of Clarence. However, Warwick did not like Louis's other suggestion, an alliance with Henry's hated foreign wife, Margurite of Anjou.

Louis went all out to convince the earl that an alliance would be beneficial to both of them and that they should put away the past animosities that had been between them. It dawned on the earl that it was the only way that he would achieve his ambition.

Margurite was a strong, determined woman. She had been sent to England at the age of fourteen to marry Henry. After their marriage it was soon apparent, that the young queen would dominate the kindly, placid King.

Now, for almost twenty-three years, she had been the power behind Henry's throne. She had devoted her spectacular energy and courage to the defence of Henry's rights and to those of their son.

Now present at Amboise and sitting on the right hand of Louis, the proud, dignified Queen Margurite glared piercingly across the room at Warwick. She was still beautiful although she eluded arrogance and Louis knew that an allegiance between the two was going to be difficult as Warwick and Margurite were old enemies and had a deep distrust of one another.

Margaret's young son, Edward of Lancaster, was there with her and he sat and studied the predicament with a wild stare in his eyes. The boy had inherited his mother's arrogant manner and had by all accounts a cruel streak to his nature. He was known to have talked of nothing but war and cutting off his opponents' heads at a very young age.

However, he was his mother's pride and joy and since his birth she had fought anyone who came between him and his birthright.

Louis sat between the two as mediator and tried to find common ground. He was an expert at negotiating and had become known throughout Europe as 'The Spider King'.

After much verbal fencing a commitment was made to oust Edward and place Henry back on the throne. Margurite's thirst for revenge overcame her loathing for Warwick and on the twenty second day of July 1470 she formally accepted his submission at the cathedral of Angers. Margurite never let her emotions cloud her political judgement. King Louis had managed to broker a remarkable agreement.

Warwick prepared, for a second time, to invade England and this time to replace Edward with Henry, with the fiery Margurite as regent. The earl would be her right hand man, they would rule together. To seal the pact Warwick promised his second daughter, Anne, in marriage to Margurite's seventeen-year-old son.

Once again Warwick aroused his supporters in England and rebellion became rife in the north. The rising began in Lincolnshire with an attack on Sir Thomas Burgh's manor house by Lord Wells.

Edward, true to form, was late in responding to the danger.

******

The hour was late when my father, together with Dickon, came to say their goodbyes. My father had at last mustered his troops and was going to do battle. His spirits were visibly down as he could not believe that Warwick, who had once been as close toward him as a father, was now in league with their old enemy. An enemy who had killed his father, brother and uncle, indeed the Earl of Salisbury was Warwick's father and he found it unbelievable that he was now preparing for Henry to sit once again on the throne of England with the loathsome Margurite as queen.

As for my Uncle George of Clarence, my father would not accept that his brother had plotted his downfall and put all of the blame of George's doings on other people including Warwick.

I remember that nigh in detail. Young Dickon stayed silent and stood looking nervous; fiddling with the dagger he kept on his belt. He had been by my father's side throughout and I had seen a lot of him in recent months.

But now on the eve of leaving to do battle Dickon looked a very different person to the one who made regular visits to the nursery. His countenance was stern and solemn with a serious nervous look forever upon his face.

Putting his arms around my mother, my father held her close as he spoke gently to her. 'You must take yourself and the children to the Tower as its walls are impregnable, for I do not know if I can defeat Warwick this time as he has much support from several quarters.'

I knew that my mother had decided to be strong, for it would not help their cause if her husband were to meet his enemies with other worries on his mind.

She kissed him and gave him her favourite pendant for luck. 'Let this stay by your heart why you are away,' she whispered as she hung the chain around his neck.

Turning from her and with assuredly, my father then lifted me up into his arms. He was the tallest and strongest man I knew. No man could ever defeat him!

'Now Bessy,' he began. 'You look after your mother while I am away. I shall return soon.'

Swallowing hard to hold back my tears, for I too had decided to be strong, I nodded and then gave him a kiss and a big hug.

Then my father turned to my two older half brothers, Thomas and Richard, who were thirteen and twelve respectively, who were stood behind our mother. 'Comfort your mother boys.'

There was a pause as my two brothers silently nodded.

'Elizabeth, kiss the babies for me.'

Then he signalled to Dickon and they were gone.

Within days my mother receives news. Although my father had forced marched from London to Leicester, Doncaster and York, by the time he arrived the rebels were already safely over the Scottish boarder under the protection of King James the Third of Scotland.

James was a staunch supporter of Henry and Margurite and my father could do nothing more but wait.

At York where my father always felt at home, he and his army refreshed themselves. He had no idea that Warwick and his followers had landed at Dartmouth and claimed land for King Henry. Warwick branded my father a usurper to anyone who would listen. By the time news of all this activity reached my father it was too late as Warwick's forces were only a few hours march away from the capital.

My mother was beside herself with worry as she learnt that in Kent Warwick's unruly troops had become a drunken rabble. They had beaten down the walls and with dreams of riches, gone mad with power.

My mother's anguishes were compounded when the very next day the Mayor of London raised the alarm that Warwick's army had breached the wall at Southwark and an unruly mob was rampaging through the street, drinking, pillaging and burning.

Holding us children close to her my mother pondered our fate. I could feel the desperation in her whole body and see the fear compound in her eyes as little Cecily cried and Mary and me preyed that everything would be all right.

******

The Mayor of London rushed to the Guildhall to raise the alarm, but it was too late the army had breached the wall at Southwark and an unruly mob went rampaging through the street drinking, pillaging and burning.

In a safe house in Doncaster Edward pondered his fate. He knew that his life was now in danger as most of his armies had deserted him. With him were several still loyal, Anthony Rivers, the queen's oldest brother, Lord Hastings, his dearest friend and of course his youngest brother, Richard, Duke of Gloucester.

Out numbered and with little hope of reinforcements Edward decided to head to King's Lynn and to catch a boat for the Low Countries. From there he would travel to the court of his sister the Duchess of Burgundy.

Riding through the night on tired horses, for fear of being caught, they reached the wash and Edward decided to cross here by boat instead of taking the longer route by road. They landed at Lynn at dawn, wet, cold and dispirited.

Young Dickon sat in the corner of a small sailing boat and wrapped his cloak firmly about his shoulders. The weather was unusually cold for the beginning of October and a fierce wind blew, that did make all about shudder and clank.

His brother Edward sat close by. Trying to make light of the dire situation his voice was upbeat as he spoke. 'Come now Dickon, cheer up.'

Edward then pressed a small jewel into Richard's hand. 'Happy birthday little brother…you did not think that I would forget?'

Richard's eyes lightened and the expression on his face change. On opening his grip he saw a small ruby clasp surrounded with gold. 'Thank you brother... I will wear it directly.' Fastening the jewel to his cloak he went on. 'Now my cloak will stay around my shoulders as the sea breeze has a chill to it.' Richard gave Edward a quizzical look. 'Where is you fine ermine trimmed cloak Edward?'

Edward, as always, made light of the situation. 'Why I gave it to the captain for payment of our passage.'

Richard was moved and hugged his brother for he knew that he could have given the jewel for the payment.

Edward continued, 'I could not let my brother's eighteenth birthday go by without giving him a gift.'

Richard's tone was determined. 'Our sister and her powerful husband are sure to support our cause. It will not be long before we return to England and rout the usurpers.'

Giving a weak smile, Edward tried to give a positive tone. 'I am sure you are right little brother.'

But secretly Edward was a desperate and worried man as he had left his pregnant wife and family in London at the mercy of Warwick.

It was a dangerous crossing. The merchants of the and Hanseactic League, owing to quarrels over trade, were at war with Edward and some of their ships espied the little fleet and chased it into the Port of Alkmaar. A low tide was the only thing that saved Edward from his enemies for he was gone before the tide rose again.

******

My mother on hearing the news of my father's fate was beside herself with worry. London had become a city under siege and high above the River Thames, inside the Tower, I could hear the screams of the crazed mob. I trembled with fear as the smell of burning filled my nostrils and not too far away I could hear the sound of cannon fire.

The Great London fortress, built by William the Conqueror, although renowned as a stronghold, was no defence to someone like Warwick who would take complete control of the whole city, including the Tower, and order its constable to do his bidding.

My mother was now almost seven months pregnant and in fear of her life. She knew that we had to flee. It had been suggested that we should go to Westminster Abbey, where the Abbot had agreed to surrender his dwellings to us.

In total desperation my mother had made up her mind to go to The Abbey with us, her daughters, her sons and her mother, to take up the Abbot's offer of Sanctuary.

I knew that from primitive times there had been a belief that anyone, even a criminal with blood on his hands, attained some degree of holiness if he passed the inner portals of certain holy places.

This had been embodied in Roman practices to the extent of establishing certain churches in all countries as sanctuaries and the Abbey at Westminster was the most famous sanctuary in England.

My voice softened as I spoke to my mother. 'Do not worry, mother,' I began, in a hope to regain a smile on her face. 'Father will make it better, you wait and see.'

My mother's expression changed and a wry smile took over where an unpleasant frown had been as she could not help but admire my faith in my father's ability to, 'make it better.'

All of us children and those faithful to her gathered round, they looked towards my mother for inspiration.

Trying her best to stay calm my mother's words quickened. 'Come children, we must go to the Abbey at Westminster, for sanctuary. We need to make ready right away.'

Without ceremony but still as queen she released the Tower into the hands of the Mayor and with his help we escaped to a small barge awaiting us on the Thames to take us down the river to the Abbey. I was afraid of the drunken mobs as our family was led to the waiting craft.

'Quickly children,' the Mayor ordered as our small party boarded the barge. 'You will be safe in the Abbey!'

I hid my eyes in my mother's skirts and I sat silently, I knew that we were all in great danger. Already many buildings were ablaze and the shouts and screams that were about me were blood curdling.

My sister Mary sat with her hands clapped over her ears and her eyes tight shut completely traumatised by what was occurring about her. Young Cecily wailed in her panic and my mother held her close to try and reassure her.

Almost unnoticed our royal party had reached the banks outside the Palace of Westminster. With my mother leading the way, all made haste to locate safely inside the Abbey before the earl found and no doubt imprisoned us.

My mother had brought the crown jewels with her and held the chest close to her body. We children also carried what we could and I had carried a bundle of my best clothes wrapped in a fine linen bed sheet.

With great haste we entered the Abbots apartments, thankful for the welcome retreat.

Within the next few hours Warwick's lieutenant entered the battered city and took total power of the Tower. We had escaped just in the knick of time.

Warwick's brother, the Archbishop of York, soon arrived and took command of the city until a few days later Warwick himself arrived.

Immediately Henry was released from his prison and paraded about the city streets to gain the support of the populace. The old King did not however raise the people's spirits. His demeanour was feeble and his skin now bore the pallor of one who had spent many months imprisoned. His thin body was hunched over his horse in his saddle. Although he was dressed in a magnificent blue gown, it was ill fitting and he did not inspire confidence or adoration amongst the people.

My mother's hopes rose at this report and we huddled together for support and prayed that our stay inside the Abbey would be short lived.

The following day the sound of trumpets could be heard and we all rushed to the small window on the south wall to see what was going on.

I was lifted by Lady Scrope to get a better view. I saw Warwick riding through the streets with his retinue trying to persuade the citizens that he, Warwick, was the right person to govern them and not my father.

For several days the earl attended meetings by the council and rode the London streets making himself seen by the people.

My mother knew that although rather short and stocky in build, when dressed in full armour and seated on his magnificent horse, Warwick was capable of being a very effective leader of men.

The crowds cheered, Ah Warwick! When they saw him riding at the head of his retinue, all of whom were dressed in crimson coats adorned with his badge, The Bear and the Ragged Staff.

Within a week the Londoner's had accepted Warwick and Henry as their new rulers.

Inside the Abbey my distraught mother tore at her hair and paced the small room that was now her home. Gone were the throngs of servants obeying her every wish. With her now were only her mother, her children and a handful of loyal brave servants to give her comfort.

News of all these events reached us in sanctuary but at only five years old I struggled hard to make sense out of the situation. Why did my mother weep so and why had my father not returned? Was it possible that my father was not the king anymore?

******

My mother blinked and stopped thinking about the past events which had brought about her situation. We had been in the sanctuary now for almost two months and I was beginning to wonder if my father was ever going to come back to claim his throne.

My distraught mother would spend hours pulling at her hair and pacing about the small room that was now her home. Weeping constantly she would hold us children close to her and pray for my father's swift return.

Through reddened eyes she would sit and watch as her young daughters played at her feet, for the rooms at the Abbey were not the vast expanses she had been used to.

Although her royal status was now gone and all the finery that went with it, my mother was some how

able to find a dogged determination not to give up hope.
She had to be resolute and give all who supported her a
positive appearance to their situation, for soon, within a
few weeks, she would be delivered, with God's help, a
prince.

In Sanctuary my mother tried to shelter us
children from the goings on outside our small
claustrophobic world. It was at this time that my mother
found closeness to us children that would never be
repeated in future years. My mother not only became
our confidant she became our teacher.

I was soon use to the daily routine of lessons as
my mother committed herself to the education of her
daughters and showed skills in many areas. As well as
teaching me to read and write in English she also gave
lessons in Latin, Spanish and French. Manners and
etiquette were also among the daily lessons and in the
evenings my mother would sometimes teach me to play
the lute.

More and more days passed and life for my
sisters and me in the Abbots house was very different to
that in the palaces. Gone were the throngs of servants
and the sumptuous lifestyle, the plenitude of long
corridors to run and race along. Now there was little
room for us children to play inside and outside was
considered too dangerous to venture.

The gloomy dwellings, which occupied a space
at the end of St Margaret's courtyard, were in complete
contrast to the luxury of the palaces that I was use to.

The summer green grass and flowers of red and
blue had given way to the gold's and russets of autumn
and the days were shortening and much time was to be
spent in the gloom of the sanctuary, illuminated by the
fewest of candles. The scent of incense constantly filled

the air and my whole family would huddle around the few fires there were for warmth.

To Warwick's credit neither my mother nor we children suffered humiliation or deprivation at his hands. King Henry would not breach the Sanctuary as everyone knew he was a most pious King.

Our needs were met even if it meant that we were not now of royal proportions. We were allowed to remain undisturbed in sanctuary and were permitted to receive half a beef and two muttons each week, from the butcher John Gould, for the sustention of the diminished household.

And then the time came in early November for my mother to give birth. As well as my grandmother and Lady Scrope, two experienced women in the delivery of babies were allowed to attend her, one of whom was Ankerette Twyenhoe and the other, a holy lady known as Mother Cobb. Also in attendance was the queen's physician, Master Sergio who had help deliver her daughters, including me.

I could not sleep; I knew something was happening in the small cramped, darkened room the Abbot had temporality given to my mother for her laying in. The small window had been closed with wooden shutters and holy relics had been placed about it. On the bed was a blue cloth to represent the Virgin Mary.

Even though the hour was late I was not tired, although Mary and Cecily slumbered soundly in their beds near to mine.

I was able to hear my mother's muted cries and people talking on the other side of the wall. Strange noises were mixed with ladies voices and then suddenly the cry of a baby.

Quietly, bathed in the orange glow of the candlelight, I left my room and tip toed to see what had occurred. The stone floor was cold on the soles of my feet as I peeked my head around the corner of the large wooded oak door.

'Come in, dearest,' my mother whispered when she realised that I was there. Sheepishly I stepped out of the shadows and walked towards her. The ladies were gone and we two were alone, except for a tiny sleeping baby in a crib next to my mother's bed.

Giving me a weary smile, my mother sighed, 'you have a baby brother.'

Widening my eyes, for the room was very dark all but one small candle on a table, I looked at the small figure that was my new brother. I could only see his small head covered with fine straw-coloured hair. My mother was gazing lovingly at the child in the cot and smiling.

This was the baby that my parents had been praying for these past years and at last their prayers had been answered. I did wonder if this baby would take my place in my father's affection, for this was the son everyone had been talking about ever since my mother's belly began to swell. I could not help but overhear my mother and father talking for hours at a time of the joy a prince would bring to the whole family.

Dressed only in my nightshirt I began to tremble. Patting the bed next to her my mother signalled to me, 'come...warm yourself,' she whispered.

Climbing next to my mother and wrapping the bedclothes about us my voice hesitated. 'Is father going to come to see the baby?' I innocently inquired.

My mother seemed to return from far away thoughts as she looked at me. 'Yes my dear. I have sent him a message and I do believe that he will soon come to save his family and his country from the usurper Warwick.'

I said nothing. I only hoped and prayed that my mother was right.

Almost at once the baby was christened, to my surprise, with no more ceremony than if he had been a poor man's son. He was named Edward for his father. The Abbot, Thomas Milling, and the Prioress were to be his God Parents.

It was now December and the shafts of light peering through the small windows were short and weak. I was beginning to wonder if living in the Abbey was going to be my fate for the rest of my life, a fate I dreaded.

In sanctuary there was not the colour and vibrancy of the palace, I only felt gloom and detested the drabness of the place.

My mother did not discuss the political situation with me and each time I questioned her about father she would begin to weep and so I thought it best to let the matter lie.

I knew that the London Sanctuaries were full to overflowing with Yorkist supporters. Stories were reaching the sanctuary about the plight of many of the Yorkist nobles who had been captured by Warwick's men and I could understand only too well my mother's fears.

Only recently, John Tipoft, Earl of Worcester, had been captured and executed on Tower Hill amid scenes of great mob violence.

On the Lancastrian restoration, Worcester had fled into hiding, but was discovered and tried before the Earl of Oxford, son of one of the many men Tipoft had condemned to death.

The weeks passed and Christmas inside the Sanctuary was a very sober affair. To the Abbot and the rest of the clergy the celebrations were extremely serious and sombre.

At my father's court Christmas was heralded as a time for celebration and merriment. The halls were decked with holly and ivy. Minstrels and jesters, actors and story tellers all came to entertain the court over the twelve days of celebration. There was music and much feasting and the giving of gifts.

I had heard that King Henry's government was not as magnificent as my father's had been and that King Henry himself was a holy man who did not relish in over extravagances at Christmas time.

As the winter days grew shorter and shorter and night fell not long after four o'clock in the afternoon, my younger sisters, Mary, Cecily and I went to bed early. All three of us shared a room and would spend hours discussing our present situation and reminiscing over happier times when we were royal Princesses.

I turned to face my sister Mary, who being two years younger than me was closest in age. Although the room was in total darkness I could tell that Mary was still awake in the adjacent bed. Over in the far corner of the room I could hear my youngest sister, Cecily, making gentle sounds of sleep.

'Mary', I whispered, tying not to wake Cecily. 'When are we going to be free from this dreadful place?'

Mary's reply was short. 'I don't know.' There was a moment's silence then Mary continued as if she had taken time to think about her next words. 'I suppose it depends…if father can defeat his enemies and rescue us from this situation.'

I nodded even though I knew that Mary could not see my nods of agreement.

My thoughts turned dark. What if our father was defeated… what if he was killed…what would become of us? Keeping my fears to myself I tried to reassure my sister. 'Father is probably on his way to England with a huge army this very night and in the morning we will hear the heralds announcing that King Edward has returned.'

There was no reply from Mary and I could hear the faint sounds of sleep coming from her direction. I looked heavenwards and sighed, I only hoped what I was telling Mary was right.

******

With every month of Henry's reinstatement to the throne the number of hangers on at his court grew. Every day many crowded into Westminster Palace seeking wealth and favours from the king who sat not in splendour but in plain course attire.

The people of London were not happy for they had lost their magnificent King Edward and in his place was a man who was more like a monk than a king. His words were feeble and his deeds were dowdy and weak and all knew that behind the scenes the mighty Warwick ruled the pliant Henry's every deed.

All this time Margurite of Anjou and her only son dawdled in France awaiting favourable winds for her cross channel voyage to England.

Apart from the weather, Margaruite also waited for reassurance from Warwick that he had secured the capital and that Henry was now safely and securely back on the throne.

Above all else she did not want her beloved son involved in any violent conflict that may arise if the country was not well secured. She did not want any harm befalling Edward of Lancaster who she insisted was Prince of Wales.

******

Meanwhile in Bruge young Richard was miserable and homesick. He had never in his life been so cold. Though the sky was cloudless there was no warmth in the wintry sun. He and his friends had to travel by road as the canals that criss crossed the city were frozen solid.

Although Bruges was a beautiful city with many fine houses and churches, Richard swore silently at his exile. Edward and his loyal band had spent the Christmas of 1470 not within the court of his sister but in the Hauge, with Duke Louis de Bruges.

Bruge was the principle centre of trade and Edward had been keen to have Louis as a friend and ally. This nobleman had formed, during a visit to England in 1466, a personal friendship with the king, which he now loyally showed.

Throughout October, November and December the duke entertained the exiled monarch and his friends with magnificence worthy of his guests' former high positions.

A servant entered Edward's presence and bowed low on handing him a rolled scroll bearing the seal of his queen. With a wave of his hand the page left and eagerly Edward unrolled the message.

'Dickon, Anthony, stop playing cards and hear my news!' Edward's voice was euphoric and the two stopped and looked at him. 'I have son!' he beamed.

Dickon and Anthony rose and each in turn embraced Edward.

Rivers voiced some concern. 'How is the queen?'

Edward clasped an arm about both of them. 'Your sister is recovered and my son is fair and lusty.'

With the news of the birth of his son a new determination gripped Edward. Constantly he begged Charles for help, but for the time being his brother- in-law seemed too busy to give such an exhibition any serious thought. He wanted the help of the king of England against France, but he did not greatly care who that king was.

The arrival of Edward had, in fact, been an embarrassment for Duke Charles. With Henry VI once more on the throne and the all powerful Warwick in control again meant the end of his schemes against France.

On the second day of January Edward reached St Pol. He and his small gathering waited outside his sister's private chamber.

A page bowed low. 'Her majesty will see you now.'

Margaret stood to greet her two brothers and the men she knew from her youth.

With distress in her voice she began. 'I have been speaking with Charles. I have put your case to him.'

Edward paced the room as he spoke. 'I need to act now…I cannot wait…each day I delay Warwick and Henry become more and more in control…I must return to England!'

Margaret was in anguish and could not answer her brother. Looking at young Richard her tone lightened as she spoke. 'Why Dickon I did not hardly recognise you for you have changed these past two years.'

Dickon stepped towards his sister and gently kissed her hand, he knew that her remark was to side step the position that she found herself in.

Margaret's tone changed to one of hope. 'I will speak again with my husband, for he knows how important it is to me to see you once gain King of England. Come now you must tell me news of our family, for I miss them dearly.'

The following day Margaret's meeting with Charles was positive and there was good news for the exiles for she had persuaded her husband to meet with her brother that very day.

Edward smiled and hugged his brother-in-law as he recalled their relationship and alliance, and the fact that they were brethren of the same order and begged for his help.

Charles needed to ponder his thoughts and Edward returned to Bruges and took up residence in the Hotel de la Gruthuyse, although a hotel it had the splendour of a palace and Edward and his band were given it in its entirety as they continued to wait for the much needed support.

Then, in February news reached the Burgundian court that Queen Margurite intended to set sail to England on the next favourable tide.

Even more alarming was that France attacked Burgundy, forcing Charles to get involved in the political upheaval that was once more taking place across the channel and finally he agreed to give Edward the men and supplies he needed, for an English French alliance Charles could not afford to let happen. He gave Edward a fleet of eighteen vessels and money totalling 50 000 florins and some 50 000 francs.

On the fourteenth day of March Edward and his party, after several weeks of hard work assembling a fleet, said their formal farewells to the Burgundian hosts, whom Edward would never forget for their hospitality.

Margaret embraced her brother Edward. 'I shall light a candle every day for your safe arrival in England and victory,' she promised with tears in her pale grey eyes.

Hugging the sister who he loved dearly Richard puffed out his chest as he tried to reassure her. 'I promise to send you a message of Warwick's defeat!'

With misty eyes Margaret watched as her brothers turned and left through the mouth of the arched doorway. She had enjoyed having them at court with her and the sight of them leaving was heart breaking.

In torrential rain they were taken first to Damme and then to Flushing where the royal party, its guns and its two thousand strong army were safely embarked onto thirty-six ships.

The weather was not favourable and the crossing was rough and it was impossible for the convoy to keep tight together.

Nine days later, after enduring over a week of rainstorms, Edward's ship, The Anthony, landed at Ravenspur, at the mouth of the River Humber in Yorkshire, alone. Edward spent the first night on English soil in poor man's lodgings about two miles outside the village.

The next day came the news that most of the other ships also landed safely and that Richard was a few miles up the coast as too was Earl Rivers. They had very few soldiers and even smaller quantities of arms, so the overthrow of Warwick was going to be almost impossible.

Within days Edward and his followers had reached York. Orders from Warwick had been specific, no one, on pain of death, must abet Edward.

On approaching the city a clever Edward declared that he had not come to fight for the crown but to claim his inheritance as Duke of York. As a gesture of loyalty to Henry, Edward wore an ostrich feather in his hat, the badge of the Prince of Wales.

At first it looked as if the city was not going to open its gates, but after a long parley with the Mayor and with the council in agreement the gates were opened.

The people came out to cheer and all its citizens welcomed Edward warmly and the crowds shouted, 'God save the Duke of York,' as he rode through the streets. Edward waved a jaunty hand and reached down to accept gifts and kisses from the giggling girls.

He did not tarry in York, with great urgency Edward began to move steadily south and throughout the north there was little resistance to him or his army. In fact followers of his cause grew daily and his forces went from strength to strength. So in an air of total jubilation Edward rode south to Coventry to confront Warwick.

Edward was further overjoyed when a disillusioned George rode into his camp at noon on Maundy Thursday, together with four thousand of his retinue.

Unknown to Edward, Richard, with encouragement from his mother, had had secret meetings with his wayward brother and had persuaded him to rejoin Edward's cause.

It was an emotional reunion. George threw himself on his knees and made a formal submission to the king. Edward immediately raised him up and kissed and embraced him. George had been totally forgiven for his misdemeanours and now the three united sons of York stood together against the mighty earl.

By now Edward had discarded the pretence of coming merely to claim his father's Duchy and outside the city of Coventry he publicly declared himself king.

Warwick was now alone, with only a small retinue of men, inside Coventry's city walls awaiting the delayed arrival of Margurite and her son. Now outnumbered, he stayed safely behind the walls and ranted about the treachery of George of Clarence.

Edward, however, seized his chance and made swift progress to London, for he may be able, without a fight, take possession of his capital city which was of great importance. Edward now realised that whoever held London was in a very strong position indeed.

******

I knew that there was something troubling my mother and every day that passed I could feel the tension mounting in her. Today the atmosphere was unbearably fraught and I could see an uneasy stare on her stone white face. 'Are you ill mother?' I asked as I readied myself to read a little Chaucer.

My mother shook her head and slowly lifted her reddened eyes to look at me and with a new vigour in her voice she answered me. 'I am quite well, thank you.'

Patting, with her hand, the plumed up cushion beside her she continued. 'Now come and sit next me'.

Hesitantly I spoke to her. 'Is it father you think about?'

My mother wrung her hands and made a deep sigh. 'He is in England… I have had news that he marches south…'

Nervously I made a replied, as I did not want to upset my mother anymore than she obviously already was, 'that is good, isn't it?'

My mother's face broke into an uneasy smile and her eyes brightened. 'Yes it is good…now shall we get on with our reading?'

The remainder of that day went by slowly, and there was not much study to be had as every thought was with my father.

The following day a messenger arrived at the main door of the Abbey. The Abbot showed him into the presence of the queen. He found my mother in the mists of her whole family, sitting with baited breath for news of her husband's progress.

The messenger bowed low and then spoke. 'Madam, I come from your husband, the king, with good news.'

My heart soared upwards as I saw, at that moment, the light come back into my mother's eyes, the light that had been extinguished for so long.

The messenger went on to give a detailed account of the last several weeks and ended his report by informing her that Edward would be in London directly.

Composing herself and taking two deep breaths, for inside I knew that my mother wanted to exude her joy, as indeed did I, she went on. 'I thank you for your swiftness in getting this news to me, now go to the kitchens and be refreshed,' my mother ordered him with a wave of her hand.

Alone with her remaining few trusted followers, my mother showed her joy. There was tremendous relief and elation as my sisters and I hugged and kissed our mother.

My mother's voice was euphoric as she addressed the small band of people, who had been with us in sanctuary, 'come everyone we must make ready to move back into the outside world, a move we have all been praying for.'

During the next few hours there was tremendous animation inside the Abbey... it became a hive of activity as my mother, grandmother, Lady Scrope and my half brothers set about the preparations to leave it.

I was washed and put in my very best clothes. My sisters and me were inspected by our beaming mother. 'You are all beautiful and like beautiful flowers you need nurturing,' she concluded.

I was puzzled by all the commotion. I needed to make sure that my presumption was right. My mother was in complete animation as I spoke to her. 'Are we then finally to leave this dreary place?'

Taking a quick breath my mother spoke in haste. 'Bessy come we must make ready for your father will return to us very soon.' My mother gushed with relief, whilst looking at the gowns she intended to pack.

'Mother... is father the king again?' Cecily questioned.

'We can only pray, my dearest, as I do not think the danger is completely over.'

Finally sitting down and wringing her hands, my mother took a deep intake of breath. It was the first time that I had seen her still since she received the good news.

She went on...'to answer your question...I believe it would be folly at this time to leave the sanctuary as we do not know yet the outcome of events.'

Seeing the disappointment in our eyes she quickly added. 'I am sure that soon we will be able to return to the life we have known...come we must now go to the Abbot and clergy and ask them to join us in prayers of thanks.'

Prayers were said all the time for my father's salvation and ultimate victory over his enemies. I was in no doubt that we were dwelling within a church as all I could hear was the constant chanting of the holy men.

Everything about the place, which was built by

saintly King Edward the Confessor, was built for the glorification of God. The coloured glass windows depicting the saints and scenes from the bible, the golden alter, the magnificent Norman arches and the mighty stone pillars were all obviously built with one aim in mind, to worship and adore God.

I felt overwhelmed by the seriousness of the place, it had an almost melancholic feel and I could not wait to be free from it.

******

Edward and his growing band of supporters approached the city with caution. Although he knew that Henry did not inspire the people of London and the city had always been Yorkist, he also knew that Warwick had some powerful allies stationed within its walls, Lord Montague for one was a very capable soldier and leader of men.

Luckily for Edward, London and its council had convinced the few of Warwick's men that the situation was useless and Edward came into the city at Aldersgate, in a bloodless coup.

He went directly to St Pauls to offer thanks to God for his deliverance and to request formally the crown of England, which was in Henry's possession.

The meeting with Henry was as Edward had imagined, for he knew that without Warwick the old King would become befuddled and lost. The ever serene and docile Henry was very amicable and called Edward cousin before un ceremonially handing over the crown and then he was returned to a single room inside the Tower.

Edward placed the crown on his head and took a deep sigh. All in his presence knelt before him, he was king once more! Then there were lusty cheers from all of his followers.

Edward did not have time to relish his achievement before he hurried off to free his family from sanctuary.

There were scenes of much passion as he hugged and kissed Elizabeth and then each of his daughters in turn, before being led, by his wife, to the room where his baby son lay. Tears rolled down his eyes as he saw for the first time the baby boy name after him. Holding the baby and with emotion in his eyes, he told all present that his baby son was his greatest joy and his most desired treasure.

The pleasure felt on the return of Edward was to be short lived as Warwick had left Coventry and was marching south and reports were reaching Edward that he was at Barnet, just north of the city gates.

Edward knew that to look secure as king he needed to show that his family was free from sanctuary. There was no time to loose and immediately the entire family were boarded onto a barge and taken down the river to Baynard's Castle.

This huge mighty fortress lay just west of the city, on the River Thames, only a short distance by barge from the Tower and Edward thought it a wise move to house his family there until the threat of Warwick was over.

The imposing mansion with its courtyards, gardens and private stairs onto the river belonged to the kings mother, Cecily Neville, Duchess of York. It was within the city walls and a safer place than Westminster, as although there was a sanctuary there it was not a stronghold and Edward did not know what Warwick would do.

He did know, however that Warwick and his army were only hours away from the city and that he and his army would make straight to meet him from Westminster.

******

My Neville grandmother Cecily, whom my sister had been named for, was Grand Duchess of the north. She was born in Cumbria, but her husband, the late Duke of York, had bought Baynard's Castle almost thirty years before when he was one of the most powerful nobles in the land.

Although she travelled the country staying in many of her other magnificent castles, since my father had become king, she had spent more and more of her time in London and residing at Baynard's and it was one of her favourite abodes.

My grandmother of York had always appeared untouchable. Unlike my grandmother Jaquatta, Cecily was rather grand and very regal. Once upon a time she was revered as a queen when her husband was made Protector of England. She had earned the nickname of 'Proud Cis' and I was a little afraid of her.

It was holy week and the bell's of the city churches were tolling solemnly, for it was Good Friday and the Londoners were making their way to mass, but at Baynard's Castle the talk was of military matters.

Warwick was nearing the capital and my father had sent out orders for his army to muster at St John's Field early the next morning.

The whole family had joined our grandmother in an evening of prayers inside her private chapel. The occasion was special for me as it was the first time I had been allowed to join in prayer with the adults, whilst my sisters remained in the nursery.

Although I was still very young, I had already learned how to behave with the dignity and serenity suitable for a girl of my breeding.

I had to kneel for hours as the priest spoke his blessings and chanted prayers in Latin.

My grandmother had become one of the most devout ladies of the realm and late in the evening my father and my Uncles George and Dickon had joined the family in divine and revenant prayer. The evening was closed with a special blessing.

I knew that my father and my uncles were going away the very next day to do battle with their cousin and that they were asking God to be on their side during the fight. They had come specifically to their mother's for the night, for all three sons of York were taking their retinues into battle early the following morning.

I too prayed that my father would soon be victorious and that I could go back to the Palaces I knew and the life that I loved.

It was a difficult time for my grandmother as on many occasions, when Warwick was on friendly terms with Edward, she would tell us children stories of the young Richard Neville as he was one on her favourite nephews.

He was the son of her eldest brother also named Richard Neville 5th Earl of Salisbury. Salisbury was six years Cecily's senior and she would reminisce of the times she would sit and play cards with his young son on her visits.

For her now to think that this boy she had known and loved was now her son's deadly enemy was hard for her to understand or to accept.

After prayers my father and my uncles once more joined the council, who had assembled in the Great Hall, for consultation on his battle plan.

As the hour grew late I sat and tried to imagine life without my father. How I loved the people about me and dreaded the thought of anything bad happening to any on them. It was a thought that frightened me greatly and I pushed it firmly to the back of my mind.

It had been a long day and I yawned and rubbed my tired eyes.

My mother approached me and took hold of my hand. 'Come along now young lady it is time you were in your bed. It has been a busy day for one so young.'

I did not argue, the day had been a long one and I wanted my sleep.

Just then my father had returned from council and seeing me he knelt on one knee and gave a wry smile, 'come and give your father a kiss.'

Opening his arms wide I ran and filled them and covered his face with earnest kisses.

My father embraced me with much passion and fervour and tears began to fill my eyes. 'Do you have to go?' I finally said with a sniffled tone.

My father's voice was strong and firm as his words echoed around the castle. 'Don't you worry my precious we will be victorious. Your father will return to you your king.'

He patted my hand and brushed his fingers over my face trying to wipe my tears before he continued. 'Now go and give George and Dickon a good luck kiss.'

I climbed off of my father's lap and ran towards my two beloved uncles. George and Dickon stood at a little distance from me and on seeing me making my way towards them, both bend down for me to kiss them.

My Uncle George looked very much like my father in looks with the same forceful, brash nature. Uncle Dickon was shorter than both his brothers with longer, shoulder length, darker hair and blue grey eyes

65

that were both mysterious and intriguing. Yes, he was quite different from my jovial exuberant father. He was quiet, retiring, speaking very little, and could be intensely serious. He was less outspoken in the company of adults, almost a different man to the one who was so full of fun when alone with the children. He treated me as if I were older than I actually was and I liked him the better for it. There was sincerity to his character.

In turn my uncles took me in their arms and hugged and kissed me and both reassured me that everything would be alright.

That night I did not sleep very well. Throughout I tossed and turned and had a vivid nightmare where my father and my uncles were killed and their heads put on spikes upon London Bridge. I awoke and sat up screaming with cold sweat trickling down my forehead and back, making my nightclothes stick uncomfortably to my body. Mistress Caux tried to wake me, but I was still in a deep sleep.

Anne Caux knew that my mother's apartments were not far away. Waking Letty, who slept on a pallet at the foot of my bed, she spoke to the girl. Anne's voice sounded agitated.

'Letty you must go and fetch Bessy's mother, tell her that her daughter has wild dreams and cannot be comforted.'

I could hear a voice. 'Wake Bessy...you are dreaming.'

On opening my eyes I saw my mother and my nurse sitting either side of my bed. My mother spoke in a calming voice, 'Bessy dear...it is going to be alright...hush now.'

Holding tightly onto my mother I was unable to speak as I was convinced that everything that I had dreamt about was going to come true.

66

After much reassurance I tried to settle back to sleep, Letty spent the rest of the night close to me in my bed to alleviate my distress.

It had been a dreadful night of horrible visions and I was never more pleased when it was the next morning and the sunlight began to stream through my tiny window. My dreams had been so real, but to my relief, that was all they had been...dreams.

******

Edward rode out of the city early on Saturday morning. There was a fine mist over the city as the dawn sun began to rise. It struggled hopelessly to burn off the mist which was to linger all of that day.

Edward was determined to meet with Warwick's army before he could meet up with the armies of Margurite; for word had reached him that she had indeed set sail from France.

A scout rode towards Edward, pulling up his horse to a screeching halt and panting for breath he spoke. 'My Liege Warwick left St Albans by the Barnet road last night under the waning murky light of evening.

'We will go forward,' ordered an ever more resolute Edward. 'Time is everything. Warwick must be forced into battle for tomorrow Margurite's troops will be arriving from France.'

With his troops enduring a forced march along the St Albans Road, Edward did manage to encounter Warwick just north of Barnet.

The sun was beginning to set as the Yorkist vanguard, led by the young Duke of Gloucester, plodded up the long slope. It was Richard's first command and he was determined more than ever to fight well for his brother.

Some way behind came the king together with Lord Hastings. Each division was some three thousand men strong.

The Duke of Gloucester had news of Warwick; he had camped just north of Barnet. Calling for a messenger, Richard began. 'Ride and tell his Grace that Warwick has made camp.' Richard's lip twitched as he continued. 'I do not think he will attack tonight...even the mighty earl will not risk a night battle. Tell his Grace I will take the advanced guard on to Barnet and wait for him there.'

The messenger bobbed a small bow and swiftly turning his steed galloped away.

It was the early hours of the morning when Richard, seated in a local house with several men at arms, heard the sound of trumpets and men shouting, 'clear the way!' 'Make way for his Grace!'

Richard went to greet his brother. Six feet three inches tall, broad shouldered and handsome, Edward, astride his white horse, dressed in his magnificent Italian armour, really did inspire all who saw him.

Inside the safe house the council of war was short. Edward's tone was urgent and determined, 'if we hesitated, the morale of the troops will drop and any other support that has not yet joined us would hesitate too. We must engage with Warwick tomorrow he must not be allowed to join up with Margurite's brother -in - law, Jasper Tudor, who marches from his stronghold in Wales or indeed Queen Margurite who this very minute approaches the south coast.' Taking a deep breath Edward concluded. 'Now try and get a few hours sleep, we engage at dawn.'

The next day was Easter Sunday. Again a mist hovered at early dawn. Quickly it turned into a thick fog and there was much confusion on the battlefield as the thick fog covered it.

As the mêlée progressed the fog became thicker and the two armies had difficulty finding one another, the visibility was down to a few feet, at one point Warwick's men fought each other.

It was a grim and savage conflict, hand to hand fighting with cursing, sobbing and screaming, with tired men hacking and thrusting at one another, at any figure that loomed out of the mist.

Warwick's army finally gave way, the Lancasterian front line was broken, Montague was dead.

In a final bid to regroup his men, the earl of Warwick hastened to find a more strategic position. In the confusion and the lack of visibility he stumbled into one of Edward's detachments, a group of knights and squires, led by Sir Richard Herbert. Immediately they recognised him as Warwick and were closing in on him like a pack of hounds.

A man-at-arms rushed to the earls aid with a horse. Warwick quickly mounted the horse and made a last desperate effort to escape, but the pack was on him. Without delay he was pulled from his horse and mercilessly killed. Herbert stood momentarily motionless as he looked at the bleeding lifeless body of the earl. At last he was avenged and the memory of Edgecoat and Banbury would no longer rankle in his mind.

The battle ended after a three-hour struggle and because the order to spare the common solider had not been given, there was an unusually large death toll.

A triumphant and relieved Edward marched directly back to St Paul's, he paraded through the streets with the captured Lancasterian banner out for all to see.

Two open coffins were also on show containing Warwick and his brother John Neville, Lord Montague. Edward wanted the people to see that his enemies were now indeed dead.

Whilst resting at Cerne Abbey in Dorset, Margurite was told of the defeat of Warwick. Her instinct was to return to France but she was persuaded, it is thought, by her son to continue with the campaign.

Realising that they would need more troops to defeat, the now swelling, Edward's army she planned to link up with additional Lancasterian forces under the command of Jasper Tudor. Their hope was that Edward be distracted by attacks on Kent by Warwick's supporter, Lord Fauconberg.

******

My father's return to his family was brief and only my mother, in her private apartments, spent a few precious hours with him.

News was reaching him of Queen Margurite and Prince Edward's progress. They had landed at Weymouth together with an army led by the Duke of Somerset and the Earl of Oxford.

Lying awake I could sense that there had been a victory as the shouts coming from the courtyard below told me that my father was within the castle.

I sat up in my bed and peered through the window. I could see the flickering of the fires that were being lit throughout the city.

'Go back to sleep,' my nursemaid quietly whispered while gently trying to coax me to lie down.

I resisted, I wanted some questions answered first. 'Is father home Letty?'

Letty nodded and pulled back over me the feather quilt. 'Your father is victorious, but he must leave soon for the foreign Queen has landed.'

Gazing at the crucifix on the adjacent wall, I obeyed my nurse and lay back down in my bed silently thinking and dwelling on what must have happened.

Warm and cosy now under my bedclothes, I imagined what it must be like to be forever fighting in some cold dirty field with bloody, maimed bodies all around. I shuddered to think of my father killing many with his poleaxe and his sword.

Just at that moment, I could sense a presence, through half closed eyes I saw a figure appeared in the doorway. At first I did not recognise who it was. Gold armour shone as the flames from the fire burning in the hearth bounced off its surface. Almost at once I knew that it was my father dressed ready in his armour to leave and fight another battle.

I pretended to be asleep as he neared me, bending forward he gently stroked my cheek. Silently he stood there deep in his thought, looking at his little girl. Then, suddenly, without uttering a word he left.

The following morning I was awoken very early by the sound of trumpet coming from beyond the river.

'It is your father's army,' Letty announced whilst re stoking the fire which had burnt down completely during the night. He is mustering his troops to meet the foreign Queen.'

******

After a fleeting visit, to reassure a worry stricken Elizabeth, Edward departed again to muster at Windsor. As he bestrode his horse, wearing his magnificent gold armour and with black plumes coming from his helmet, everyone who saw him agreed that Edward looked every bit the warrior King.

The royal trumpets blew and with his standard, The Sun in Splendour, fluttering in the breeze, Edward rode at the head of his army. Flanked by his brothers and followed by Hastings and Rivers, he marched out of London to meet the last of his enemies. Each soldier wore a badge of the white rose and carried a flaming torch; hundreds of priests sang hymns of victory as they escorted the army out of the city.

A reluctant Marguerite had landed at Weymouth, on the very day of Edward's victory at Barnet. On hearing the news of Warwick's death Magurite's army first headed towards Bath and then onto Bristol where she anticipated receiving both more troops and additional funding.

She quickly realised that she had to hastily unite with her ally, Jasper Tudor.

Being Henry's half brother Jasper was half Welsh and had his stronghold in the west of England and in Wales.

Queen Katherine of Valois was the young widow of King Henry V. Her son Henry was only eight months old when his father died of dysentery.

Scandal broke out at court when the queen began an affair with her keeper of the wardrobe, Owen Tudor. Some say that they married, but never the less they went on to have at least four children, a daughter who died young, and three sons.

Edmund, the eldest died in his early twenties of plague, leaving an infant son also named Henry. The second son of Katherine, Jasper, had now become young Henry's guardian and was Edward's enemy.

It was imperative that Edward reached Margurite before she could join up with Jasper, for their combined armies would be an overwhelming force for Edward to defeat.

King Edward once again forced marched his weary men and with vital news from his network of spies he knew that the queen was heading west and was near to Bristol.

Edward called a council meeting it was almost certain that his army would meet with the Lancasterian one between Bristol and Gloucester.

On the third day of May he made contact with the enemy at Tewkesbury.

Edward had no time to lose and attacked the following day at dawn. The weather was going to be hot, one of those early May days of sudden and unexpected warmth.

Once again the fighting was fierce with the shouts and screams of rage and agony of the eight thousand men closed in a ferocious hand-to-hand battle.

Slowly the Yorkist pushed forward. The end came suddenly and with little warning with a mob or running men. The Yorkist trumpets sounded their cries of triumph.

A group of Edward's men surrounded a figure with a white cross on his surcoat and a tall feather on the side of his helmet. It was Edward, Prince of Lancaster, the only son of Henry VI.

Knocking the young Prince to the ground they rained down on him many dagger blows. This was the end of the house of Lancaster as there were no direct heirs left alive.

A blood soaked Richard of Gloucester stood outside the great west door of Tewkesbury Abbey. Edward was there too with several other leaders of his army. Many of the Lancasterian leaders, including the Duke of Somerset had taken refuge there. On Edward's orders they were dragged out to face trial. Tewkesbury Abbey is not a sanctuary Abbey and therefore Edward was within his rights to enter it.

Once again Edward was victorious. The threat from Jasper was also over when Edward received news that he had fled abroad to self imposed exile, taking the only remaining Lancasterin heir, his fourteen year old nephew, Henry Tudor, with him.

After a few days of avoiding capture, Margurite and Warwick's younger daughter, Anne, who was now the widow of the dead Lancaster Prince, were found hiding in a nunnery and brought before Edward.

The hall was crowded with people who had come to witness the fate of their former queen, although defeated a look of defiance emanated across her thin pale features. All inside saw a strong face, stamped with pride and an arrogance that seemed natural as if she had never been anyone but a woman who expected immediate obedience from all around her.

King Edward sat on the dais beneath a canopy of gold silk. Edward looked with intensity at Margurite. All present could not fail to be dazzled in the presence of such a man. Lifting himself to his full height, Edward spoke directly to the woman standing in front of him. 'Your son has been killed and your husband is a prisoner languishing in the Tower.'

There was a silence as the chaotic pain in Margurite's mind built up. Her voice, although weak, was full of emotion. 'Non…non…non, it cannot be true, my beautiful son…dead.'

Edward's tone was insistent. 'It is true; his body lies in Tewkesbury Abbey. One of my men at arms will take you there directly to prove to you that what I tell you is true.'

Swooning to the floor Margurite had to be carried out of Edward's presence.

From that day onwards Marguerite's spirit was broken and all she ever wanted from then on was to be reunited with her father, Duke Rene of Anjou.

In triumph Edward rode quickly back to London for he had received a message that an army, led by the Earl or Warwick's illegitimate cousin, the son of the late Duke of Kent, Sir Thomas Fauconberg was nearing it.

Fauconberg had attached himself to Warwick's fortunes and was trying to breech London's defences. Fauconberg had arrived at Southwark on the twelfth day of May with an estimated force of 17 000 men.

The deceitful Fauconberg sent a letter to the Lord Mayor asking that he might be allowed to enter and pass through the City unhindered saying that he would cause no disturbance to the city or to its citizens. The Lord Mayor, John Stockton, and his council knew of Fauconberg's reputations, the burning and pillaging he had been doing in Essex and Kent had reached the Mayor's ears. The council refused his passage through the city.

The Mayor was well prepared. He ordered that watch be kept on vulnerable parts of the city and where defences were weak, they should be reinforced.

Fauconberg was furious. He decided on a three-pronged attack on, Aldgate, Bishop's Gate and London Bridge. Attacks were also made upon Aldersgate and Cripplegate and many houses were set alight around these gates. Bombardment was to continue from the Surrey side of the Thames at the city where the wall had long fallen into disrepair.

******

My mother had received news that Warwick's bastard cousin, Lord Fauconberg, was burning and pillaging in Kent with a force of up to 20 thousand men.

With news of his cousin death he had landed at Sandwich. He had then sent ships to Kent and up the Thames estuary and they were now heading towards London.

The Mayor bowed low and spoke as the council looked on in the Great Hall at Baynard's Castle. Lord Scales joined my mother in the parley as he had been left in London with a small retinue by my father to protect his family.

'Thomas Fauconberg, your grace, wishes to enter the city.' The Mayor began.

My mother's face was stern as she pondered her reply. 'I have it on good authority that King Edward has defeated the foreign Queen and he is on his way back to the capital as we speak. I ask you to hold firm and continue to deny Fauconberg entry to the city and await my husband to come and rid us of this threat to our peace.'

There was no argument from the council and the Mayor concluded. 'I will reinforce the weaker parts of the city wall and keep a vigil night and day. I will send a message directly to Fauconberg with our decision.'

Inside Baynard's Castle my mother gathered us children about her as Fauconberg was now bombarding the city day and night with heavy artillery from his ships anchored along the Thames.

We could see from the windows the fires burning and people frantically trying to put them out. The guns along the south bank fired barrage after barrage of heavy cannon balls which made the castle shake.

My mother held us to her and clutched at her crucifix as we heard the blood curdling screams and cries coming from the streets below.

My younger sisters began to cry and sob as panic began to grip them.

My mother and my two grandmothers tried to calm them with words of comfort and I tried my best to show resolve as I spoke to my mother as I knew that she had just received new information of my father's whereabouts. 'Mother is father nearing the city...when will he arrive with his army to save us from this ordeal?'

Wiping a tear from her eye my mother gave out a long sigh and replied. 'I hope it will be very soon...one day or two at the most...London must hold out to this man!'

I forced a smile and hugged her, 'it will hold...father will come soon and defeat this terrible man.'

The following day the noise from the guns stopped.

Coming to us late in our chambers my mother gathered us to her. She had a glowing look on her face as she spoke to us. 'Your father is outside the city gates. Fauconberg has fled and the people of London cheer and give thanks that the city did not yield. I have it from Lord Scales that Fauconberg has returned to Blackheath.' She looked heavenly and crossed herself before continuing. 'Thankfully the capital has held fast and did not let this terrible man and his army through its gates.' Taking three deep breaths she went on. 'When the news reached him that your father had been triumphant and was returning to London and was only a few hours march away he decided to head for safety.'

At last the sparkle in my mother's eyes had returned as she had been told of a great victory and that *she would within hours be reunited with my father. And that finally we could all return to our lives as The Royal family.*

Once again my father had been triumphant and returned to a city that appeared to be totally his.

My father made his way to Baynard's Castle by barge. My uncles were with him and the people also lined the river bank to wave and cheer. My father and uncles waved back as they made their way to be re united with their family.

There was much anticipation as we waited to welcome my father back. All us children were lined up to greet him in his triumph, my two half brother, Mary, Cecily and myself together with my baby brother who was being held by his nurse.

There was little spoken as we all in turn hugged and kissed my father.

That very same evening in great pomp and ceremony and with the blowing of trumpets our family was once more reinstated into the Palace at Westminster and to the apartments we all loved and missed. The people lined the banks and waved and cheered as we all made our way back down the river.

Whatever the political situation which had brought us back I was overjoyed that I was to return to my apartments and to the life I had missed so much, a life of pampering by the throngs of servants and waiting ladies.

The very next day there was a proclamation that the old King was found dead in his single room at the Tower. The official reason given was that he died of melancholy.

I could feel the tension and hear the whisperings amongst the many attendants, who once again would pamper to my every wish. Some believed that he died of despair, but many believed that there had been foul play.

Whatever the reality, I was overjoyed that finally I had returned to the Palace and to my apartments that I had missed so much.

A de-moralised Margurite was paraded through the London streets in an open litter and was pelted with stones, mud and verbal abuse by its citizens. They had always despised the foreign Queen and had only tolerated her as loyal subjects of King Henry.

My father mercifully spared the life of Margurite and she was imprisoned firstly in the Tower and then in Wallingford Castle.

After ordering Dickon and his royal troops down to Kent to settle matters with Fauconberg, who was eventually captured and executed in September, my father breathe a deep sigh in the knowledge that he was now the undisputed King of England.

To the many who watched that day they must have thought that they were witnessing the end of the house of Lancaster, the only remaining heir was the fourteen year old, Henry Tudor, Earl of Richmond, now in self-imposed exile in France with his Uncle Jasper.

******

Happy in the knowledge that all my father's enemies were no more, I returned to my daily life as one of the most loved princess in the land. Re housed in our Palaces and once again I had the attention of the hoards of servants that made up the vibrant Palace of Westminster.

Over the next few days I heard the triumphant sound of the many trumpets that marked the king's arrival and the shouts of the crowds of, 'Ah Edward!' whenever his people saw him.

Now warm and content in our private chambers my sisters and me swarmed round our father, each one of us trying to position ourselves in his generous lap and to make ourselves comfortable ready for him to tell us stories of his time in Burgundy and relay to us the splendour of Aunt Margaret's court.

At this time my Uncle Dickon always seemed by my father's side, there was no one who my father trusted more than my Uncle Dickon.

During that summer Dickon made many prolonged visits to my sisters and me telling his own tales of travel and adventure and before long I began to idolise my uncle and he became a hero in my eye, and at the end of each of his visits I could not wait until the next one and I began to love him even more.

After spending Christmas with his family at Westminster and most of January at Shene, Uncle Dickon went away.

I found out that he had gone north, married the sixteen year old widow of Edward of Lancaster, Anne Neville, and settled at Middleham, capital of Wensleydale in the North Riding of Yorkshire.

I had learnt that those loyal to my father had been handsomely rewarded no one more so than Uncle Dickon. He had already become Constable and Admiral of England and Chamberlain and Steward of the Duchy of Lancaster beyond the Trent.

The seat of Uncle Dickon's power, up until now, had lain in Wales, but now it was quickly transferred to the North, where my father needed a trusty lieutenant.

As always my father's authority ran weak up there and once again the Scots were giving trouble. So Dickon resigned the office of Chief Justice and Chamberlain of South Wales receiving in return

Supreme Command in the North. He was granted all Warwick's estates in Yorkshire and Cumberland.

Dickon being now married to Anne Neville could earn the trust and respect of the men of the north and soon he would become one of them. A much loved lord who was wise and just

For the next two years I did not see my Uncle Dickon and I began to miss him very much.

In the April of that year my mother gave birth to another baby girl, who she named Margaret and there was joy and excitement, especially amongst us three girls who had now grown to four.

Our happiness was short lived as the following month our grandmother Jacquatta died suddenly and there was great sorry felt by my mother's kin. I especially cried for her as she was kind and loving and had always been there for me.

There was no time for me to be gloomy for in the autumn, my father invited his benefactor, Louis of Bruge, Lord Gruuthuse, to be his guest at Windsor. He wanted to honour the man who had fed and clothed him and lent him ships and money, and without which he would never have been restore to his country or his family.

It was dawn; the day was cloudy with slight drizzle in the air when my nurse woke me early. It was the day of Lord Gruuthuse's arrival.

'It is on orders of your royal mother that you must dress in your finest clothes today.' She told me whilst laying out the items on the chair nearby.

Inside the Great Hall my mother and her court together with us children waited for Lord Gruuthuse's arrival. His ship had landed in Kent and Lord Hastings was escorting him to Windsor.

By 10.30am the weather had cleared and an air of excitement could be felt as we waited in the hall.

Louis was announced with a fanfare of trumpets as he entered the hall next to my father dressed in all his finest regalia. Behind them came Lord Hastings and other nobles and gentry.

Louis, I noticed as he walked towards my mother's gold gilded chair set high upon the dais, was quite a demure man with kind smiling eyes. He gave a small bow of his head as my mother held out her hand to him.

'I am pleased to be here to meet Edward's beautiful wife and family,' he told her.

We girls stood at the side of our mother as if we were her treasured prises. Our small brother was held by his nurse and baby Margaret was left in the nursery fast asleep.

He did not linger in our presence as Lord Hastings led him to the far side of the quadrangle to three chambers where he was to be housed during his visit. These apartments were very richly hung with cloth of gold. They contained wall-hangings, fine furniture and richly embroidered furnishings. His bed had a counterpoint of gold furred with ermine.

Over the next few days Louis went hunting with my father who gave him a crossbow with silk cords and a gold headed bolt.

Throughout his stay there was much feasting and dancing. On one occasion my mother ordered a grand banquet to be held in her own apartments. I was allowed to sit beside the Duchess of Exeter.

After the food was cleared away games were played and the minstrels filled the rooms with jolly music. To my great joy my father led me out onto the *floor and danced with me while my mother played marbles with some of the ladies.*

On the thirteenth day of October Louis rode with my father to Westminster where he was created Earl of Winchester and was granted an annuity of £20 a year.

A few weeks later he also received a coat of arms.

It was now late December and after the magnificent Christmas festivities there was again sadness as little Margaret, only eight months old, had suddenly become ill and within days had died.

Everyone tried to hide their grief as Duke Louis was still my father guest and it would not do to go moping about.

After months more of feasting and celebration Louis prepared to return to Bruge in the late spring.

I watched with my mother and siblings as my father hugged him and called him brother on the day he finally departed from Windsor.

******

Little by little King Edward achieved, with good government, enormous wealth and utilized it to the advantage of himself, his expanding family and the kingdom.

At this time the court was continually on the move as Edward and his family made progress throughout the country. Showing himself to his people who lined the street and cheered their magnificent King wherever he went.

The king liked to travel at the head of his cavalcade with the queen sitting beside him and not far behind would be litters and their bearers in case they should get tired of riding. Following them were their ministers, knights, courtiers, musicians, entertainers and the rest. Then would come the wagons filled with bedding cooking utensils and favoured pieces of furniture and tapestries.

Throughout the year of 1474 Edward went on progress. He was away for many months collecting Benevolences, gifts of money to the king.

He visited towns the length and breadth of the country; Leicester, Nottingham, Derby, Coventry, Daventry, Guildford, Bury St Edmunds, Woodstock, Worcester, Gloucester, Bristol, Bedford and Lincoln. As he rode he treated the people in such a fair manner that he raised a notable sum of money.

His methods were not those of intimidation. One amusing story was circulating the court of how he asked a rich old lady what she would give him for the war in France. For thy lovely face I would give £20. The king thanked her and kissed her, whereupon she doubled the sum she had promised to £40.

In the spring of the following year, with his coffers full, Edward strengthened his position with an invasion of France. Edward had not forgotten the help King Louis had given to the Lancasterians especially to Warwick and Margurite.

Also the persistent rivalry between France and Burgundy had given him an opportunity for political advancement. Edward, together with sixteen thousand men, set sail from Calais in June with the intention of joining forces with Charles of Burgundy.

For two months he waited at Peronne for his Burgundian allies. At the last minute Charles pull out of the agreement.

Instead of sailing home Edward took advantage of France's weakness, for it was already in a war with Italy.

During all this inactivity Louis sent Edward and his army three hundred wagons full of his best wines. Louis organised a gigantic alcoholic party for the whole English army at Amiens that lasted three days.

Edward invited Louis to parley, for he realized that Louis had no stomach for war, and the Treaty of Picquigny was reached.

Richard of Gloucester and many of the other nobles were not pleased with the turn of events. Richard was especially angry and vented his anger to his old friend Francis Lovell as they watched from a distance the meeting of the two kings.

Richard bit his lip and grimaced as he spoke. 'Our King Harry V would be turning in his grave,' he whispered to Francis as the, Lord Hastings and his brother George, amongst others rode off to meet Louis.

Richard continued to vent his grievances. 'I refused to be part of the signing ceremony. The people of England did not give their taxes for this and I did not come here to see my men belittled by this French King.'

Richard made no attempt to hide his indignations at such an end to an expedition. Richard continued, his voice was now raised, 'the people of England did not give their money for such a peace...again and again they had responded to the appeal to support their king in the hope that the territories lost under Henry VI would be recapture.'

Francis nodded his head in agreement, although surprised at Richard's stand, as it was the first time he had known his friend to go against his brother's council.

Francis spoke in support. 'Most of the nobles and their supporters expected to come to France to profit from the wars, win lands and wealth and now no one is to win except maybe Edward. It is a dishonourable peace.'

The two kings greeted one another over a barrier, which had been especially erected. They laughed and joked for all to see.

Edward came back from the meeting very satisfied indeed. He came back to England with 75 000 gold crowns and a promise by the French King to pay him 25 000 each year.

In return Louis ransomed Queen Margurite of Anjou and he received a pledge of peace and to bind the agreement Edward offered him the hand of his eldest daughter in marriage to Louis son, the Dauphin.

A great reception awaited the king on his return home, the people didn't hold Edward responsible for the fiascos in France, and they blamed his ministers.

All along his route, from Calais to London, people came out onto the highways to cheer their king.

In London the bells rang, candles were lit and hundreds of wine barrels were broken open to toast the king's success.

He was met at Blackheath, by the Mayor and Alderman and 500 commoners and conducted, as a conqueror, to Westminster.

******

No one was more excited than me on hearing the news of my father's return.

'Dauphiness!' He shouted whilst swinging me round in his arms.

'What does it mean to be Dauphiness?' I asked him after getting my breath back.

Laughing loudly at my naive remark he answered me. 'Why it means that one day you will be Queen of France and what a lovely queen you will be,' he teased.

86

My eyes widened as I questioned him. 'When I go to France will I take many fine clothes and jewels with me like Aunt Margaret?'

My father laughed ever louder. 'First things first my dearest you must begin to learn the ways of the French court... we must commence lessons in foreign etiquette straight away.'

I had a blissful childhood from that time onwards, growing steadily into womanhood, every day a little more grown up than the day before.

During the long summer days I would spend time with my sisters exploring the Palace gardens and the winter hours would be spent storytelling, with tales of King Arthur and his knights.

With every year I became more beautiful with a regal bearing inherited by all us Plantagenet women. However, there was less talk of me becoming the Dauphiness and negotiations for a wedding were postponed time and time again.

Being the king's daughter I was honoured and privileged and as I grew older I began to share the pleasures of my father's court. I would play backgammon or chess, dance and sing or play my lute.

There were many festive occasions, which gave the opportunity for pageantry when minstrels and actors would come to entertain.

The family grew, my mother seemed always to be with child and by January 1476 another sister, Anne, and to everyone's delight, another brother, Richard had been added and my mother was soon pregnant again.

The people of England loved my father and most of his large extended family was loyal to him and the country began to live in peace and prosper under his rule.

As well as the wool trade, there were several other lucrative businesses that were most profitable. There was much trade in tin, wood, alum, wax and writing paper.

With my father's newfound wealth he set about updating his castles. As well as refurbishing Westminster he made Windsor one of his main residences and decorated it with oriental tapestries of rich colours and intricate stitch work. He commissioned fine wall paintings of religious scenes from both the Old and the New Testament. Every room was adorned with the finest of furnishings.

At Windsor I would go hunting. I loved the chase and was, by the age of ten, an accomplished rider; in the breakneck of the chase through the forest I tempered my horsemanship.

In the summer of that year most of my family travelled north, for there was a solemn ceremony that we had to attend.

My mother tried to explain. 'Your father needs to bury, with dignity, his kin that were brutally murdered at the battle of Wakefield.'

I needed some questions answered, 'when was the battle of Wakefield mother?'

Taking a deep breath my mother began to try and explain. 'It was a long time ago but your father is still haunted by it.' She paused and took in another deep breath. 'It is time you knew the details of your grandfather's death'

She went on... 'your grandfather, The Duke of York, your great Uncle, The Earl of Salisbury and your sixteen year old Uncle, Edmund, Earl of Rutland, were all brutally killed at the battle of Wakefield in 1460, their heads were cut off and placed on spikes, wearing straw crowns on Micklegate Bar, the main entrance of the city of York.

Your father remembers, every day, the humiliation of his love ones last hours.'

I looked at my mother and could see a tear in her eye as she thought of my father's hurt. Swallowing hard she continued to explain. 'He has ordered a re-internment as the bodies lie in paupers' graves.'

The bodies were exhumed at Pontefract on the twenty third day of July and lay in state in the choir of The Collegiate Church, a wondrous building, almost as lavish as a cathedral.

The next day the cortege headed for Fotheringhay, in slow progress, taking a week to reach the castle and the church.

Twenty thousand people lined the street to get glimpse of the procession. The bodies were in a magnificent chariot, bearing the arms of England and York, being drawn by six beautiful black horses, all were richly decorated in black and deep purples. A huge crucifix was carried a few paces in front of the funeral procession.

Dickon as Duke of Gloucester, dressed entirely in black, together with several other dignitaries followed the hearse until the procession reached its destination.

On the expected day of the arrival of the cortège, my father had gathered his family including his older children at the Church of St Mary's and All Saints at Fotheringhay and stood regally with the rest of the family.

I waited together with my sisters, mother and other dignitaries, my grandmother, Cecily, did not attend as she had already wept bitter tears for her dead husband, brother and son. It was an unexpected side to my haughty grandmother whom people had called proud Cis.

The ceremony was solemn and my father kissed my grandfather's image before it was taken into the church and the assembled clergy.

After the prayers and masses were said for the dead, the hymns of the choir began.

Later in the day, my sisters and I distributed gifts to the large crowds who had gathered to witness the sad event. Money was scattered to some five thousand people and there were cries of joy as they scrambled for the pennies on the streets.

After the days events our royal family went back to Fotheringhay Castle where a meal had been prepared for over two thousand people. A village of pavilions where another 20,000 people were fed and my father gave alms to all who asked him.

My father sat on the dais dressed in black, solemn splendour, flanked by his two brothers. All three remembering the loved ones they had lost.

The occasion was a very heart-rending one and there was no bemusing entertainment; only gentle mournful music filled the hall played from the minstrels in the gallery.

To our delight Mary and I were allowed, for the first time, to sup with the adults during a state occasion and I was rather over whelmed with the amount of people who attended the banquet.

As the evening wore on huge candles were lit throughout the Castle. Their orange glow filled the hall and made strange shadows appear.

I began to study the people gathered. The many that congregated sat and talked freely as the very best continental wines flowed. I had been allowed a little of the wine and I liked the feeling it gave me.

My eyes found my Uncle Dickon, engrossed in conversation with my father. He had been given overall responsibility of the whole affair to rebury, with great pomp and respect, his dead father, uncle and brother.

My eyes moved further along the board and found Dickon's new wife Anne, talking to her elder sister, George's wife, Isobel.

Anne Neville was small of stature and did not have the baring of a blood royal, although at the age of fifteen she was betrothed to Marqurite of Anjou's proud young son, Prince Edward of Lancaster and had spent much time in France, at the court of Amboise, in the company of the fearsome Margaruite.

I knew that Anne Neville had had a turbulent life. She had adored her great and glittering father and when he turned traitor to the crown she became terrible torn, for on the one hand it was impossible to think ill of him, but on the other she had been through a terrible miserable time when he was allied to the French Queen.

On his death at Barnet, Anne's father, The Earl of Warwick, was declared a traitor and his lands were attained.

The earl's wife, Anne Beauchamp, through whom Warwick inherited his title, was deemed privy to the treason and therefore exempt from his lands.

Afraid of what my father would do to her, the Duchess had fled into the sanctuary at Abbey at Beaulie.

I had learnt much about my Uncle Dickon through the court gossips. The adults seem to speak freely in front of us children as if we did not have ears. I knew that Dickon had married Anne soon after the battle of Tewksbury, where her Prince was slain.

Looking now at his insipid wife, I could not imagine why such a charming, handsome man like

Dickon would have married such a small, sickly specimen of a woman.

There had been rumours that Richard had married Anne for her inheritance. Indeed there were stories of how Dickon and his brother George had argued bitterly over the disgraced Warwick's fortune.

Isobel and George had the entire estate and were reluctant to share it, so determined was George that his younger brother should not marry Anne and share in the earls fortune he hid Anne in a cook shop in the city.

After several weeks of frantic searching for Anne, Dickon did find her dressed in the attire of a kitchen maid in a residence belonging to one of the Duke of Clarence's retainers.

Dickon then placed a thankful Anne in the safe keeping of the monks at the sanctuary at the Church of St Martin le Grand.

An outraged Dickon then went on to protest fervently to my father. He begged the king to intervene. My father, to George's annoyances, sided with his youngest brother and gave his blessing to him marrying Anne. The cousins were married in haste.

Dickon and his new wife immediately move north to the earl's lands, which my father had granted him, and there making their main residence at Middleham Castle.

I continued to listen to the servants' gossip and knew that Dickon had gained a reputation as a good and honest lord and my father loved him more than any man. He was now my father's representative in the north of the country and I expected that their conversation to be about the policies and government of the region.

With intensity I gaze across the room, unable to tear my eyes away from my uncle. My thoughts began to wander...they were out of my control as if in a dream *and my imagination began to run wild, pictures whirled in my head of Dickon and me walking together arm in arm with passion in our eyes. I was pulled back to reality by the sound of Mary's voice.*

'Bessy...what do you think?'

I turned to face my sister. 'I'm sorry I did not hear your question.'

'It was not important...I just remarked that grandma has gone to her room the day's proceeding have all been too much for her.'

Just at that moment I turned to find my Uncle Dickon standing between Mary and myself. It had been over two years since Dickon had spoken to me and I knew that my attitude towards him had changed.

When younger I would have spoken to him with ease, but now, at the age of almost twelve, I had become awkward in his presence.

My body too was changing, as well as experiencing my first monthly; my breasts were beginning to form as I could feel the tiny buds on my chest start to swell.

I had become self-conscious of my every action and when he smiled at me I felt my heart flutter and increase its beat. I began to blush when he looked towards me and could not hold eye contact with him. I swallowed hard. Could he tell that I thought him to be rather attractive and indeed found him the most handsome man in the room?

Dickon's tone was soft but deliberate. 'I have come to speak to my two lovely nieces.'

Mary smiled and thanked her uncle, but I did not answer instead I lowered my eyes and blushed deeply.

'It gives me great pleasure to see you again Lady Mary...and...you Lady Bessy... how you two have grown since we last met. I hope to see more of you both in the

93

next few days.' Within the next moment he was gone, pulled away by a message whispered in his ear by his friend Francis Lovell.

Mary gave me a quizzical look, 'did the cat get your tongue sister?'

I smiled weakly and skilfully changed the subject, hoping that Mary would not probe me too deeply.

Our time at Fothringey was short and to my disappointment my uncle did not make my acquaintance again.

All too soon, goodbyes were being said. A feeling like no other before came over me when Dickon kissed me on both my faintly flushed cheeks as he left to return to Middleham. It was a mixture of embarrassment and exuberance and I felt sure that he knew my newfound feelings towards him.

There had been a change in me that I could not help, for although I tried hard to ignore my feelings I could not control my thoughts. A searing shock ran through my whole body whenever he spoke to me now.

A week later, after Dickon and his entourage had gone, preparations had been made for the royal party to return to London and the royal cortege set off on the long journey back to the capital.

During the months that following life continued at court for me in the usual manner. My mother had given birth to another son, who was named George, but he was not a strong child and worries for his health began not long after he was born.

Over the next few months I constantly thought about my uncle and wondered when I would see him again, but my Uncle Dickon stayed in the North of England and I began to think of him less and less.

******

94

It was a bright chilly winter's morning, the court had just returned to normality after the long celebrations, when sadness enveloped my world, with the news of two deaths in the family; My Aunt Margaret's husband, Duke Charles, had been killed during the battle of Nancy fighting the Swedes and my Aunt Isobel had died in childbirth.

Her husband George of Clarence had taken the loss of his wife and baby very badly and retired to his estate at Warwick Castle.

Although I had seen very little of my Aunt Isobel and had never met my Uncle Charles, my sisters and me were dressed in black mourning clothes like the rest of the court and jolly music had been banned.

Everyone walked about with a solemn look upon their face and my sisters and me were afraid to laugh in the presence of the adults who accompanied us everywhere. A Lin waiting sometimes spent the night in my room and I ached to be jolly again.

Then to my joy the unpleasant atmosphere at court came to an end when it was announced that there was soon to be a wedding and the strict mourning was to come to an end.

In brighter spirits my sister Mary and I sat chatting and giggling ensconced in a window seat, in the recently refurbished Westminster Palace.

Mary had become my constant companion and we had begun to do almost everything together.

Here, beside the newly ensconced window we could get the best light, which flowed in through the stained glass and made pools of radiant colours on the floor.

We two sisters had been spending most of our time at our studies but this morning we had persuaded our tutor to allow us some time for private reading. Both were sitting with books in hand, but we were not reading as we were full of talk of our little brother's wedding.

Mary swung her legs and closed her book. 'I cannot believe our little brother will be married in a few days time.'

Lowering my book I weighed up the situation. 'You see Mary, father thinks that little Richard's marriage to the country's richest heiress will be a good match, even though he is not yet five years old and his bride, little Anne Mowbray, is only seven.'

Mary nodded in solemn jest and added, 'who are we to argue?'

We then began to snigger, showing no understanding for our tiny brother's fate.

'We must control ourselves Mary we are, after all, royal princesses.' I announced using my most regal of voices.

There was a pause of several minutes as the two of us stopped our fool hearty behaviour and re established a much more sombre mood. Our books were reopened and our study continued.

I was restless; I was in no mood to study. Lowering my book once more I spoke again. 'Father has promised that he will take us to see the newly installed printing machine.'

Mary stopped reading and gave me a wry look. 'If we were to go secretly to the Abby we would see it set up in the yard below by the sign of the Pale where I believe the printer, William Caxton has his printing press.'

My breath was excited. 'Yes... I want to know how it works, to make the words appear like magic onto the paper.'

Mary's tone changed. 'We are not really allowed in the Abbey yard un supervised, you know how cross the abbot gets if any of us children are seen there alone.'

We were interrupted in our conversation by the sudden appearance of our Uncle Dickon walking towards us. I was astonished to see him for although I knew that he was in London to witness the marriage of my brother, to the heiress, Anne Mowbray, I thought that he and his family were staying at Baynard's Castle with my grandmother.

Dickon stopped, for he was surprised to see his two young nieces alone. Catching my gaze momentarily Dickon inquired, 'why are you here?' His voice was soft as his face blossomed into a smile.

I lowered my head for I was sure that my uncle could see my rekindled feeling of desire for him.

'We wait for Lady Greenfield to come and read with us,' Mary replied.

However hard I tried I could not stop myself from blushing. I began to feel my face go red. My voice had deserted me as I tried desperately to regain my composure.

Mary continued. 'We were just saying how good it would be if we could see the printing machine of William Caxton's in the Abbey yard... were we not Bessy?'

There was a moment's pause and then, surprising myself I stuttered a question, 'would you take us to see it, Uncle Dickon?'

Our uncle raised an eyebrow and studied us girls, and then the smile returned to his face. 'I suppose I could spare the time. Your father is busy with other things at the moment and has told me to come back later for an audience and so I am at your disposal. I would be glad to take my two favourite nieces to see the new printing machine.'

Both my uncle and my father had become fascinated with the machine when they were at the court of Louis de Bruges. Both my Aunt Margaret and my Uncle Charles had been supporters of Gutenberg's printing machine.

I knew that William Caxton had brought Johannas Gutenberg invention back to his native land only last year and had been printing many books at the press that my father had allowed him to set up at Westminster.

Without hesitation we two girls jumped up and speechless we each took hold of our uncle's hands and hurried him along the corridor towards the Abbey and the machine.

When we reached the part of the yard, where the machine was installed, my eyes widened. All three of us watched in amazement at the ink stained men who worked the new wonder of the age, printing pages of script.

There was a hive of activity as the men worked the machinery. In the centre was a large timber frame held together with iron. It resembled an enormous cheese press.

The sight and sounds of the workmen handling the newer thinner parchments, the inking balls, which were dipped into large vats of ink ready to be presses and rubbed on the type blocks and the sound of the large screw wound downwards to give the necessary pressure, was a real delight for us to hear and see.

'Come girls,' Dickon said after we had watched enough of the printing. 'Let us go into the marquee for I intend today to buy each of you one of the newly printed books.'

Next to the machine there was a small marquee where Caxton sold the many books he was now able to print in the English Language.

When William first set up his machine he found, to his surprise, that the Guild of Stationers was strongly against the new method of making books by machinery. What would become of the scriveners and text writers who made their living by making copies of books by hand? They asked.

The Church at first considered printing an unholy practice. It was the work of the devil reaching out to spread the evil thinking, it preached.

Without the support of the king, Caxton might have found angry mobs ready to destroy the ungodly instruments of printing.

There was none more in support of Caxton than the Duke of Gloucester and together with Lord Rivers they persuaded my father to allow the work of Caxton to be conducted unabated at Westminster.

In a scurry of feet we entered the make shift shop, there to find an Aladdin's cave of books. Chaucer, Malory and Aesop were but a few of the books on offer. I had never seen so many books in one place. There were up to thirty copies of a single title and I was fascinated by the fact that now many books could be made so quickly, where only a few years ago it would have been impossible.

The few books that I owned were hand written and very valuable. My father had given them to me on special occasions. Several had belonged to him and I treasured them.

The atmosphere was relaxed now and although I tried hard to hide my true feelings in my uncle's presence my heart was beating hard at Dickon's nearness to me.

'Now... which one is your favourite, Lady Bessy?' He began, pointing at the array of books on the nearby shelves.

After Mary decided on, Malory's King Arthur, I chose Caxton's latest book to go into print, 'Recuyell of the Historyes of Troye,' for I had a fascination with its heroine, Helen.

Dickon chose himself a book that looked far too studious to me. I knew that in his library at Middleham were books both hand written and those printed by his friend, William Caxton all in handsome bindings.

How I longed to go to his library and sit and share his wonderment in reading, for it was something I would find exhilarating.

Taking three deep breaths I exhaled deeply. 'We thank you uncle,' I began, giving Mary a quizzical look.

'Yes we do,' Mary added.

Dickon laughed aloud and I could see that he loved to be amongst the books. He really was a cultured man. He had been one of Caxton's greatest benefactors and owned many of his newest printed manuscripts.

Dickon slipped his arm through mine and must have wondered why I was trembling, but did not comment. With Mary on his other arm, he escorted us excited girls back to our tutor.

'Master Ashcroft I do apologise for taking away the princesses all afternoon...I hope you will forgive me...we have been to see the printing machine.'

Ashcroft bowed. 'Why of course your Grace is forgiven...I do hope you had a nice afternoon?'

Turning towards Mary he kissed her hand and then turned my way and took my hand and brought it up to his lips. I closed my eyes and felt his warm mouth kiss the back of my hand.

'Goodbye, sweet girls,' he said on leaving us.

I sighed deeply as I watched him walk out of sight.

'Bessy...Bessy!'

Blinking my eyes I realised that Mary had been trying to get my attention. I had been miles away in delightful thought.

'Bessy what a kind and delightful man our Uncle Dickon is.'

Sighing deeply again I nodded in agreement.

The rest of the day was spent reading our new books and arguing on whom had chosen the more exciting story.

That night, alone in my room, I reflected on the afternoon's events. Dickon was indeed a most noble man who was both chivalric and courtly. Although he looked very strong I thought of him also to be kind and gentle. He was wonderful; he had become a champion in my eyes.

I stretched out my arms and then wrapping them about me sighed; I had become energized by Dickon's attention to me and what's more I was to see him again at my little brother's wedding in a few days time.

The wedding ceremony was to take place at Westminster and together with the banqueting of fifty or more dishes a tournament had been arranged to dazzle the beholders.

The preparations had taken months and I was especially excited, for I was to wear a brand new gown for the first time. It was the most lavish I had ever worn, it was sky blue velvet, trimmed with pearls and other precious jewels. It was a lady's dress, cut low at the front to show my now blooming womanly figure.

My auburn coloured hair was brushed until it shone and adorned with tiny white silk flowers attached to a dark blue velvet hair band. Whitening makeup was

101

applied to my face emphasizing my plucked eyebrows, arching over my large hazel coloured eyes, and my sensual lips reddened with cochineal.

The day was bright but cold. The ceremony took place at St Stephen's Chapel Westminster. The young couple were led towards the Archbishop whilst the choir sang. The pair did not know quite what was happening, but my father looked happy in the knowledge that little Anne was one of the greatest heiresses in England.

After the ceremony, in the weak January sunshine, my family gathered on a platform especially built to watch the events of the tournament.

My father dressed in fine velvets with The Baton of State in his hand and The Order of the Garter on his leg resided over the events. My baby brother and his infant wife sat and mused over the proceedings.

I sat wrapped in my furs and watched the jousting and other fine spectacles that had been arranged.

At the end of a long eventful day, when the winter's sun had dipped over the horizon, I was invited to give the prize to the tournament winner, who was none other than my Uncle Anthony Rivers.

There followed a most spectacular week full of delights. Most of which were inside the palace where I could discard my furs and reveal my new grown up dress.

I danced and played games and talked to the ladies of the court, I really did feel grown up. Many young noble came to make my acquaintance and Lady Scrope commented on what a beauty I had become.

Although my Uncle Dickon was in attendance he did not make contact with me. He was too busy talking politics with his male friends.

Then at the end of the first week of celebrations, Dickon and Anne were most eager to travel back to the north. They had left their sickly infant son Ned, at Middleham, and begged my father's permission to leave early.

Accompanied by Anne, Dickon came to say his goodbyes early in the morning, just after breakfast and before matins. My father had gathered us in the solar, a small room behind the dias.

My uncle and aunt hugged and kissed us all in turn.

Closing my eyes as Dickson lips briefly brushed against my soft cheek, I relished the brief moment of nearness.

All hoped for a safe journey. Then together with the rest of his household and servants he began his long arduous journey back north.

In the privacy of my chamber, I slumped on my bed. Looking up at the decorated ceiling I let out a long sigh. The time spent with my uncle was all too brief. I was frustrated and a little discouraged for I knew that the young men of the court looked at me with desire in their eyes, I could feel the sexual tension in their every fibre. But as for my Uncle Dickon, he probably thought of me as nothing more than a delightful, little girl. He could not possibly know the intense love I bore for him and that my every waking moment I thought about him, thoughts, which I was too ashamed to share with anybody.

*** * * ** *

My mother was a worried woman and paced up and down the room, pulling at her clothes and wringing her silk kerchief she held in her hand. There was a secret that had come out into the open and the person responsible for her anxiety was my Uncle George.

The death of his wife seems to have unhinged his mind and his behaviour had become most outrageous and threatening. All at court were whispering that George was now pronouncing himself as... King of England!

I could see the stress on my mother's face, as she dismissed the ladies of her chamber.

Alone with me she began to ranted and rave. 'He is out to destroy us! He will not stop telling these lies until he gets what he so desperately wants...to be king.'

I sat in silence, deciding it was wise just to listen to her, for I could tell that she was in great need to vent her anger and I knew that my mother could get herself worked up into an excitable state where she would swoon and faint.

In a nervous state, with her hands tugging and twisting the gold crucifix she had around her neck, she went on. 'He blames me for the death of his wife...I was not even there when she gave birth... he then accuses Isobel's midwife, Ankarette Twyenho, of poising her on my orders because he knows that the poor woman has worked for me in the past and had helped to deliver all of my children.'

Squeezing and wringing her hands together and pacing the room she continue. 'Without any authority or legal writ he put the unfortunate woman on trial, and had her quickly convicted and executed at Warwick Castle.'

Narrowing her eyes in disgust she continued to rant. 'If this was not enough for his vengeance he also accused another of his household, John Thursby, of poisoning and he suffered the same fate.'

I looked at my mother I could see the lines of anguish crisscrossing her forehead and kept silent as she continued her angry outburst. 'I have learnt from my spies that George's servant, a Thomas Burdett, has been working his magic for the death of not only myself but for your father and your brothers...this is treason!'

At that moment a dark and menacing look came over my mother's face as she began to sway back and forth in her anger. 'He cannot get away with taking the law into his own hands... Ankarette was a good woman... your father now holds his brother in the Tower to answer for his crimes.'

I went forward and put a comforting arm about her. 'Calm yourself, I am sure that you are getting yourself in a swooning state for nothing mother,'

Kissing the crucifix that she had been clutching she held it against my lips. 'There is more...you must swear that what I tell you will not be repeated to another living soul.'

I nodded in agreement and kissed the wooden Christ.

A little calmer now she sat next to me and took a deep breath. 'George claims that your grandmother had an affair and was intimate with an archer, which resulted in the begetting of your father. He, George, is therefore the rightful king as your father is a bastard.'

I looked at her quizzically, 'I remember you telling me such a story a few years ago. You said that grandma told this story when she found out that you and father had married in secret. She then went back on it saying it was said in spite and rage.'

My mother had indeed told me the story of Cecily's Archer. At the time everyone thought that Cecily had made up the account as a result of her anger when my father announced that he had married my mother and then my grandmother almost immediately denounce it. No one since has taken the ranting of my grandmother seriously.

Standing once more, my mother again began to pace the room. I knew that there was more that my mother had to say and listened as she went on.

'George now says that he has found proof in Rouen Cathedral that your father is the archer's son and what is more he is threatening to produce the man, a certain Edward Bleybourne, who is willing to confirm the fact.'

She paused and took another deep breath. Her words were deliberate as if to grasp the true horror of the situation. 'George also says that he has evidence of a previous marriage between your father and a woman called, Eleanor Butler and there was a son…he was never divorced from her… when he married me; therefore our union is bigamous and not recognised in the eyes of God or the Church.'

My mother shook her head as if she could not believe what she was about to say. 'You and your brothers and sisters will be proclaimed bastards and your father would face mounting pressure to abdicate in favour of his brother George.'

I was shocked at these revelations and in urgency took hold of my mother's hand. 'There is proof of such a union?'

My mother's voice was stricken with panic. 'Eleanor and her child are both dead but there may be witnesses who would come forward if George is allowed to make his feeling public.'

Collapsing into a chair my mother looked to the heavens. There was silence now all except for the faint weeping sound coming from my mother's bowed head. Dabbing her redden eyes she rose and came next to me.

I was as still as stone with the shock of the news I had just been given. Looking into my eyes she stroked my cheek and tried to force a weak smile.

Her mood had changed and she straightened her body and lifted her head. Defiance had take hold of her. 'I am confident that your father will not allow this situation to jeopardize your future. We must not let this state of affairs get out of hand.'

I gave my mother a reassuring smile and swallowing hard she continued. 'We must look to the outside world and to the court as if nothing has changed within the family. 'We must put a good face on the situation and smile whatever the cost.' She paused and I could see her mind at work...thinking of her next move. 'My dearest daughter, you are nearly a grown woman. Your birthday is in two weeks time. We will not let this crisis spoil your special day.

A whimsical look came upon her as she remembered. 'It is a special day for me also; for it was on that day that I gave birth to the daughter I had secretly prayer for... We must not let George destroy what we both have.'

Straightened her dress once more for she had regained all her composure, my mother went on in a much calmer tone. 'I intend to make your birthday my first concern and leave George of Clarence for your father to deal with.'

******

As promised not another word was spoken about the allegations being made by my uncle. My mother kept to her word and a small gathering was organised for the eleventh day of February 1478, my thirteenth birthday. The celebrations were not to be formal and my sisters and half brothers were amongst the close family members who attended in my mother's private rooms.

My mother approached me at the beginning of the festivities. 'It is with regret that your father cannot be with us. He hopes to come and wish you a very happy birthday later, as he has pressing business to attend to.'

My reply to my mother was instant. 'I do not fret mother, as father presented me with a beautiful new palfrey early this morning. One of father's grooms took me to the stable where they had the horse adorned with colourful ribbons and gold and silver hangings from its new reins.'

As we spoke the food was being put onto a buffet and the tables were removed in readiness for the games me and my guests were about to play and the children whooped with excitement at the prospect.

Mary, Cecily and my younger brother Richard were among the guests together with several of my cousins. My mother and Lady Scrope were in overall charge and the servants were standing discreetly by to attend to their commands.

My brother Edward was now almost eight years old and being Prince of Wales, could not attend as he was resident in his castle at Ludlow on the Welsh boarders.

My uncle, Lord Rivers, was in overall charge of the prince while he was there learning how to govern when he became king, hopefully in many years time. My brother Edward had sent me two wonderful gifts of a falcon and a red velvet cloak lined with fur together with a heartfelt message.

Although the gathering was small there was much merriment. I was having a lovely time and enjoying my birthday banquet.

A single trumpeter blew a fanfare and there in the doorway, to my immense delight, stood my Uncle Dickon. A tingling sensation went through my whole body the moment I saw him.

As I took a sideways glance at him, as he made conversation with my mother, I knew that I had lost none of my admiration and desire for him and my attraction towards him was as strong as it had ever been.

He was in London for a special reason. He had travelled to the capital at his mother's request. Grandma Cecily's eldest daughter, my Aunt Anne, had died after a short illness soon after Christmas, and I knew that Dickon had made the journey south to comfort his ageing mother. He had returned from the north after almost two years of being away.

Throughout the evening I took secret glimpses towards my uncle, but I was much too nervous to speak to him.

I saw from my periphery my mother approached him whilst we younger members were engaged in singing a well loved song which I accompanied on my lute. With snatched glances, I could tell that the two adults were engrossed in their conversation, something important perhaps?

Dickon's eyes watched the younger members of his family enjoying themselves as my mother spoke to him.

'It lightens my heart to see them enjoying themselves.' she began in a wistful tone.

Dickon was also wistful. 'I am glad to see them all having such a good time, unaware of the political situation that is brewing. They are celebrating with great gusto and enjoyment.'

I watched my mother move towards a servant and brought short the conversation.

To my disappointment Dickon did not join in the fun but stayed quietly in the corner of the room observing while the rest of us play games, blind man's bluff and closhey. We told stories and sang songs. My mother had musicians in attendance and we even danced.

After almost an hour Dickon began to mingle about the room and move towards his nephews and nieces.

I felt myself become hot as he stood near to me and I was sure that everyone in the room had guessed my feelings.

I noticed how relaxed and casual he was, he always seemed happiest when in the company of the younger members of his family away from the rigid protocol of the court.

To many he had a reputation of being dour and solemn, but I had, on several occasions, seen another side to him, one that was merry and carefree. As the company tired and began to quieten, Dickon approached me. I could almost hear my heart beating as he got close and I was sure that he too could hear it.

Looking directly at me he spoke. 'I come to wish you a very happy birthday Bessy and to present you with this gift.'

Nervously I made eye contact with him and I could feel an uneasy smile emanated from my face as I took the small box from my uncle's hand. On opening it I found a wonderful broach made of gold and decorated with pearls and other fine stones.

'It is lovely...thank you.' An over whelming feeling came over me to hug him and before I could stop myself I was embracing him. I had never been, in recent memory, that close to him, and I could feel his hot breath on my cheek and the tingle of his unshaven skin.

Within seconds the embrace ended with Dickon kissing me on both hands and smiling.

His voice was soft as he spoke to me, 'a lovely jewel for a lovely young lady.'

He then went and sat on a corner chair with a glass of red wine in his hand. He sat quietly watching his young relatives celebrating like only young people can.

Candles were lit as the night came early and the celebrations went on. Then my mother called for silence for she was about to speak. 'I am afraid the hour is late and you must all retire back to your rooms. I hope you have all had a merry time.'

Spontaneously we all clapped our mother and each in turn thanked her for the wonderful time we have had. She spoke again. 'Your Uncle Dickon wants to speak to you all.'

There was silence as we waited in anticipation for Dickon to speak. Stepping a little forward and taking a deep breath he began. 'I thank you for a most enjoyable afternoon. I have not had such a good time in ages...it was wonderful seeing you all again...how you all have grown.'

I stood motionless, listening to him speak. His tone was always soft and gentle with a hint of humour and with a gleam in his eye he went again to speak to my mother.

Although, I felt that he was sure that my mother was behind my father's attitude towards his brother George he engaged in more polite conversation with her before he made his excuses to leave. 'I must take my leave now,' he told us and with a bow to my mother he was gone.

******

Duchess Cecily's distress was to be heightened over the next few weeks and she was only too glad to have her son Richard with her.

Thing between the Duchess's two eldest sons had deteriorated and there were new accusations of treason.

George of Clarence had become too outspoken about his feelings towards his elder brother and his queen.

His violent outbursts and allegations when under the influence of too much of his favourite Malmsey wine had gone too far and now Edward was determined to bring him to book.

Richard approached his distraught mother behind the dais in the solar of Baynard's castle. A grave look was upon her face as she spoke to him. 'Is it true what I hear that Edward intends to put George on trial for treason?'

Taking hold of his elderly mother's hand Richard swallowed hard and nodded. 'Yes the court convenes in two days time.'

Cecily held on tightly to her son's hand as if to give her strength as she continued to speak. 'I cannot go to the trial as I fear that my heart would break to see my two sons as bitter enemies. You must go Richard to oversee George's trial and report back to me each night.'

Richard tightened his jaw as he answered her. 'I will do as you ask mother, I only hope that I can stay neutral as the situation unfolds before me.'

The next few days were stressful ones; there was an ominous tension surrounding the Palace, there was a frosty coldness without as well as within. Elizabeth Woodville was visibly wracked with worry as the trial of George of Clarence got underway at Westminster.

The evidence was heard and it did not look good for George. Throughout Edward's reign he had continued his role as troublemaker. As early as 1472 there were reports that he was in a plot with Louis of France to depose Edward and foolishly, he made no secret of his distaste for the queen and her family.

There were rumours that the Duke had become insane with wild and dangerous plots against his brother. There was even proof that Clarence had employed a dealer in the black arts, Thomas Burdet, to use incantations and other devices to cause the king's death.

Evidence showed that he had been taking the law into his own hands and acting as if he was already king.

The young Duke of Buckingham delivered the court's verdict. There could be no other verdict than guilty.

Although there was much pleading for mercy from Richard and Cecily, Edward was now convinced that his brother was totally deranged and should no longer be allowed to display his lack of scruples. He was far too dangerous to Edward and his children and so less than one week after he was found guilty of treason Edward condemned his brother to death.

There would be no public execution it would be a private affair and on a cold moon lit night on the eighteenth day of February, George was put to death inside the Tower walls, drowned in a vat of his favourite Malmsey wine.

Richard was stunned at Edward's actions; he could not believe he would go that far as to kill his own brother.

Richard stayed with his devastated mother for the rest of February, but was eager to return north.

At the beginning of March Richard approached his mother soon after morning prayers. 'I am keen to return north my lady mother.'

Cecily looked at him with love in her steely grey eyes. 'Yes, my son I understand you need to see your Anne and the family you have gathered around you at Middleham.'

Richard smiled and Cecily could not help notice how he reminded her of her dead husband. Of all her sons Richard was his father's look alike.

Richard took hold of her hand as he continued to speak and stroked it gently. 'The people of the north will always be behind you. There is loyalty given and faiths are unbroken. Here in the south it is all deception and betrayal, fine words covering foul thoughts.'

Cecily nodded and added, 'I too was always happiest in the north. How I long for the Cumbria countryside and the pleasant way of life. Your father came south many years ago to steak his claim to the throne and when he was killed… Edward became king and I stay in London' …her voice trailed off and Richard kissed her on the forehead.

Although Richard too was stricken with grief he put on a brave face. He rubbed his eyes wearily and his mind went back to his dead brother, the brother he was brought up with and was so close to.

Richard's words were heartfelt, 'I will never come back to London unless I am called back specifically I will stay at Middleham with Anne and live quietly.'

Cecily's looked strained, her face was in constant pain and Richard knew that she was thinking about George…

Richard went on, 'I will take George's two children, young Edward and Margaret, with me to Middleham…it is Anne's wish to have her dead sister's children near her.'

114

Smiling a strained smile, Cecily nodded in agreement. 'God's blessing be upon you my dear son.'

Richard kissed his mother tenderly on both cheeks before leaving to prepare to go back north.

******

A stunned silence enveloped the whole court when news reached them of my Uncle of Clarence's fate. Rumours and whispers could be heard in the corridors of Westminster, as the lords wondered what secret my uncle took to the grave.

I too was shocked at my father's actions, and I was not surprised when I heard the news that Dickon had travelled back to the north disgusted in the decision my father had made to kill his own brother.

Stunned by the change that had come over my father, Dickon stayed firmly in the north of England away from his brother's court.

Alone at night I began to wonder, if the allegations made by my Uncle George were true; was my father an incurable philander? I began to think in a way I had not done before.

When I was younger my father could do no wrong, but now, growing up, I was beginning to see my mighty father in a different light. I was no longer the little girl, wide eyed in wonderment at his magnificents, for now I was well aware that he had bedded many women before and after he wed my mother and that as queen my mother was good at ignoring the things that upset her.

For years my mother must have known that her husband was unfaithful to her with a number of different women but she said nothing of her indignities to anyone.

I thought on, I had other half brothers apart from Thomas and Richard Grey, and sisters. These

*children were bastards of my father's and when I began
to think of the circumstances of their births a cold
shudder went through my body as it began to dawn on
me that Uncle George could have been right. Now I was
beginning to realise how these other brothers and sisters
came into the world. Everything points to the story
being true, in fact I wondered how many other women
my father had secretly married.*

*I thought on...Lady Eleanor Butler no doubt had
gone through some sort of wedding ceremony with my
father and had given birth to a son, who I later found out
to be called, Edward de Wigmore. There was also Lady
Elizabeth Lucy who had given birth to a daughter who
she also named Elizabeth. Then there was Elizabeth
Waite who had two bastard children, Arthur and Grace.
Yes my father had many bastard children.*

*This knowledge was devastating for me and I
tried hard for it not to compromise my love for my father
especially as one of his bastard daughters had the same
name as me.*

*Looking skywards I could feel tears filling my
eyes; I had thought that I was the only daughter named
Elizabeth that my father had and somehow I now felt
cheapened in the knowledge that I was not unique.*

*Patting my eyes I composed myself and thought
on... I was the only Elizabeth who was a royal princess
and I could now recognise why my mother's fears over
my Uncle George were so serious. I liked my position
and everyday from now on I will thank God for it.*

*Although these were events of the past and these
ladies were either dead or far away from the court I
wondered if my father had change his ways and ceased
taking women to his bed.*

*I blinked as a thought rushed into my head, a
thought a few years ago I would never have had. I knew*

of one lady who was a regular visitor to the palace. She was the most beautiful woman I had even seen and I would often sneak a passing glimpse of her walking the corridors late at night, now it was obvious to me, the lady was just coming or going from my father private chamber. The woman's name I had learnt was also Elizabeth but she was known as Jane, and she must be my father's current mistress.

Now I was spellbound with the sexual deception, which all the court seemed to know.

Jane Shore was a shadowy figure that I would now watch from afar or from a concealed position for Jane held a fascination for me that was to grow over time.

******

I continued to mature into a most handsome young woman. My fourteenth and fifteenth birthdays passed and my Uncle Dickon stayed away from the London court. Each month I would develop a little in my body and in my mind, a mind that was becoming now most active.

Each day I would think and wonder in silence about the hypocrisy that surrounded me and swore that I would never be untrue to myself.

There had been happy times, the birth of a new sister, Catherine. There had been sad times, my little brother, George, had died just before his second birthday. The whole household was moved to tears as preparations were made for his funeral at Windsor Castle and he was laid to rest in a tiny tomb.

Although as a princess I enjoyed many privileges of my royal status, one thing I did not have was freedom, I was accompanies almost everywhere I went. Now at fifteen I longed to have a romantic encounter. I

117

desperately wanted to invite the attention of the young men of the court, but being the king's eldest daughter did not allow me to fraternize with boys of my own age. In fact I was kept apart from all male attentions, closeted in one palace or another, waiting until my father found me a most suitable political marriage, one that would be both beneficial to my family and to my country.

All this waiting for a vibrant young woman like me was not easy. Most girls my age were already married and even had children. My own mother was married at fifteen, and had experienced the knowledge of a man's body. Anne Neville had married Edward of Lancaster at fourteen and was not yet sixteen when she married Dickon.

Alone at night, in my darkened room I would imagine myself in love with a mature, knightly man. I imagined myself in love with my Uncle Dickon!

Although I had not seen him in over two years, news of his heroic deeds in beating the Scots and his just and wise northern parliaments had reached my ears and made his image irresistible to me.

My head told me that this union could not be but my heart was telling me otherwise. Every thought of him made my pulse quicken and a feeling of excitement come over my whole body.

Night after night I tried hard to get his image out of my mind but on sleeping I had many dreams where I was with him on an intimate basis, riding through the countryside laughing and…kissing his face which was looking at me with lascivious eyes.

Knowing that I had to keep these feelings to myself, not even my favourite sister could know my secret, was becoming a burden to me and played heavily on my mind and I became noticeably quiet and withdrawn.

Confused by the emotions that I was experiencing, I wanted desperately to talk to someone about them, but who?

My idea of a confidant came in the most unusual and bizarre person, none other than my father's mistress, Jane Shore. Surely I could confide in this woman my innermost thoughts and feelings and be safe from judgement. But how was I going to meet this elusive woman? I had to hatch a plan.

The hour was very late and I was alone in my room, except for my lady of the chamber, Veronique de Salle. It had been a long and tiring day and Veronique slept soundly on a pallet in the small-screened partition.

Standing with my door slightly ajar, I could hear the slightest movements along the corridors outside.

I knew that Jane Shore was with my father as I had seen my mother retire to her own apartments earlier in the evening and this was a sure sign that Jane was making a visit.

The dawn light had just begun to trickle into my window when I heard footsteps softly coming towards me. In an instant I opened my door fully and was face to face with my father's paramour. Pressing my finger to my lips, as a signal for her silence, I motioned Jane into my room.

'My lady,' Jane panted and made a small curtsey when she realised who had accosted her.

I gestured for her to come in and put my finger to her lips in a plea for silence.

Jane's whisper was laced with questioning, 'why do you bring me here so?'

In an urgent murmur I spoke. 'I wanted to meet you… for you intrigue me.'

Jane's reply was just as urgent. 'I have no time to spend here, for the hour is late and it is my duty to be gone before the dawn rises. It is you father's wish.'

Jane Shore flashed her cat green eyes at me as she was becoming quite agitated. She did not want this liaison with the king's daughter.

I tried hard to pacify the lady as she continued to talk in whispers. 'As you want, but I would really like to talk to you Jane.'

Jane shore momentarily studied the young girl who stood before her. 'I will come tomorrow after dark and you can tell me then what is on your mind.'

I nodded and opened the door. It was the signal for Jane to leave.

With her black cloak covering her flame red head of hair and sensual body she hurried out of the palace, down to Westminster Pier to a waiting boatman.

Exhausted by my nights work I lay on my bed and drifted off to sleep.

I dreamed of the day that I would be with a man who was brave and just, that was honourable and pious… a man I could love… a man like my Uncle Dickon.

All the following day I was nervous at the thought of having a heart to heart talk with my father's mistress, I only hoped that my mother would not find out.

Veronique and my sister were told that I had a malady of the head and needed to be alone to get some quiet and rest. I was just beginning to regret my actions when I heard a light tapping on my door. On opening it, Jane Shore stood in front of me visibly nervous.

'Come in,' I said quickly.

Almost at once the two of us were together in my bedchamber. Jane tossed her head and her hair leaped like a red flame.

Jane spoke first. 'Why do wish to speak with me? I cannot divulge anything your father the king has said or I could be arrested for treason.'

I lowered my eyes as I remembered the true reason that Jane visited the palace. 'I do not ask you here to talk about my father. I ask you here to talk about you and maybe to help me with a dilemma that I have.'

Jane looked puzzled and waited with baited breath for me to explain.

Signalling for Jane to sit, I cleared my dry throat. 'You fascinate me Jane...I want to know why you do what you do.'

Taking a deep breath, Jane began to explain her actions to the daughter of the man she had sex with at least twice a week. 'I was married to man who did not know how to show love.' She hesitated before continuing. 'He was much older than me and he found it difficult to... satisfy me. I was married to him when I was only twelve years old.' She paused and then finally added. 'He is a goldsmith and when he was seconded to do some work for the King, Edward and I met and because your father was already married I agreed to become his mistress.'

'What of your husband? What does he say?'

'I have left my husband these past three years.'

'And what does my mother say?'

Jane flashed her green eyes at me and crossed her legs, revealing her ankles that disappeared into calf soft leather boots. 'Your lady mother knew of your father's reputation when she met him. She probably thought that she could change him, but it was not to be. For a while she was his only love but soon after he took

121

other women and in 1473 I became his mistress and your mother knew it. She accepted the situation but insisted that we conduct our affair discretely and so I make my visits in the dead of night, leaving before morning, back to the house your father has bought for me.'

I was not shocked, for now I knew the true nature of my father's sexual habits. 'That is very interesting, but what I really want to know is do you feel guilt in what you do?'

Jane did not answer but a grimace appeared upon her beautiful features.

'I have not really thought about it. Your father is the king and I must obey him.'

There was a long silence while I summed up the courage to pose the questions I knew that I had to ask.

'What would you say if I told you that I was in love?'

Jane remained silent. She had decided to hear me out; she no doubt could tell that there was something troubling me that I could not tell anyone of my family. In choosing her as her confidant I concluded that Jane had guessed that the problem facing me must be of a sexual nature.

Jane's answer was long in coming. 'I feel a little troubled as I do not think it quite right talking thus with an innocent girl, especially when the girl is the king's daughter.'

I looked about myself to make sure that no other person was privy to our conversation and continued. 'Do you know that I have just turned fifteen and have not yet had the knowledge of a man?'

Jane sighed and fixed me with her eyes. 'Your father wants the very best for you; he is in negotiation, as we speak, for you to wed.' Jane bit her tongue and lowered her gaze; she was not supposed to repeat anything the king might tell her during their lovemaking.

Seeing that I was beginning to tremble Jane approached me cautiously, there was no protest from me, and so Jane put her arms about me. There was at this point an explosion of tears and I began to sob uncontrollably.

Jane's voice was soothing. 'Now sweet girl it cannot be that bad! Dry your eyes; come tell me what troubles you so'

The two of us sat close together on the edge of a velvet clad bed as I tried hard to tell Jane of my feelings; I found it almost impossible to put how I felt into words.

Taking a deep breath I looked into Jane's eyes and blurted it out. 'I think I love my Uncle Dickon and I am ashamed of the thoughts that I have about him. I know that he is married but I fantasize about becoming his mistress.'

Jane smiled, 'you do not have to be ashamed. It is quite normal for young girls to have a fixation for older men.' Jane patted my hand as she tried to reassure me. 'Your uncle is handsome and noble and has made an impression on you at a young age. When you do find true love this infatuation with your uncle will pass.'

I sniffled into my kerchief and a faint smile began to take over my face and my tone lightened. 'Do you really think so?' Jane noticed that my expression went vacant as I went on. 'He cannot escape my thoughts. Every day I contrive to be near to him. I have dreams where we are together as husband and wife.'

Jane gave a laugh. 'Why yes... there are many girls who share your feelings towards older men in their family... I should not be telling you this, but your Aunt Margaret, as a young girl, had an infatuation for your father's friend and confident, Sir William Oldhall.'

I was perplexed as I continued to pour my heart out to this woman who had quickly gained my confidence. 'I am afraid that my thoughts are sinful and I will go to hell for them.'

Jane placed a reassuring hand over mine, her tones were soothing, 'I do not believe that love in any form is sinful. It is those who do not love that sin.'

I nodded, Jane had convinced me that all would pass; I only needed patients and everything would be well.

Urgency suddenly took over in Jane's voice. 'I must go now, but do not hesitate to talk to me again if you have any other need for my council.'

I nodded; I had taken a liking to Jane, even though her continuing presence at court was a constant hurt to my mother.

Quietly and swiftly she left me and alone I began to think again about what she had said. I felt much better; for all I had to do was wait and my feelings towards my uncle would change.

My choice of confident had been justified, as Jane had been the perfect person to talk with as she was neither mute nor full of babble and I began to realise why my father enjoyed her company so much.

I had spoken freely to her and she had been a very good listener, one who did not judge or scorn. Yes, I was thankful that I had spoken to Jane and a weak smile began to emanate across my face.

******

The winter was especially long and hard that year; chilling rain gave way to icy sleet and snow. The peasants huddled indoors to ease their aching bodies before their fires and drank measures of warm ale and milk.

The spring thaw was most welcome; the countryside was rejuvenated into lush green, flecked with the colour of primroses and bluebells.

The king had continued to work determinedly by day to educate his children, to give good and just government and to spend time hunting with his close friends and family.

But during the nights he revelled and entertained his court, eating too much, drinking too much and whoring too much. Gone was the lean powerful body and in its place was a fat, rotund man who was easily out of breath.

Bessy continued having secret meetings with Jane Shore and was beginning to think her right about everything to do with her feelings towards the opposite sex, until one day news reached her that Richard was travelling south to join the rest of the family at the newest and most splendid Palace at Greenwich.

A week previously Edward had gathered his children in his private chamber, for he had the most wonderful news, their Aunt Margaret, after twelve years abroad, was paying her relations a visit and the whole family was to gather at Greenwich to help make the Duchess's return to her family and her country a visit she would not forget.

Sadly, Margaret, since the death of her husband and having had no children of her own, was becoming rather lonely in her Burgandian court of Malise and so she had jumped at the chance to represent her step son - in- law, in negotiations with her brother.

The powerful Maximillian wanted an alliance with England against France and had sent Margaret to parley with her brother.

Edward had pitched high terms to Maximillian for his support. He wanted Burgundy to replace the

125

annual French pension and his daughter Anne was to marry the young heir of Burgundy without being paid any dowry. All Edward would offer in return was to allow Maximillian to recruit six thousand archers to be paid for at Burgundian expense.

Now Margaret was to try and negotiate a farer deal for Burgundy.

To the Dowager Duchess her blood bonds were of great importance and so a much welcomed the trip to England was arranged.

She was to travel to the English port of Calais, where she would sail to England in one of Edward's finest ships and would arrive in July at Greenwich and hundreds of people would be striving away to make the visit a success.

From the beginning of May the court was a hive of activity getting everything perfect for the visit. Rooms were cleaned and aired and new furnishings put into place.

It was the end of June when Richard arrived in London. He had a few men accompanying him but apart from that he was alone. He was to stay at Baynard's Castle with his mother while the final lavish preparations were being made at Greenwich and when the news reached Edward that Margaret had landed in England, Richard together with the rest of the family and dignitaries were to gather at Greenwich to meet her.

******

I knew that Dickon and his mother had deliberately stayed away from my father's court since the execution of my Uncle George. Grandma Cecily had been crushed by the news and she was finding it hard to come to terms with what had happened. She could not

126

accept that her sons had come so far as to plot one another's deaths.

Dickon, however, had been a blessing to his mother at her time of need and had stayed with her for several weeks after George's demise before returning north.

He had, through his wisdom, decided to keep away from the London court in fear of his own life as my father was now, it seemed, unpredictable in what he was capable of doing.

All who knew him had noticed that my father was a changed man by the summer of 1480, he had aged visibly through the stresses of kingship and he awaited his sister's visit with much apprehension for the death of my Uncle George gnawed at him constantly as he had cut into the flesh of his family and was stained with fratricide.

What was more George was Margaret's favourite brother and my father knew that the meeting would be fraught with tension.

At one time, soon after Isobel's death, Margaret tried to arrange a second marriage for George with her stepdaughter, Marie of Burgundy, a daughter from Duke Charles's first marriage, and the news of his death at the hands of my father, a few months later, shocked her tremendously.

Oblivious of the political implication of Margaret's visit, I had no such qualms about meeting the aunt I had heard so much about, for I had not seen her since she left for Burgundy all those years before.

I was eager to ask Margaret all about the Burgundian court and to hear stories of courtly love and knightly deeds that was so prevalent at her court in Mailas.

I knew that there would be weeks of festivals in which I would be able to see and talk to those I had not seen in many months, if not years.

I was also intrigue to see if Jane Shore had been right about my infatuation with my Uncle Dickon, for news had reached me that both Dickon and my grandmother Cecily would be in attendance.

The day of Margaret's arrival finally came and the people gave her a rousing reception throughout her route from Margate to London.

Once in London she was put on a magnificent sailing barge, lavishly decorated with pendants and other fine ornaments. It sailed majestically along the River Thames for all to see before reaching Greenwich Palace.

By this time my whole family had gathered on the banks of the river, waiting to welcome her.

As the flotilla came into view my eyes found Margaret. She looked magnificent in the most exquisite gown that I had ever seen. The barge drew close to the Palace steps and a fanfare of trumpet blew to announce the Duchess's arrival.

The summer evening air was still and there was a buzz of excitement as well as an overwhelming feeling of anxiety as it neared its moorings.

Dickon stood by my father's side, still and emotionless, he had always been a man of few words.

I studied him carefully. He had not changed much over the past few years if anything he was more handsome, unlike my father, who had put on a great deal of weight making his features red and blouted.

I knew by the sudden rapid beating of my heart that my feelings towards him had not abated, they were definitely stronger than they had ever been.

Each one of the family made Margaret welcome with nervous hugs and kisses. Grandma Cecily was overcome with emotion on seeing her daughter again after so many years. Margaret too was overcome and tears of joy began to appear in her eyes before she and her melee of attendance and ladies in waiting were escorted into the apartments that were going to be hers for the next several months.

I followed the royal party, flanked by Mary and Cecily. Looking about me I could not help but notice that everyone of my age seemed to be with someone of the opposite sex. Why was I still without a future husband? My betrothal to the Dauphin was annulled as Louis tried to make allies elsewhere.

I thought on...my father was now trying to bond his family to princes of other countries. My sister Mary had been promised to the King of Denmark and I had recently learnt that my five year old sister, Anne was soon to be betrothed to Maximillian's son Philip. I thought on, my parents seemed to be making many beneficial marriages for my younger sisters, so for what reason did they dally in finding me a suitable husband?

On retiring to my chamber I sat tentatively as pangs of guilt washed over me like a spring tide, for I knew that my love towards Dickon had not altered. I shook my head to try and clear my sinful thoughts as I prepared for the evenings events.

Looking in my mirror I gave a smile for the reflection, which shone back at me, was most pleasing. My auburn coloured hair was thick and covered my shoulders like a luxurious cape; my skin was fair and luminous. My eyes were the most intriguing pale hazel brown and my mouth was full with soft lips that were ripe for the kissing. Indeed I was the most beautiful girl *in the Palace and tonight I intended to be noticed by all the men who would be present.*

With the help of my ladies I prepared to make a grand entrance. I dressed in my most lavish green velvet gown with fine gold embroidery, brushed my hair until it shone like silk and plucked my brows to emphasise my large eyes.

I arrived at the Great Hall to be to shown my place on the top table. There was strict etiquette as to where I was allowed to sit.

My father and mother would take centre position upon the raised dais with them would be my grandmother, uncles, and aunts and of course Margaret. I was to sit a little further along the table next to my sisters, my half brothers and other younger dignitaries. The rest of the guests were to be placed on strategic tables throughout the hall.

Discreetly I glanced at Dickon who had arrived with Cecily. It was difficult to see him clearly because of the positioning of the table. I did not want to make my interest in him obvious to my sisters and for them to unravel my secret and so I quickly averted my eyes and made casual conversation with Mary. My voice was soft and calm; although my pulse was racing with an anxiety I had not known before.

Everyone waited for the king, queen and their guest of honour to arrive, for the festivities could not begin until my father gave the several hundred servants who slaved away in the kitchens the word for the food to be brought in. Finally, after about fifteen minutes, with much grandeur and to the fanfare of trumpets, the party arrived. Taking their places, my father nodded to the Chief Minister for the festivities to start.

The banquet was lavish indeed with at least twenty-five courses. The tables were laid with hundreds of dishes of every type possible; wild boar, baby swan, goose, pigeon, oysters and tarts and pies of every kind imaginable. There were jellies placed at intervals, set in the shape of castles and animals, amongst the other splendid table decorations. My father had spared no expense in making Margaret feel welcome.

At the end of the meal my father gave gifts to all the trumpeters, players and heralds who had made the feast so enjoyable.

Then the entertainment began; the entire hall was delighted in the playacting of The King's jester, Scoggins.

The evening wore on and I indulged in polite conversation with the people about me.

Discreetly, my eyes found Dickon further along the table, talking with intensity to Margaret and my grandmother. Margaret's faced looked strained and tense as she talked with them. My aunt's manner appeared to be cold towards my parents. There was obviously much talking and healing to be done and I hoped that my father would be forgiven for his actions against my Uncle George.

The wine flowed and as usual my father drank too much, and his voice became louder and more raucous as the evening went on.

Serenely Margaret ignored my father's gesturing and chatted freely to the company she was in. Margaret's tone intensified. 'What has become of George's two children?'

Cecily smiled an uncomfortable smile. 'They are at Middleham with their Aunt Anne.'

Margaret turned to her brother, the brother she had not seen since he was sixteen. 'Where is your Anne, Dickon?'

Dickon gave an awkward look and began to twist the ring on his little finger. 'She stays at home with the children as she has no liking for the city as it has too many bad memories for her.'

Margaret sighed, 'that is a pity as I would like to have seen her again.'

'She sends her love and her apologies,' Dickon continued.

Margaret let out a deep breath and wistfully looked about her. 'Where have all the years gone?'

Their conversation was brought short by a fanfare of trumpets. The next moment the king stood up and announced that the musical entertainment would now begin.

This was what I had been waiting for. Now, I hoped, an opportunity would arise for me to be able to speak at length with my lustrous aunt and of course my Uncle Dickon.

My mother, who was pregnant again, retired to her apartment almost at once.

As the evening wore on, I went unnoticed and sat in my mother's vacant chair, as all the other hall furniture had been cleared away and entertaining stations had been set up where one could play at cards, marbles and other such games.

I could hear the conversation clearly now and sat in silence while a dynamic scene unfolded before me.

My father's voice was raised as he continued to drink large measures of wine and his countenance was noticeably much the worse for drink as he approached his family.

His voice was loud and strong as he began, 'are we to live the rest of our lives as strangers, mother?'

The Duchess Cecily stopped what she was doing and looked at her eldest son. Lines of anguish were

132

clearly visible on his face and an uneasy atmosphere prevailed.

Swallowing hard and with his tone even louder he went on. 'Would you go to your grave denying me the love that I bear for you both?'

His bleary eyes were now looking at both Margaret and his mother. His outburst left the two women momentarily stuck for words. Finally, with ashen face, Cecily spoke. 'I will try to forgive, but it is hard to come to terms with...my two sons...' she broke off her sentence as she saw tears beginning to appear in my father's eyes.

Margaret's voice was charged with emotion as she spoke next. 'I know that George did deceive and disappoint time and time again and you forgave him...but why did you not banish him from the country? He was your brother.'

There was an eerie silence before Dickon, his voice trembling, broke it.

'What is done is done. Only God can judge us now...' His tone then lightened as he desperately tried to raise their spirits. 'Come, this is a celebration for tonight our beloved sister has returned to us.'

I could see that my father was desperate to be forgiven for what he had done. Ever since that cold February day he seemed to have abandoned the will to live and had deliberately set out on a path of self destruction.

Hesitantly I left the place at table and went to my father's side to try and lighten his heavy heart. After everything I had learnt about him, he was still my father and I could not bear to see him suffer in this way. Without a second thought I came to the aid of my distraught father. 'I love you father,' I said suddenly.

The trio were so engrossed in their conversation that they had not noticed me standing amongst them. My father turned to me in surprise and stroked my cheek. In quieter tones he spoke. His words were blurred but sincere. 'You are a sweet, dear child.'

Dickon got to his feet and stood before me, his voice was laced with irony. 'Why this cannot be little Bessy?' he teased, trying to ease the atmosphere that had now become very tense.

Blushing bright pink, I lowered my eyes. The conversation did indeed change as Margaret took hold of both my hands and began to inspect her niece. 'Why you have grown into a beauty...how old are you now?'

I felt myself go redder as I answer her, 'fifteen and a half.'

'I cannot believe it, why it seems that only yesterday you were a babe in arms.'

Margaret was now smiling and the tension that was between her and my father seemed to have abated.

Cecily got to her feet and all about her rose in respect for this granddame of the family. 'I must return to my chamber.' she announced. 'I am not as young as I used to be, I seem to tire so quickly these days.'

Dickon kissed his mother on the cheek as did Margaret and lastly my father before he ordered several of the ladies of the court to escort Cecily to her rooms.

My father then turned to look at me. 'Now young Bessy is it not time that you were retiring too?'

I arched my eyebrows. 'Please can I stay here a little longer?' I pleaded.

My Uncle Dickon turned out to be an ally in my cause, 'let her stay a while Eddy. Your daughter is nearly full grown and does light up the room with her presence.'

134

My father swayed and smiled. 'I do admit you have become a woman full grown and are as beautiful as any I have seen. All right, as it is a very special occasion, you may stay a little longer, but you must go when the hour reaches midnight.'

My father then left us in favour of a card game that had just begun on one of the tables of entertainment. William, Lord Hastings, his chief associate in over indulgence, quickly joined him.

I sat between my aunt and uncle, the aunt and uncle I had always loved and admired most.

An embarrassing silence followed, where Margaret looked and smiled at her niece. Dickon sipped a little wine and then broke the silence. He began to tell us about his life at Middleham. How he enjoyed his court there, how much he loved his son and how he worried so about the young boy's health.

I listened with great interest and my eyes could not but help study his every move and gesture. He had such a noble and dignified face without exuding an untouchable superiority that so many of the other lords did.

Margaret stood up and left us. She wanted to talk with some other members of the family she had not seen in years. Where ever she went a bevy of ladies followed pampering her every whim.

Just at that moment Harry Buckingham joined Dickon, who now was left standing at his sister's departure. Buckingham's heavily pregnant wife, my Aunt Katherine, had also retired early.

'Dickon!' Buckingham was all smiles as he approached.

I did not like Buckingham. Not only was he outspoken he was too concerned with his own importance. He surrounded himself with companions who applauded his actions. He dressed flamboyantly and strutted about as if he was everyone's overlord. He was arrogant and greedy and was known to have a violent temper. He had refused, at first, to marry my Aunt Katherine on the grounds that she was not a noble enough match for him. Feeling that my mother had forced the marriage with her interception with the king, he had an intense disliked for my mother and spoke of his views about her openly with his cronies with intense venom. I had the feeling that he did not like me very much. He did not even acknowledge me and began to converse with Dickon as if I did not exist.

He was, however, cousin and friend of my uncle and before long the two of them were in deep discussion, a conversation in which I was not included.

A little drunk with the giddiness of the evening, I sat quietly with my gaze firmly focused on my uncle. My eyes had become heavy with wine and made me feel dreamy, voices became distant and a far away look took over my features. I was looking into the future and my imaginations began to run wild…

My thoughts were interrupted and I returned to reality in an instant by the sound of a male voice and a gentle hand upon my shoulder.

'I do believe that the hour is late. Your father commanded that you retire at midnight.'

As my eyes slowly opened, I thought that I was still dreaming as Dickon's face came into focus.

'Come now Bessy you are much the worse for wine and you should be escorted to your rooms.'

Shaking my head for the feeling of some kind of reality, gripping the table for support, I got unsteadily to my feet. My head began to swim and the room seemed to whirl before me.

136

'You are right...I do believe it was time I left you.'

Harry did not acknowledge me and deliberately avoided my glance.

Signalling for two waiting ladies to attend, Dickon held tightly onto my hands. 'Lady Bessy, it has been a pleasure,' Dickon announced, taking one of my hands and placing it to his lips. 'We must talk again soon.'

I nodded, smiled serenely and with concentrated sure footedness, left the hall.

After helping me to dress into my nightwear, I dismissed my servants. In the privacy of my room, my heart soared and I whooped for joy as I slumped onto my bed.

Dickon had made me feel special and I loved him all the more for it. He had said that I lit up the room. Maybe for the first time he had seen me not as a little girl but as the beautiful woman I had become. My tiredness was unbelievable and within moments I drifted off to sleep.

******

The following morning I woke with a searing headache. My mouth was dry, there was a feeling of needles scratching my throat each timer I swallowed and I felt awful.

I could not remember in detail the previous night's events, but I had a warm feeling inside and I could memorise practically all the words Dickon had spoken to me.

One of my favourite waiting ladies, Lady Veronique, drew back the curtains around my bed and curtseyed. Veronique had been my lady of the bed

137

chamber ever since I left the sanctuary at Westminster almost ten years earlier.

The girl was full of energy and mischief and I was a little jealous of her carefree manner, behaviour that I was not allowed to display in public on any account.

My head throbbed as I sat up. 'Veronique, what is the time?'

'You have missed morning prayer my lady, as it is close to midday.' Veronique busied herself in folding some of my discarded clothes and went on. 'Many of the Northern men still slumber in the hall as they revelled well into the early hours of this morning.'

My ears pricked up. Could it be that Dickon stayed at Greenwich last night? Could it be possible that my uncle was now staying at the palace and not at Baynard's. Biting my lip to silence my thoughts, I considered...my father had planned many pursuits and festivities during my aunt's visit and maybe he had requested Dickon's company, he may have asked him to act as a go between for him and his estranged sister.

My thoughts were further considered...my father knew that his younger brother had a persuasive manner about him, was it not he who, still a teenager, successfully re united him with his brother George years before.

Looking at Veronique I knew that I had to be discrete, I could not afford to show her my true emotions, absolutely no one must know my heart's secret. I could not question Veronique further, as she would be full of probing questions for Veronique had a woman's intuition and would surely guess that some secret dwelt within her young mistress's heart. Fearing that if I told her within days all would know my shame, I was especially quiet as Veronique helped me dress.

138

The girl could not stop talking and went on in length about the extra people who were staying at the castle. *'I have seen the men's' livery; they are men of Northumberland and Westmoreland.'*

I wanted desperately to ask if any wore the White Boar, Dickon's livery, but I dared not. Facing the girl squarely, I spoke my orders. *'I will not be in need of you for the rest of the day, as I would like to be alone.* My voice was soft and Veronique did not question her mistress's motives. With a short bob of a curtsey she was gone.

My mind was active throughout the rest of the day. I was desperate to know if my Uncle Dickon was staying at Greenwich. I concluded that my mother would surely know who was now staying at the palace, as the queen made it her business to know everything that went on at court. Without delay I hurried to my mother's private chamber.

My mother smiled when she saw her eldest daughter enter her inner chamber, as she had not had a private audience with me in quite a while. Sitting on her grand chair in the middle of the most luxurious room, dress in a surcoat of cold and red brocade, its great sleeves hanging near to the ground my mother gave instructions and orders to the multitude of servants and waiting ladies who surrounded her.

My mother loved the pomp and ceremony she received as queen and I knew that she would do almost anything to keep that rank and power.

With arms outstretched she greeted me, *'my dear, please do come and sit with your mother.'*

Studying my mother closely, I noticed that she was still a strikingly handsome woman, although she had lost some of her youthful beauty. At forty-three she had given birth to twelve children and the thirteenth was *due to be born in a few months time. With the birth of each child I had seen less and less of my mother and this had left me a littler in awe of the woman who had born me.*

My mother continued to smile at me and her jewelled throat sparked with a hundred gems and her fine cause veil, which hung from a velvet and pearl head dress, shimmered in the light breeze that prevailed.

Sitting comfortable she began to speak. 'I get the feeling that there is something on your mind, something that you are a little shy in discussing with me...am I right?'

I blushed, I did not realise that my mother knew me so well.

Feeling my uneasiness, my mother turned to the multitude of servants and signalled them to leave.

I stepped closer and away from viewing eyes knelt and lay my head in my mother's lap. 'I come to talk of our family, for there is much I am confused about. There seems to be a number of father's relatives who do not like your kin very much. I felt it when I was little but it has grown into hatred these last few years.'

My mother stroked my cheek and took both my hands in hers and patted them. 'Let me try and explain.'

There was a pause as my mother sensed that she could be treading on sensitive ground. 'Your father's family blame me for all the ills that befall the realm. They say that I insisted that he... well...did away with his brother.'

My mouth fell open and unwittingly I let out a small gasp. 'Is it true...did you?'

My mother's voice was defiant. 'I only do what is best for my husband and for my children. George of Clarence was threatening all that your father and I had worked for. If what he was claiming would have gained

140

credence your father's future as king was doomed as was yours as a royal princess.'

I was beginning to realise the political turmoil that surrounded my family and as to why my Uncle Dickon avoided being in London. I was now beginning to realise that my mother would stop at nothing to advance the power of her immediate family.

My mother took a deep breath and went on. 'Your father's family, especially his mother and his sister have a dislike for me, that is why I retired early to my room, I am uneasy in their company.'

I hesitated before answering her. 'What of father's brother Dickon, what are your feelings towards him?'

Biting her lip my mother's expression changed. 'He is your father's favourite brother, he adores little Dickon.' My mother's tone was rather sarcastic. 'I have no qualms with him as long as he stays north and does not interfere with the politics at Westminster.'

I knew instinctively to keep quiet about my feelings as the gravity of my mother's words hit me. Not being able to bring myself to inquire whether my uncle was lodging at Greenwich, I decided to pursue the subject of a suitor. 'I come here in truth to ask if father has found me a fitting suitor. Mary and Cecily have been found suitors and they are younger than me.'

My mother's tone changed. 'Be patient, your father has been in negotiation with several foreign powers, he only wants the very best. He is determined to see his eldest daughter a queen.'

The thought of being a queen was a desirable one to me, but why was it taking so long? Surely there was some foreign prince who needed an escort. I raised my eyes to the ceiling and let out a long slow sigh. 'How much longer have I to wait?'

141

There was no reaction but a smile from mother and I realized that she was not going to enlighten me any further. Graciously I asked to be excused. Gently I kissed my mother's cheek before leaving her presence.

Back at my own apartments the hour was getting late, I had eaten a little light supper in my rooms and was now sitting, talking over my day's events with my sister Mary.

We were in good cheer as our aunt's visit was continuing to be a great success. We girls had been excused from our daily lessons and had been allowed on adventurous pursuits and exciting exploits.

'Mary's tone was fanciful. 'Tomorrow I believe there is to be a great hunt in the nearby woods and we are to go!'

'That's wonderful, I do enjoy the hunt and I have a new pony I would like to try out.'

'I believe that our sister Cecily has not been given permission.'

'Well she is still too young.' I concluded.

My ladies maid busied herself while we sisters talked. Veronique coughed and interrupted. 'Begging your ladies pardon...the Palace is full of guests from both Burgundy and from the north.' Veronique gushed at Mary.

On hearing this I could not stay silent any more, I had to find out! Trying to sound nonchalant I posed the question. 'Do you know if my Uncle Dickon stays at the Palace, Veronique?'

'Well I was talking to one of the nice young men who accompanies your Uncle Dickon and he says that he stays until the new month.'

I could feel my pulse rising, but I kept a calm voice. 'Out of curiosity... do you know where they have been billeted?'

'They are sharing quarters with the serving men and women but I hear that your uncle stays in a room quite near to your father's private quarters.'

I was thoughtful for this indeed was interesting news. 'Veronique... I would like to be alone now with Mary.'

Curtseying, she left the apartments.

Mary and I were then joined by our twelve year old sister Cecily whose betrothal had just been announced to Sir Ralph Scrope.

In the privacy of my bedchamber I talked with my sisters. Both my sisters were kind and sweet and hung on my every word. To them all I did was right. They both had never forgotten my strength to them in the gloom of Sanctuary. Our conversation soon centred on the men of the court, their virtues and their vices. But I could not bring myself to mention our uncle.

Mary yawned and stretched. 'I need to say goodnight dear sister, for our father has many activates planned over the next few days to celebrate the return of our aunt and we need to be rested to keep up with his punishing schedule.'

Mary rose and kissed me on both cheeks and then left to make her way back to her rooms. Cecily followed her elder sister's lead and said her goodnights.

I knew the corridors at Greenwich to be long and endless and ran throughout the Palace like mazes. Many of them I had never been in as there were stories of ghosts and ghouls that roamed them late at night.

Alone now my thoughts quickly turned to Dickon. I was wide awake with the knowledge that he was under the same roof as me and was only a short distance away in one of the castles guest chambers.

My mind went into overdrive... could I make up an excuse as to why I needed to see him, alone and so late?

What would he think of me? My mind was now in complete turmoil with the feelings that were rushing through my head; his rooms are close to my father's, too close...what if my father were to come into the room...what could I say? What if my mother found out that I paid my uncle a visit so late at night?

Then my mother's words came flooding into my head, I had to think at all times who I was and act accordingly.

The idea of roaming the palace in the dead of night to meet a paramour thrilled me and I desperately wanted to go fulfil my flights of fancy. But an emotion strong inside was keeping me in my room. It was fear, fear of rejection, fear of ridicule, fear of being sent away in shame and disgrace, and so I did not go that night to Dickon's room.

For the rest of his stay, I felt that Dickon seemed to be avoiding me. There was a brief encounter, just after breakfast, one morning, just before he left to go hunting with my father. But his words were brief and formal. I was beginning to wonder if I would ever get the chance to speak to him alone before he left to go back north.

Then on the very day he was about to depart, whilst I was walking in the garden, for I loved to walk amongst the newly laid lawns and ornamental bushes and trees that my fathers army of gardeners kept immaculate, I noticed him sitting alone on a stone seat next to the rose scented flowers, deep in study, reading.

How splendid he looked, he had grace and an elegance that thrilled me. There was a physical attraction I felt for him that I felt for no other. Mustering up all of my courage I sat next to him.

Within seconds he knew that I was there and lowering his book he then looked deep into my eyes. 'Why Bessy...I did not realised that you were there.'

My throat was tight and I could hardly speak because of it, there was a tremble in my voice. 'I come to walk in the garden for the day is lovely, too nice to sit and study and to make embroidery pieces. I have escaped my waiting ladies for a few moments, for I do at times love to be alone. I like sometimes to be by myself with my thoughts and just wander in the fresh morning air.'

Dickon's face exuded a smiled and he closed the book he was reading and began to speak to me. 'You are right, my thoughts exactly. The air is fresh and the fragrance of the garden makes my spirits rise. I also love to be alone from time to time with my books and my innermost thoughts.'

His eyes seemed to look into my soul and read what was there. I felt as if he could tell what I was thinking and I blushed bright red. I smiled as if to agree and looked about at the wild array of shapes and colours. My heart was beating wildly in my chest, was it so loud that he could hear it?

There was awkwardness between us and at last I broke the silence. 'Do you leave soon?'

His answer was short and direct, 'tomorrow.'

I looked down into my skirts and Dickon could see by the look that suddenly appeared on my face that something was wrong.

Lifting my head in his hand he looked deep into my face. 'Why do you look so miserable?'

With my heart all of a flutter I began to speak, 'I...I do not want you to leave.'

I had revealed something of my true thoughts before I could stop myself.

To my relief, Dickon did not appreciate my true meaning. He tried to explain. 'I have to return north… I have had a good time seeing everyone… I promise that I will return soon and bring my wife Anne and my son Ned with me.'

There was another awkward silence where I changed my expression. I had to make light of my words now for I feared that Dickon would guess my true feelings towards him, but had I already revealed too much to him?

Taking a deep breath I answered him. 'That will be nice,' and nodded in agreement.

With his tone relaxed Dickon continued. 'It is a shame that we did not spend more time with one another, I feel at ease talking with you my dear Bessy.' He paused and let out a deep sigh. 'What a joy it is to talk to you alone. I know that I appear different alone than when I am in the company of others? I can relax when the pressure of government is not upon me.'

Inside my stomach was churning but I knew I had to keep a calm exterior. 'Yes, I realise that you are not yourself when in the presence of many people; I myself take on a different countenance when in the company of the court.'

Dickon nodded. 'I feel that we have a lot in common, not least that we both love to read and we could have discussed our favourite books.'

There was another moment's pause, where I could see his mind thinking. 'I do not leave until tomorrow maybe we could get together tonight after evening prayers?'

My tone changed to one of euphoria. 'That would be wonderful!'

146

'Lets say here at this very spot, as the day is long and the air is sweet, I think it a perfect place to discuss poetry and literature.' He got to his feet. 'I must take my leave of you now sweet girl for I have much to do. Farewell until tonight.'

He then took both my hands and kissed them lightly, before giving me a single white rose he had picked from the garden, and then he was gone.

For the rest of the day I reined in my excitement, although my heart was racing and my palms were sweaty. I had to act in my usual fashion in front of my sisters and my ladies; I did not want them asking any awkward questions.

The time ticked by slowly, but finally, when the hour approached I managed to slip away discreetly after evening prayers.

A churning feeling was in the pit of my stomach as I walked towards the rendezvous seat, clutching a most recently printed copy of Chaucer's Canterbury Tales. The ornamental stone seat was situated in a most private part of the garden, with high walled climbers and beautiful rose covered trellises.

The garden at Greenwich was one of my favourites with an exquisite pond and marble fountains with ornamented sea creatures spouting water into it. There were many magnificent plants with hundreds of flowers omitting their wonderful smells. The late evening light was magical and I felt as if I was in a dream.

I was early Dickon had not yet arrived. What was I to talk about? Should I let my felling be known to him?

At that moment a messenger bowed low and handed me a rolled scroll baring my Uncle Dickson's seal. I carefully broke the seal.

It read...Dearest Bessy; by the time you read this I will be many miles away. Just after our meeting this morning I received grave news about my son's health and I left within the hour to travel north. I hope that you are not too disappointed and understand my motives? I will return when my little Ned is well and we can read to him together. My deepest love and fondest wishes... Dickon.

The months passed and Dickon did not return to London and I wondered if he ever thought of me, for thoughts of him had filled my every waking moment and my dreams.

My mother gave birth to a fine healthy daughter that she named Bridget. A daughter that my father deemed should go to the church and become a nun, no doubt to try to make amends in the eyes of God for all his misdoings.

I continued to mature into a most strikingly beautiful woman and negotiation dragged on to find me a suitable husband. Just when I thought I would be betrothed something would happen to change the political landscape and the talks would fall through and I began to wonder if my father would ever find anyone suitable to become my husband.

My mother's kin and my father's kin sustained their dislike for one another, although Margaret went back to Burgundy on much more friendly terms with my father than when she arrived.

******

My sisters and I were grief stricken and sat close together silently weeping as our mother entered the room. Mary had contracted a fever and on the twenty third day of her conditions she had died.

148

Our mother looked tired and drawn as she spoke to us, for she also had shed many tears. 'The good Lord has seen fit to take your sister to him,' she whispered with tears once more filling her eyes.

I was beside myself with grief, as I had not been allowed to go to Mary during her illness. It was deemed by the doctors that her ailment was contagious and now I would never talk again to my beloved sister.

Wiping a tear I swallowed hard, I could feel a burning sensation in my throat and I could not speak. Lowering my head I gave out a deep sigh. Mary had died so suddenly. It was only a few weeks ago that the two of us were running and laughing together in the grounds of the Minster, sitting discussing our futures while playing chess beside the fireside.

At the onset of her illness, Mary had been taken to Greenwich, as the air was thought better, more conducive for a recovery. But my dear sister did not recover and now she was gone.

Although I had lost siblings before to malady, they had been only babes, George, who was just over a year and little Margaret who died within eight months of being born. Mary was almost fourteen and she had become so close to me not only as a sister but also as a friend and confidant. If I was ever to have reveal my true feelings towards my uncle to anyone it would have been to Mary, but now she was not here and how I missed her.

Over the next few weeks the loss of my sister and companion of many years overcame me. My throat continued to burn as I choked back my tears and squeezed my mother's hand for comfort.

There was venom in my words as I struggled to speak to her. 'Why... why Mary...why not take me?' Then losing control of my emotions I burst into deep

149

sobs. Before long Cecily was crying too, indeed the whole household had a love for Mary and most shed many tears at the news of her departing.

Everyone was devastated by her untimely death. Her funeral at Windsor was a very sad occasion. A very solemn Prince of Wales had come from Ludlow to attend his sister's funeral; even my mighty father was seen to have a tear in his eye as his second daughter was laid to rest.

Our only comfort was the thought that she would sit with God in heaven, as she was one of the sweet, dear innocents.

That summer was a miserable one for me, without my beloved sister. Each day I would wake as if Mary's death had been a dream and that my dear sister would come rushing into my room at any moment. Then I would come back to reality, Mary was with the angels. Every day I would pray for Mary's soul and light a candle in the family's private chapel.

I began to question why God would do such a thing, what had Mary done? It was me who had the unholy thoughts; surely it should have been me who was taken not my dear innocent Mary.

The winter came all too soon, with the November winds and icy rains and my spirits were at an all time low.

It was then at the beginning of December, with great joy, that I received the news that Dickon had come back to London.

He had bought a fine new residence in Bishopsgate called Crosby Hall, built by Sir John Crosby in 1466 it was well appointed and modern in appearance.

Dickon and his extended family had travelled from the north, together with many of their northern *followers, to stay there for the whole of the Christmas season probably returning northwards in the spring.*

My life had meaning once more and my heart soared with the thought of seeing Dickon again after all this time.

Would he remember his promise to me and spend some time with me, time together reading to his young son?

Looking at myself in the silver edged looking glass, I called for Veronique, for now I had to dress in my very best clothes and make sure that everyday my hair and skin were in pristine condition.

Holding the mirror to my bosom I swung around for joy. I was now a woman grown and I had made the decision that the time had come to let Dickon know my true feelings towards him, but how was I to do it?

******

Almost immediately, before Richard had had time to settle in his new abode, an urgent message arrived. Two horsemen entered the courtyard at a gallop, their clothes covered in mud. Dismounting, almost before the horses had stopped, they approached the Duke who had arrived into the courtyard on hearing the cries of the grooms and the neighing of the horses.

The messengers panted and breathed deeply. One stepped forward and bowed. My Lord, the herald began, I bring bad news.'

Richard squeezed Anne's hand; she had followed him into the yard, and both prepared themselves to hear the worst.

Richard's tone was urgent. 'What is it? Out with it fellow!'

'It is the king,' the messenger paused to take in a deep gulp of air... 'he has taken to his sick bed and John

151

Howard had sent me in great speed to bring you to his Majesty's bedside.'

Knowing that Jack Howard would only send such a message if the situation was serious, Richard turned to his wife. 'I must go my love,' he gasped, looking at Anne.

Anne nodded; she knew that her husband had no choice but to obey the summons.

Within minutes, together with two most trusted members of his retinue, Richard boarded a barge to travel to the Palace. It was his favourite way to travel when in London, as most of the streets were dark and narrow and strewn with danger. It was also the quickest and the boatman made the trip in less than half an hour.

The boat docked silently, only the sound of the brown tide of the River Thames lapping against the algae covered stone steps could be heard.

On docking Richard was met by Howard. Jack looked distressed, as he strode out to meet him. 'Thank God you have come…'

Quickening his stride, Richard followed Jack up the stairs from the dock and into a small side entrance. Hurrying along the winding corridors Richard gasped his words as they went. 'What has happened?'

Jack swallowed hard; he was a little out of breath, as he began to report the day's events. 'It was about two hours ago; your brother was reading a message from one of his spies in France when he began to rant and rave about the despicable Louis. Suddenly his breathing became erratic and he began to cough. He could not get his breath and almost collapsed.'

Richard bit his lip in frustration. 'How is he now?'

'I left him in the capable hands of his doctors who believe that he over heated his blood during his rage against the French King.'

With great haste, the two reached the king's bedchamber. On entering Edward's bedchamber Richard was met by Queen Elizabeth's far away glance. She was sitting by her husband's bedside silently, gently rocking her body from side to side, and clutching a crucifix. She fixed her eyes on Richard. 'He sleeps.' She muttered.

Quietly Richard sat next to her and studied his brother. Edward did indeed show the strains of a lifetime full of the pressure of kingship and the constant over indulgences he had put on his body.

Although Richard had assured Elizabeth Woodville that all would be well, looking at Edward now he was not so sure.

Elizabeth voice was now a whisper. 'His doctors have assured me that he will live.' She then shook her head and took a kerchief to staunch her tears. 'But for how much longer if he continues to pursue his debauched life style?'

Richard nodded in agreement. Although he thought Elizabeth guilty of many of his brother stresses and strains he was of the same opinion as her regarding Edward's other over indulgences.

Just at that moment Edward slowly opened his eyes. He was awake and with a croaky voice uttered, 'ah, Richard.'

Richard smiled nervously at Elizabeth and patted his brother's hand. 'Do not stress yourself Eddy. I will come back later when you have regained your strength.'

Edward nodded and closed his eyes.

Richard gestured his pleasure to Elizabeth and in silence, left the room, glad to see that his brother was now strong enough to talk to him.

The following day bright and early Richard decided to pay another call to his ailing brother.

******

As Dickon prepared to enter my father's chamber, I came out in a complete state of distress. On seeing him, with intensity, I threw my hands around his neck and buried my head in his shoulder. Finally I faced him, my auburn brown hair flowing about freely and my eyes noticeably red from weeping. I looked at him through my watery gaze.

'Oh Dickon, how glad I am that you are here.'

Dickon squeezed my hand; he could feel my body gently swaying as I had spoken to him.

An urgent tone took over Dickon's voice as he stroked my hair. 'Now...now... calm yourself...I am sure your father will be alright...Howard tells me he is over the worst...how is he now?'

Uneasiness crossed my face as I tried desperately to compose myself. My voice was weak and trembling as I answered. 'He is much better now, but at one time mother and I thought that he was going to... die...I dread to think what life would be without my father.'

Dickon put his arms around my shoulder as my tears once more began to flow. He looked skyward as if to ask for some divine intervention, as he tried to find words to ease my distress. 'I am sure that he will make a full recovery for Edward is strong, the strongest man I know. You look exhausted so now go and lie down, for you must try and get some rest while I sit with your father.'

I nodded in agreement, as I felt emotionally and physically drained, and I went directly to my rooms for some much needed rest.

I had my ladies with me when, sometime later, Dickon entered my chamber. I had been tidied, and my demeanour was much improved as I sat glumly in the middle of the room ashen faced. I knew that Dickon could see the distress in my eyes as he approached me.

'Bessy, I come to say that I have seen and spoken to your father and his doctors say that he will make a full recovery very soon.'

With a wave of my hand I dismissed my ladies, as I did not want them privy to our conversation.

Much more composed than an hour ago and thankful for Dickon's concern for me I began to speak to him. 'I was afraid...afraid of what would become of me, of us all, if my father were to die.'

Dickon knew exactly what I meant as he probably had the same dreadful feelings when first informed of his brother's state. He too would then dread to think what would happen if my father were to die now.

Taking a deep breath I continued. 'The rest of the family, including my mother, do not seem to appreciate the importance of my father being here as our king. They do not realise that everything we have would be jeopardised if my father were to ...die.''

Kneeling in front of me and taking both my hands in his Dickon tried to put my mind at rest. 'You must not fret; your father is good for at least another ten years.'

There was a moment between us that was both tender and loving and it lifted my spirit and my countenance began to lighten and a slight smile started to appear on my forlorn face. Tiredly gazing up to the heavens I sighed, 'you are probably right.'

155

A dogged determination had entered Dickon's tone. 'I know that I am right. Your father is the strongest man I know.'

There was a pause and Dickon got to his feet. 'Now I must get back to Crosby Place...I only arrived in London late yesterday.'

I looked into his eyes and I knew that my love for him was stronger than ever. There was urgency in my voice. 'Come back soon... you promised that we could read to your little son Ned. Why not bring George's children, Margaret and little Eddy with you as I know that they also love to listen to the stories of monsters and heroes.'

Dickon smiled and kissed me on my forehead and promised to visit me in the next few days. He could feel that I needed his support until my father gained his full strength. 'That is a wonderful idea. Maybe your sister Cecily could join us and we could make a family occasion of it?'

My smile broadened, 'yes I would like that.'

Dickon nodded, turned and left the room.

Over the next few days my father's health did improve and the court gradually got back to normal. It was amazing how quickly he made a recovery and was back to his old ways. He took no notice what so ever of his doctors' warnings to slow down.

I reflected on the two weeks that had passed and could not believe what had taken place in such a short time. It was as if my father's illness had not happened at all and in one way I was thankful for it.

On my father's insistence, the Christmas celebrations were going ahead as planned and there was to be much feasting at Westminster. A throng of activity was present from early dawn, servant and courtiers hurrying and scurrying throughout the Palace.

156

The Great Hall was decked out in the grandest way for tonight there was going to be a banquet for over a thousand people. It was to be the most spectacular banquet ever to have been held at Westminster as my father intended to show the foreign princes that he was indeed fit and well recovered.

Preparations were made to dress us young princesses in our finest gowns and special cloth had been ordered of the finest materials to do so.

My father was proud of his daughters and wanted everyone to admire them, especially his eldest.

My chamber was a bevy of activity as my ladies spent all day preening me for the evening's banquet. I was excited; it was thrilling. I took extra care to make myself especially beautiful, although, I had been assured, by Veronique, that I was the most desirable woman in the entire kingdom.

'My Lady, you look stunning,' Veronique began. A giggle entered her tone as she went on. 'I cannot see anyone that my Lady desires refusing her his attentions tonight.'

I blushed brightly at the thought, I was almost seventeen and my beauty was radiant.

My natural beauty was enhanced by the pale blue gowned I was wearing and around my tiny waist was tied a belt glittering with jewels. I had decided not to wear a fashionable head dress, as I wanted to show off my long, luxuriant hair with a jewelled hair band.

My ladies chatted with great excitement while they waited for a messenger to come with a summons.

It was tonight, that my mother had said causally, that many of the family would join her and my father at Westminster. As well as my grandmother Cecily, my aunts and uncles on my mother's side, my Uncle Dickon was due to attend with the rest of his extended family.

157

Ever Since Dickon's visit to my private rooms I had relived every word and gesture we hadshared between us. I had not seen or heard form his since then and could not help but wonder if he had guessed how I felt about him.

Veronique continued to taunt. 'The king, your father, may well see tonight that he cannot keep such a beautiful woman without a man for much longer.'

Veronique raptures were brought to an abrupt end by the sound of fanfares and we all knew that it would soon be our turn to take our place at the banquet. Within minutes the messenger did arrived with the request that we had been waiting for. With my two ladies at my side I entered the hall. An officer of the household escorted me to my appointed place.

Many trellis tables had be erected and I quickly scanned the people assembled and my eyes found Dickon sitting next to the Lady Anne, who was sat next to Dickon's fourteen year old son, John.

It was common knowledge that Dickon already had two children from a previous liaison with a girl named Katherine Haute. I was not too sure of the details, as I was a small child at the time, but I had learnt from the gossip of the court, that Dickon, at the age of sixteen, fell deeply in love with one of my mother's ladies in waiting. He desperately wanted to marry this girl, for she had already bore him a son, which they named John.

With great relief to everyone, not least my father, Dickon's amour died the following year whilst giving birth to his second bastard child. Katherine had delivered a healthy daughter, which was named in honour of her dead mother. Dickon raised these children as befitting their royal status and when he married, Anne she accepted these children graciously, becoming a second mother to them.

They sat talking quietly to the distinguished group they had been seated next to. Dickon was in deep conversation with his friend, Francis Lovell, and Lovell's wife also named Anne, *in fact the two Anne's were linked through their respective marriages, they were cousins.*

The page of the table showed me to my place. There was a temporary arrangement of tables that ran the entire length of the four walls of the Great Hall at Westminster. Although I had been seated at top table, together with the rest of the close family, I was to be nowhere near my uncle. To my annoyance I had, as usual, been given a seat amongst the younger members of the family, one, which my mother thought more suitable. Did not my mother realise that I was a woman grown and should be at the very heart of the court? I sighed; at least I was allowed to attend the banquet, unlike poor Cecily who was deemed a little too young. I had made a promise that I would give my young sister a minute-by-minute account of the evening.

At last a fanfare of trumpets blew, there was a hush fall over the congregation and my father, together with my mother regally walking beside him, entered the hall. Both were a glitter with jewels; pearls, rubies, sapphires, diamonds and dressed in the most expensive of cloths.

A flock of servants stood behind the king ready to satisfy his every whim. With a wave of the king's hand and a nod of his head the festivities began.

There were hundreds of other people seated on every side of the large hall with the entire middle a vast empty space where the entertainment was to take place.

I soon realised that there was not going to be any chance of conversation with my uncle and wondered if Dickon even knew that I were there?

The food was served from golden carts and whilst the nobles ate, players acted out the story of great deeds and mythical beasts. The evening was full of exquisite entertainment from both England and from the continent. I let out a squeal when the blow of Saint George's sword finally killed the magnificent red dragon.

'It is wonderful how real it all looks.' I commented to my young cousin Henry who was seated on my right.

'Wonderful!' He agreed and the entire hall began to clap and cheer the actors who had now taken off their costume finery to reveal themselves.

Surrounded by all the merriment I did not notice when Dickon and several of the people accompanying him left the hall. When I did become aware of their absence a feeling of frustration and infuriation came over me for once again I had been unable to talk, or to even be in the presence of Dickon.

'You look anxious my Lady.' It was Veronique, who stood behind my place at table and whispered in my ear. Her voice sounded momentarily distant as I almost forgot where I was and what I had been doing.

Veronique's questions were probing. 'Why do you stare so across the room?'

My reply was scolding, 'you ask too many questions. I...I just noticed that my uncle and aunt have appeared to have left the proceedings, that's all.' I tried to be trite.

Veronique began to raise her voice as the musicians in the gallery had once more started to play. 'Your uncle is a very busy man perhaps he has been called to some political issue that needs his immediate attention.'

It was common knowledge that Dickon's military skills had forced the Scottish lords into talks with my father, but the peace was fragile and many Scots still continued their border raids.

I nodded, trying not to show Veronique my disappointment. 'Yes you are probably right. Now shall we continue to enjoy the evening for it is, indeed, still early.'

The entertainment went on well into the night and although I was enjoying myself, my thoughts constantly turned to Dickon. He was so unlike my father, he did not indulge in excess and always kept control of his behaviour even when the wine flowed freely.

That was one of the many fine qualities that I loved about him. He put duty before pleasure and if there was a good reason for him to leave the festivities then he would.

That night I scarcely slept, I was restless thinking of Dickon all night long. Resting my head on my pillow I sighed at the hopelessness of my plight.

******

The war against both Scotland and France had reached complications and Edward had called a meeting of parliament, for all the nobles to attend.

The month that followed was full of meetings at Westminster Hall and at the beginning of February a treaty was signed with The Scottish Lord, The Duke of Albany.

Richard came in for much praise for his part in the proceedings and was given more land by Edward who now regarded his brother as his greatest asset. The following week Richard and his family left London to travel back to the North.

Negotiations were still going on with several foreign princes for Elizabeth's betrothal in marriage, but there was no real progress on that front.

There were no more congregations and grand celebrations to be had for several months; her family went back to going about their daily routines.

Bessy continued in her lessons, sat with her ladies, chatting, signing and making fine pieces of embroidery.

The new year brought with it icy winds. Although December had seen a spell of mild weather, by January the winter was back with vengeance.

The air and everything around hung with the fine midst of winter. Days were spent wrapped in furs and heavy damasks to try and keep warm in the stone draughty castles.

Bessy wore thick woollen tights beneath her dress and extra layers of linen to try and keep out the bitter cold. There was still abundant snow on the ground by the end of March.

Whilst at Winsor the king had gone out on one of these unusually cold, damp mornings at the end of March. He had mustered some experienced fishermen and had gone onto the river in a small fishing boat with them.

Soon afterwards news had reached the court that the king had taken to his bed after he had joined a small fishing party early one morning on the River Thames, Edward had caught a chill.

It came as a shock to everyone however, when several days later, instead of getting well there were fears that Edward was going to die.

******

My mother bit her lip and pulled at her skirts as I entered her private chamber. My mother's tone was serious. 'I have called you here Bessy because I believe you to be old enough to understand what is going on.'

I sat down in silence; I had never seen my mother look so worried, she had visibly lost weight and her face was pale and drawn.

Trying hard to keep control of her emotions, my mother went on. 'Your father is seriously ill. His doctors say that he will not... recover.'

My tone was one of defiance. 'This cannot be true! Father is strong! Surely he will not let a little chill ...'my voice tailed off as I saw that my mother was losing her composure.

A chaotic panic gripped me, I would not, could not, believe that my father was going to die. His doctors were wrong and he would recover. I wanted to cry out but I knew how volatile my mother could become and stayed calm.

'Sit down mother,' I continued. 'Father is not going to die.'

My mother took me by the hand and squeezed it tight and I could feel the anxiety in my mother's whole body as she began to weep. 'He wanted to live to see you a queen and his sons old enough to fight by his side and now...'

With our emotions getting the better of both of us, my mother and I began to cry uncontrollably and hugged one another tightly for comfort.

My mother tried to compose herself as she looked at me with bleary eyes. 'Come we must be brave for your father's sake, for he has summoned his family to go to him. He wants to speak with us...to tell us what he wants us to do after...he is gone.'

163

I watched as all the people in attendance, mournful, obey and gathered at my father's bedside.

My father then called each of us children to him, excluding my eldest brother who was at his own court in Ludlow.

I was holding my nine-year-old brother's hand. My sister Cecily held his other, with six year old Anne, four year old Katherine and two year old Bridget standing behind us with a nurse, weeping softly.

With his dying breath and in a whisper my father spoke to us. His breathing was short and laboured. 'Be faithful to your brother Edward... help him to be a good king...be strong for you were all born to serve a nation.'

Each one of us in turn was then summoned forward and our father then kissed each of us before we all were led, crying, out of the room.

I could not help but notice that my father looked less like a king and more like a man very weary and worn of life.

******

With doctors surrounding him, Edward had been talking, with some difficulty to his councillors. He had, without his wife Elizabeth knowing, changed his will. He wanted his brother, Richard, to be Protector of the realm after he had departed this world and also made him guardian of his son and heir, young Edward, while his son was still too young to rule. To everyone's surprise, he was not giving his wife any real power.

When she was finally told of the change of plan, Elizabeth was seething with silent rage; Richard of Gloucester had not even left his home in the north to travel south to see his dying brother.

Elizabeth bit her tongue and kept silent and held her husband's hand, as tears silently flowed down her cheeks.

With his whole family assembled, including Elizabeth's eldest son Thomas Grey, Edward's best friend William Hastings and his chief ministers, Edward, with his dying breath, urged everyone to embrace and pledge that they would all work towards reconciliation, to unite their differences and to issue harmony and peace in any future government.

The following day, on the ninth day of April 1483 King Edward IV died. He left both a family and a nation stunned. They could not believe that their magnificent warrior King was dead at only 40 years of age. It had been a complete shock to everyone and the people at court did not know what to do next and an air of complete confusion prevailed.

The days that followed were indeed traumatic. Edward's body was taken to rest in St Stephen's Chapel, Westminster.

They had dressed him in his gold armour and placed him in an open silver coffin with the orb and sceptre placed in his hands and a crown was placed on his unmoving head. Prayers and masses were said daily and offerings made.

On the morning of his internment he was placed in the Abbey for the dignitaries to pay their final farewell. Bishops, abbots, priests as well as knights came all dressed in black and caring black candles. All who attended the funeral were overcome with grief.

The dead king's nine-year-old son Richard, Bessy and her sisters stood close to a mournful Elizabeth as prayers' came to an end. Elizabeth was overcome with grief and had decided not to attend Edward's final internment and all could well understand why. The sight of her husband being entombed in the royal vault for eternity was too much for Elizabeth to bear.

The king's coffin was placed on his bier, which was draped in black velvet and drawn by six black horses. An image of the king preceded his bier, and the whole cortege moved slowly towards Windsor.

The populations lined the streets in silent respect as their king's body made slow progress through the streets.

At St Georges Chapel, amidst the spring rains, the king's body was given to his marble vault. Standing there at the grave were the men of the household who broke their staves and dropped them into the tomb and royal banners were hung above it.

Bessy together with her young brother and sisters, retreated into a secret corner of the palace and grieved in private.

******

My mother began to rely heavily on me, her oldest daughter, to give the necessary orders to the household, comfort to the children, calming the grief amongst my father's royal retainers and soothing the complaints amongst the stewards and servants.

With servitude, I tried hard to ease and to bring reassurance to my younger siblings. I tried to explain to them the best way I could the awesome finality of earthly death and the everlasting quality of spiritual life. That our father was now with God and that we to were in God's hands.

My father's end came suddenly and my mother was full of worry, mainly because of my father's change of will to put Richard of Gloucester as regent and guardian of his eldest son until the boy became old enough to rule in his own right.

My mother knew that the king's youngest brother had never liked her and that he had deplored his brother's marriage to her and she wondered what her fate may be when Dickon arrived in the capital.

But Dickon was in the north and my mother knew that by the time a messenger reached him with the news of my father's death his arrival into London would take several weeks.

Although Dickon had written, as soon as he received the dreadful news, letters of sympathy to my mother, consolation and promises of loyalty to the new king, my mother did not intend to give her loyalty to her husband's youngest brother and began almost immediately plotting his downfall.

My father's heir, my brother Edward, was with my mother's eldest brother, my Uncle Anthony Woodville; at Edward's court in Ludlow on the Welsh boarders and my mother decided to write to him urging him to get to London with the young King in great haste.

She made other arrangements too. She took possession of the crown jewels and ordered another of her numerous brothers, my Uncle Edward Woodville, to take control of the Royal Fleet.

Having been totally engaged in prayer and other spiritual matters every day since the death of my beloved father, I was completely unaware of her actions and so it was to my surprise when I found out what she, together with my maternal uncles, had been scheming.

My mother summoned me to her. 'Your brother has left Ludlow and travels south,' she began.

Looking at my mother, I could see that she was visibly wracked with nervous tension, but posed my question. 'When does Uncle Dickon arrive?'

My mother lowered her head. 'I...we intend to crown your brother immediately and then I intend to act as his regent.'

My tone was laced with anger. 'That is not what father intended. You were there at father's bedside when he called us to him.'

My mother's eyes turned to ice as she studied my face. 'Your father was delirious, he did not realise what he was saying.'

I was insistent. 'The Lords heard his wishes...we all heard his wishes...you will never get away with this.'

My mother's voice was now raised and an argument almost took place between us. 'I do not intend to let Richard of Gloucester become protector. I intend to fight for my rights as the boy's mother.'

Taking three deep breaths my expression changed to one of distain, 'what do you mean?'

My mother too began to breath deeply and nervously wrung her hands. 'Your Uncle Anthony has loaded carts full of weapons, in case Richard does not agree with my plan.'

I shook my head woefully; I could not believe what was happening. The death of my father had revealed the true nature of my mother's family to me and I did not like them for it.

Biting my lip for I was thoughtful and fearful. What would be the result of these treacherous acts and what would become of my beloved Uncle Dickon?

The next few days were to bring chaos to my world. My whole family were wrought with the tension of their deeds.

I withdrew from them and shied away when my mother approached me for I felt that my mother's fears were exaggerated and not based on any of the facts.

Within the corridors of Westminster there were people assembling in corners, speaking in lowered tones. Passing among them innocently I listen with great interest to the conversations going on around me.

'Your Uncle Anthony has met with Richard of Gloucester at Stony Stafford,' I overheard my mother telling my half brother.

I listened with great attention hidden in the half-light, behind a large stone pillar.

Thomas's voice was at a low whisper, 'does all go well?'

My mother's tone was just audible, 'the messenger brings me news that they have spent the night talking and drinking. I can only hope that Anthony has told Richard of our plans and that he does not intend to resist. I have given my brother instructions of what to do if he does.'

Swallowing hard and trying not to breathe too loudly, I listened with intense interest to their words, which were chilling enough. Were they planning on killing my Uncle Dickon if he did not go along with their plans?

That night I weighed their words carefully. But what could I do? I felt so helpless. The only thing I could do was to pray for an agreeable outcome. Clutching at my rosary I knelt and prayed alone before the crucifix in my room for most of the night.

The following morning the spring dawn had just appeared when I was woken by the sound of voices mixed with the twittering of songbirds outside my window in the sweet mellow air.

But inside there was a frenzy of activity. My mother appeared full of desperation and panic, she was weeping as she burst unannounced into my room. 'Quickly my daughter, we must leave the Palace.'

169

I got up at once and steadied my mother who looked near to collapse, 'why...what has happened?'

'Your Uncle Anthony, your half brother Richard, together with Vaughan and Haute have been arrested and taken to Pontefract Castle to stand trial for treason against The Protector.' Panting for breath she went on, 'those villains Hastings and Howard wrote to Richard and told him what was happening. They have been keeping him informed of our every move.'

I was stunned and lost for words, although I was relieved that Dickon had found out about the treason that was being hatched.

I had learnt that as well as Hastings and Howard, Richard was reputed to have some very good spy masters who could and would have kept him informed of the developments in London.

My mother dabbed her eyes as she continued to race around in alarm. 'Richard rides south together with Harry Buckingham and your brother Edward. God only knows what will happen to us when Richard arrives for he is sure to know that I and the rest of the family were in the plot to kill him.'

My disgust for my mother deepened. 'Mother stop this now! You must ask for Dickon's forgiveness and hope that this terrible feud that is developing can be averted.'

She was not listening, she continued to rant and cry. 'I have also news that your father's partner in debauchery, William Hastings, has urged the Londoners to accept Richard as their Protector and incites the people against me and my kin.... I am surrounded by enemies.'

I continued, without success, trying to calm my mother, as she continued to race about in a whirlwind of panic.

A messenger awaited her in the Great Hall and my mother together with another of her brothers; my Uncle Lionel and half brother Thomas hurried to get the latest news.

Richard was only hours away from the capital and what was more distressing was that the young King was reported to be his prisoner.

On hearing this news my mother fell to her knees and cursed and wailed so loud that I could hear her groans as she raced to the hall.

'We must return to sanctuary,' my mother finally said, clutching my arm. 'We have but a few hours,' Lionel added. 'Our brother Edward has taken command of the fleet.'

My mother nodded, her brother had indeed taken control of the ships and loaded with finery and treasure had set sail.

The now twenty four year old Thomas Grey took control of the situation and began to order everyone of the household, ladies and gentlemen as well as a small body of servants to carry chests, packs, trusses and coffers into sanctuary. To hasten the move the walls were broken down and windows were ripped open.

The packing overflowed and servants were buzzing about like bees and the noise level was loud enough to hurt sensitive ears.

Arch Bishop Rotherham of York arrived in the Queen's apartments to find much rumble and haste. He too tried in vain to comfort the queen to no avail, even after he placed the Great Seal into her hands, my mother's frenzy did not cease.

With a heavy heart I helped my distraught mother across to the Abbot's chambers and once again my family and I were in sanctuary.

171

I remembered the grey damp walls devoid of tapestries or any fine art works. Only the religious pieces and wooden crucifixes decorated the walls of our rooms and my future was once again uncertain. I remembered too that the earlier time in sanctuary had been both gloomy and dismal with endless days and nights spent in cramped cold rooms.

I thought on… my father had sent my brother Edward to his own Court at Ludlow when he was but three years old. My mother's family surrounded him in his castle there. Anthony Woodville was in overall charge of making his nephew a prince, skilled in the art of all that would be needed to make him a fine king.

I had seen my brother very rarely since then, only on very special family occasions when he had made the long journey from the Welsh borders and now at twelve years old he rides to London with Dickon.

At eighteen, I was only too aware of the political game now being played and I shuddered to think of the outcome.

That very night I heard the shout of the men who were in Gloucester's livery filling the streets near to the Palace.

News of Gloucester's movements soon reached our confinement by the unusual means of Jane Shore.

I was shocked by the news that this former mistress of my father's had become a confidant to my mother. I had always been under the impression that Mistress Shore was hated deeply by my mother.

I had also learnt that since the death of my father the sensual Jane had become the mistress of my half brother, Thomas and William Hastings and it was Hastings who believed it was his duty to keep the queen informed. It was also he who was giving Jane the news she was now about to report.

172

I was puzzled by the actions of Sir William for he was thought to be allied to Dickon. I thought on, maybe he was now trying to bring the two sides together?

I knew of the contempt for Hastings shown by my mother for when my father was alive she held the charismatic and dashing Hastings chiefly responsible for my father's debauched lifestyle which ultimately led to his early death.

Jane curtsied low before my mother gave her permission to rise. 'Come girl tell me what you know of Richard's plans.'

Jane talked freely to my mother and to her lover Thomas Grey. I stood by and listened with interest as the conversation progressed.

Jane's voice was audibly nervous, as she looked the queen in the eye. 'My Lord Hastings has informed me that Gloucester has made all the lords swear an allegiance to young King Edward and the council, at this very minute, are making arrangements for your son's coronation.'

My mother put her long white fingers to her face and thought.

Jane finished her report by repeating what Richard was telling the council. 'The Duke of Gloucester has promise that they in the sanctuary have nothing to fear from him and that he wished with all his heart that they would come out of sanctuary and attend Edwards coronation.'

I believed my uncle as he had never lied before and had always been loyal and true to my father.

But my mother would not listen; shaking her head wildly from side to side she spoke with venom. 'Tell the Duke of Gloucester that I believe that he wishes to rule the country himself and use my son as a puppet king.'

When Jane had made a final curtsy and left our presence, there was predictability in my voice as I spoke to her. 'Mother,' I began, 'why do you act so?'

Looking at me with rage filled eyes, she answered. 'I am surrounded by enemies who have bided their time, waiting for your father to die. With my son as king I have a protector, without my Eddy as king I will be at the mercy of my many enemies.'

I knew that my mother believed this with all her being and she felt that her fears were very real and it was these feelings that were leading her to destroy her own family.

With this in mind I concluded that nothing would change my mother's mind about Dickon and she would not stop in her scheming until one of them was completely destroyed.

Rocking her body from side to side and chewing her lip my mother went on. 'I do not want Gloucester as Lord Protector.' She thought on. 'If we could have crowned your brother quickly, there would be no need for a protector as his authority would cease as soon as my son would have been crowned.'

I sighed and tried to make my mother see reason. 'But it is what father wanted. I am sure that father would not have wished it so if he thought Edward would be in any danger. Dickon loved father very much and would want to carry out his last wishes.'

With motionless eyes my mother looked at me and spoke with even more venom. 'Not danger...power!'

It was then that I began to understand my mother. It was her power as Queen of England that she desperately wanted to retain no matter what the outcome. The futile gestures that needed to be made to

174

her as queen she did not want to lose and was prepared to do anything to keep them.

I did not pursue the conversation. In great despair I retired to my small dark room inside the sanctuary that I was to share, this second time, with my sister Cecily and prayed that all would be well with my family and that reconciliation would soon be made with my Uncle Dickon.

It was the last week in May and I had learned from the people who kept my mother inform that my brother's coronation had been set for a new date, the twenty second day of June and all of the nobles wished, above anything else, that my mother would come out of sanctuary with us, her children, and make peace with our Uncle, The Duke of Gloucester.

Both sides were nervous and a tension could be felt throughout the capital and the people began to ask why the royal family were shut away in side the Abbey.

Dickon had my brother lodged inside the palatial rooms of The Tower for fear of plots to undermine my dead father's wishes, although the majority of the nobles were in favour, and Dickon was officially made Protector by way of a small ceremony with all the London dignitaries in attendance.

He immediately set about having weekly meetings in the Great Hall at Westminster with the council and the first thing on their agenda was the task of crowning his young nephew.

My mother would not hear reason and for me the days in sanctuary dragged on. The rooms were even drearier than I remembered, with damp walls and darkened hallways and I could not help but think that because of my mother's scheming ways I would not be in this predicament.

The situation got much worse when I learnt that there was another plot being hatched, which involved killing Dickon.

I had overheard voices, my half brother talking in a small side room with Lord Hastings. Glancing about to make sure there was no one in earshot, I pressed my ear to the door. What I could make out was that Hasting had changed allegiances and now wanted my mother as his ally, no doubt my mother had persuaded him that he could have some powerful position in the government if he put in with her.

I knew that I could not let this happen, I had to get word to Dickon of the treachery going on for he trusted Hastings implicitly, for I remembered that it was William Hastings who had sent Dickon the message of my mother's treachery in London and had urged him to capture the Prince and travelled quickly to the capital.

As I thought on my head throbbed with the urgency of my problem. I could not leave the sanctuary and go directly to my uncle for fear that my mother would find out, as my mother had her spies everywhere. I needed a discrete way to make contact with Dickon but how?

Then an idea came to me. One of my uncle's friends and most loyal and trusted council members was John Howard. The Howard family had been loyal to the Yorkist cause longer than anyone could remember. He was also housed very close by and was often in the Palace Hall at Westminster on official business; my thoughts were that he would act as a go between for me with my uncle.

After deciding that he would be the perfect person to contact, I went about writing a letter setting out my fears.

In my dingy room by the light of a single candle I began to write my warning letter. With trembling hands I began to set down the words.

My trusted Howard... it has come to my attention that there is a plot to kill the Lord Protector...the main perpetrator being Lord Hastings...from one who cares.

I justified my actions as I thought of my mother's devious scheming. With trembling hands, I placed the hot wax on the rolled parchment to seal the letter. I would not mark it; I did not want Howard to know who the sender was.

I would need a trusted messenger to take it to Howard one who would deliver my words to no one but him and would keep my identity a secret. There was one that I trusted more than any other inside the sanctuary a young man named John Gillies. With great caution I summoned him to me.

'Master Gillies, please take this letter to Lord Howard. Do not give it to anyone else and do not reveal who the sender is.'

In silence Gillies bowed, he had been my personal messenger for over eight years and luckily had come into sanctuary with the family. I knew that if I could trust anyone it would be him.

When he had gone I wondered if I had done the right thing. My concerns soon abated for I knew that more than anything else I could not bare it if Dickon were murdered and I had done nothing to stop it.

******

It was the hottest June day anyone could remember, the temperature soared into the nineties and the weather made the confines of the Abbey even more intolerable.

Inside there was nervousness as everyone was holding his or her breath waiting to see what Dickon would do next, as he had been angered by the news that my step brother, Thomas Grey, had at the dead of night, escaped the sanctuary and was now in Paris with the exiled Lancastrian, Henry Tudor.

It was late afternoon when my mother called for a meeting of the family as she had some important news.

Waiting for my mother to begin her address to us, I could see that she was trembling and her beautiful face had begun to show the strain of the past few years.

Taking in a gulp of air my mother began, 'Hasting has been executed!'

There were gasps of disbelief. My mother swallowed hard and carried on. 'Hastings was taken from the council meeting by the Protector's men and beheaded on the Tower Green.' I lowered my eyes and crossed myself at this news.

After a small pause my mother continued. 'Hastings showed his disapproval of the plan by the Protector and his cohorts to side line my son, Eddy, and make The Duke of Gloucester King.'

Taking a deep breath my mother tried to keep her composure as she carried on. 'Whatever Lord Hastings faults he would never let Edward's son be robbed of his birthright.'

My mother looked totally shocked by the news as she continued. 'Bishop Morton, one who is also for our cause, has been arrested together with Thomas Rotherham and Sir Thomas Stanley.

Gloucester's men go about the London streets calming its citizens. They say that there was a plot against the Protector's life and it came to light when he questioned Mistress Shore.'

Laced with fear, I kept quiet about my part in the plots discovery even though Jane Shore was being blamed for the uncovering of the plotters. I had learnt that Jane had confessed, under pressure, to being involved and had informed on her fellow conspirators.

I felt pangs of sorrow for my former confidant especially when the very next day she was forced to walk through the London streets dressed in only her under garments, bare footed and carrying a lighted taper as a sign of penance for her deeds and then she was sent to the prison at Newgate.

My mother had now broken down and was weeping and her reddened eyes were beckoning me for my support. I went to her and helped her retreat to the relative calm of her room to rest.

Clutching my hand and staring wildly my mother's voice was strained as she spoke to me. 'I fear for us all,' she moaned as she was laid on her bed. A bed that was not the grand one she was use to. It was plain oak with the coverlet made of course wool.

My tone was calming, 'mother please rest now. We will talk again in the morning when your strength has returned.'

There was no comforting her; almost immediately, the very next day, my mother was now involving others in more plots. She had gained the help of her physician Dr Lewis Callian.

Then three days after the execution of Hastings, on the sixteenth day of June, I was awoken by increased activity on the river. Still in my night attire I ran to the small window and looked down onto the gentle flowing summer Thames. A great army of men, eight boats in all, were rowing towards Westminster.

With straining eyes, I could make out some of the men. I saw John Howard and his son, Thomas, the Duke of Buckingham, Thomas Bourchier, Arch Bishop of Canterbury, John Russell, Bishop of Lincoln and at the head of them in the leading boat I saw my Uncle Dickon. Quickly I dressed and hurried to my mother's rooms.

The Arch Bishop had already an audience with the queen in the presence of a small delegation. I could see that my mother was greatly flustered and holding her youngest son near she began to speak in firm tones. 'I will not let my son out of sanctuary.'

On seeing me, his eldest sister, young Richard of York ran to be next to me. I put out my arms and held him close. I could feel that my brother was trembling and I could hear his muffled crying.

Shaking his head in despair the Arch Bishop replied in lowered tones. 'You have no choice.' There was a momentarily pause and then he added. 'The Duke of Gloucester is adamant to the point where the armed men will intervene. He is insistent that York must be present at his brother's coronation and Gloucester has promised that the boy would be restored to you after the coronation. '

My mother motioned to her son. Hesitantly my brother left my side and sheepishly went to our mother.

'Nothing untoward would become of him.' The Arch Bishop reassured. 'I have The Duke's solemn promise. He only wants the younger brother to be in support of the elder'

The Arch Bishop watched as my mother hugged her son, her eyes were full of sadness as she spoke. 'Farewell my child.'

Then in turn we, his sisters, said our tearful goodbyes. With a kerchief to her face, to stifle her sobs, our mother handed him over into the care of the Arch Bishop who pledged body and soul as security for the boy.

Weeping with emotions my little brother left sanctuary. As I watched the boy go, tears flooded into my eyes, although I was sure that the giving up my brother to my uncle was a step towards the bringing together of our family. There was no way the wounds could be healed with my brother in the sanctuary; he belonged in the stateroom of the Tower together with my brother Edward.

However, there was no consoling my mother after her son's departure. She would recall her young sons as little angles and blond haired cherubs.

Then, after the first week our mother stopped talking about them as she spiralled even deeper into despair.

The next few weeks were long and fraught with tension and everyone was in a sombre mood, all too afraid to speak, in fear of the queen's tears.

Our formal lessons had stopped and my sisters and I sat for hour in our rooms, fervently predicting our fate as we finished off our embroidery pieces.

During the days that followed northern armies began to appear in London.

It was on Sunday, after morning mass, when my sister Cecily and me talked in the privacy of our shared room.

Cecily reverberated to me what she had heard. 'Our uncle has declared us bastards and that we are no longer royal princesses. He called the Londoners' to St Paul's Cross and there he had The Lord Mayor's brother, Dr Ralph Shaa, read out a most extraordinary statement.'

Cecily's tone was serious, more than I had even known, and I knew that my younger sister was nervous. Clutching Cecily's arm to give her courage, I began to speak in whispered tones. 'Go on Ce, tell me all you know.'

Swallowing hard Cecily continued; her pace was quick in quiet hushed tones. 'Firstly Shaa claimed that our father was a bastard... our grandmother was unfaithful to our grandfather with a common archer. He then continued to tell the crowds gathered that our mother and father were not actually married because our father was already married to another lady... Eleanor Butler and had a child. The poor lady was committed to a nunnery to keep her away from public life and died in 1468...no one knows what became of her child.'

I listened with interest, although I knew that this undisclosed news was what led to Uncle George's demise.

I could only stare in bemusement. 'How is our mother?' for I presumed that she knew of these developments.

Cecily's eyes widened and she shook her head, her blond locks waving from side to side. 'She is moved to hysteria, for she has been told that Uncle Dickon intends to declare himself the rightful King of England.'

There was only one thought in my mind at that moment...my brothers...what would become of them?

It was the very next day that my mother's fears were to come true. Harry Buckingham, Richard's close ally, had assembled a group of nobles to reinstate Shaa's accusations and insisted that there was only one man fit to rule England...The Duke of Gloucester.

The suffering for my mother continued, as she received news that her brother Anthony and her twenty seven year old son Richard, who were prisoners in the north, had been executed for treason. They had apparently admitted plotting to kill the Protector.

More bad news reached her when the fleet under my Uncle Sir Edward Woodville had been brought back to an English port. Mercifully, Dickon had offered a free pardon to all but the leaders. Sir Edward managed to escape to Brittany with all but two ships.

I could do nothing but, with my sisters, try and comfort our mother the best we could.

Everything that our mother had worked so hard for her entire life was now slipping away from her and she had taken to her room in an exhausted state of despair.

Her plans for us became wild. She begged me to try and escape to France or Scotland. She could disguise me, dress me as a servant, I could slip out of the sanctuary without being noticed.

The idea was not one to please me. I did not want to leave my family and my country especially as I knew that no harm was going to come to us.

In the days that followed, conciliatory messages from Dickon came frequently to my mother. He insisted that he meant no harm to her or her daughters and that he was merely assuming his rightful responsibility for the crown: a crown under God's law must pass through the true, not the bastard line of descent and as for the execution of her kin he spoke of regret but reiterated that he had uncovered certain treasonable act that had to be meted out the ultimate punishment.

In the privacy of my mother's room I approached her. Holding her hand tightly I uttered words that had to be said. 'Could George and now Dickon be right?'

Biting her lip and looking noticeably nervous my mother did not answer. I lowered my voice to a whisper. 'You know that you and father were married in secret. He could have married this Eleanor Butler in secret as well. Robert Stillington, Bishop of Bath and Wells,

183

swears on oath that he witnessed such a marriage. He felt that he had to conceal the fact as long as father lived, for fear of the king's displeasure.'

My mother lowered her head as a flood of tears trickled down her cheeks. I hugged her and kissed her forehead; I could feel the pain that she was going through.

I again broke the silence. 'We cannot stay in sanctuary for ever...think about what I have said.'

Leaving my mother lying quietly in her room, I walked the corridors of the Abbey alone. There was a nagging in my brain; I could not help thinking about my young brothers, where were they and why had no one been allowed to see them? There was only one thing to do, I must write to my uncle enquiring about their plight.

In my room I thoughtfully composed a letter, which I hoped on a swift reply, an answer, which would put my mother's mind at ease.

Dear uncle, I hope this letter finds you in good health...I ask about the well being of my brothers...would you send us some reassurance that they are safe and well.

I signed my letter, your loving niece Bessy.

Finding Master Gillies I slipped the scroll into his hands and whispered my instruction. 'Give this letter to John Howard without delay. Tell him it is for the Duke of Gloucester.'

More than a week went by and there was no reply to my letter.

＊＊＊＾＾

The day before his coronation Richard had created John Howard, Duke of Norfolk; no doubt my warnings of treason had something to do with it. Also honoured were, Sir Thomas Howard and Francis Lovell.

More interestingly the conspirator, Thomas Lord Stanley was delivered from the keep of the Tower and restored to favour, like wise Bishop Rotherham was freed and returned to his ecclesiastical life. John Morton, Bishop of Ely, however was kept in captivity at Buckingham's castle in Wales.

On the fourth day of July the activity about the Palace began to intense. All along the river preparation were going on for Richard's arrival at The Tower.

Music from the Royal Barge drifted towards sanctuary and could no doubt be heard by the family cooped up inside. Elizabeth Woodville could only imagine the scene taking place downstream... Richard, calling himself King Richard III, would land with his wife Anne at the Royal Stairs, next to the wharf at The Tower of London.

Together they would be saluted by all the important dignitaries as well as being welcomed by the commoners. Together they would proceed to the Tower, hear the cheers of acclamation, and bathe in the glow of well-being. For in two days Anne would be Queen of England and Richard, the most just and righteous man would be the king.

The only news that reached sanctuary was that Richard had named the day of his coronation, on the sixth day of July. Richard had decided to place the crown on his own head. It had taken him days of agonising, but finally he had made up his mind.

After accepting Bishops Stillington's story of Edward's children being illegitimate a proclamation was made by parliament declaring that Richard was the rightful King and he had been ordained with the consent of both the Lords and the Commons.

Once again a delegation came to the sanctuary and pleaded with Elizabeth that her and her daughters should attend the coronation but their pleading fell on deaf ears and the family stayed firmly housed in the sanctuary.

The morning of the sixth day of July was bright and sunny. Every street was lined with banners bearing Richard's emblem, The White Boar. With the sound of trumpets blowing and drums beating, Richard and Anne were brought from the Tower to the Abbey.

In the king's procession, behind the bishops was Cardinal Bourchier, followed by Duke of Northumberland with the Sword of Mercy, Lord Stanley with the Constable's Mace, and the Duke of Suffolk with the Sceptre and the Earl of Lincoln with the Orb. The newly created Duke of Norfolk carried the Crown and his son held the Sword of State. Following theses came Viscount Lovell and the Earl of Kent bearing the Swords of Justice. The Duke of Buckingham held Richard's train, and behind him walked the remaining earls and viscounts.

After the king's procession came the queen's. Her regalia were borne by two earls and a viscount.

At the high alter Richard and Anne stripped to the waist and were anointed with holy oils. They then changed into cloth of gold and Cardinal Bourchier set the crowns upon their heads. A te dum was sung and the royal couple received communion, before returning to Westminster Hall for the coronation banquet which lasted for over four hours.

For Richard the coronation was a triumph. Not only was it a brilliant spectacle, but also it had been attended by virtually the entire peerage of England, including Henry Tudor's mother, Margaret Beaufort, who carried Anne's train.

The city celebrated with costumed tableaux, parades of knights and dignitaries, music, food and conduits flowed with free wine.

The people of London talked about nothing else for weeks afterwards. Richard left the capital on the twenty second day of July with his wife and son. They had set out on a progress to show themselves to the populace.

Everywhere he went he was cheered and townsfolk danced in the streets, boys and girls with flowers in their hair accompanied by fiddlers and pipers. Some began to call their new monarch, Good King Richard, as they were ever thankful to him for preventing the treacherous Woodville plans and plunging the country once more into civil war.

On the twenty fourth day he reached Oxford and he dined at Magdalen College. The following day he travelled to Woodstock Palace and gave the nearby forest back to the common people, for King Edward had annexed it for his own pleasures.

Richard then spent a few days with his close friend Francis Lovell. Throughout August the king remained on progress contenting the people wherever he went.

By September he had reached York and there was a great deal of excitement amongst the pomp and pageantry. The city streets were hung with cloth of arras, tapestry work and other colourful banners. Here again he received the crown and on Sunday the seventh day of September an even more magnificent sight took place. This was the day that Richard's his ten year old son was made Prince of Wales and Earl of Chester in York Cathedral.

After the ceremony the young Prince walked the streets accompanied by his parents meeting the ecstatic citizen.

Richard addressed the crowds telling them that coming to York was like coming home.

York was very much the king's city and Richard and his family loved it and its people, staying there for several more weeks, joining the townsfolk's pageants, and watching several of their mystery plays.

******

While Dickon was busy impressing his subjects with the majesty of his office, inside the sanctuary life was very different for me. No merriment only the drabness of the ecclesial corridors and the constant weeping and moaning of my mother, for she was absolutely uncompromising; she ignored all petitions for her to leave sanctuary.

I had noticed that an armed guard had been placed around The Abbey and the place was beginning to look like a fortress.

There were also stories circulating that my brother's had been murdered as no one had seen them at the Tower since mid July and my mother's conditions got worse. She would go days without eating or taking sustenance and would make herself faint and weak.

My mother gulped her sobs and with reddened and swollen eyes would focus on us, her daughters. Cecily and I tried with great effort to comfort her, but she would not be calm and would not listen to my words of reason. My two younger sisters, Anne and Catherine wept and little Bridget knelt and prayed. I tried in vain to give hope and solace to my mother.

My voice was strained and I took in a gulp of air, 'mother you must not believe these wicked rumours.

Dickon would never harm those boys! Please talk to the men who come from him to offer you an olive branch.'

My mother was obviously not listening; she had already made up her mind as to what had happened to her sons. Taking a deep breath, my mother spoke in harsh tones. 'May God bring vengeance on those involved in my innocent babes' murder!' Taking another deep breath she went on, 'I fear for us all… my daughters… you must make your escape before the same fate befalls you also.'

I felt myself shudder at my mother's blind reasoning. Looking closely at her I could see a faraway look in her eyes. She had lost all sense of logic and had begun to rant and rave at the slightest provocation. A kind of madness had possessed her.

That night I reflected on all I had heard, the rumours and the accusations. If only I could talk to my uncle and hear his side of the story. It was true that he had not answered my letter, but there may be some reasonable explanation why he had not. He had been extremely busy these last months. I made up my mind to try and speak to him as soon as he returned to London.

The months dragged on and the summer turned into autumn and Dickon and his family lingered in the north. The people there adored him and he was finding it hard to leave. With every month he stayed in the north I knew that his enemies in the south of the country were spreading the heinous rumours about the fate of my brother…the two boy princes, that they had met a violent death at the hands of Dickon's servants.

Inside the sanctuary I was at an all time low, my life had become unbearable and I had to get out and get out soon, for it was now over seven months since I had entered these dismal confines. The air was becoming increasingly stuffy and for the sake of my sanity I

189

decided to stay away from my mother, who had become insufferably neurotic.

I had concluded that my mother had enough doting family around her and I wanted above all else to keep well away from the plots and devious schemes that she was always hatching. She made plans to escape, to incite the citizens of London to revolt, and to employ someone to kill Dickon. There were always men whispering in corners and unknown women walking the corridors in black cloaks passing coded messages.

Then one evening whilst I was reading quietly in my private chamber, for I was now spending hours at a time alone, a message came to me. I was to attend my mother immediately. Closing my book I hurried to my mother's private room and waited there patiently for her presence.

There were many people within whom I did not recognise. A low murmur went around as the ensemble waited for Elizabeth to be with them.

My mother finally made her entrance, several family members accompanied her, but I was surprised to see her physician, Dr Callian by her side.

With elegance my mother sat down and in a strained voice began to talk. 'The people who I have summoned here today I trust implicitly. Not one word spoken here tonight must go beyond these walls.' The people in attendance looked at one another and nodded.

Taking a deep breath and sitting tall and majestic, the look she had at the time she was queen returned to her countenance. Her voice was strong and steady. 'My dear doctor has been working hard on our behalf. He has been the go between with those outside sanctuary who want to help us. Margaret Beaufort, Thomas Stanley' wife, has been a staunch ally. She has, with the help of Bishop Morton, managed to get the

190

weak headed Duke of Buckingham on our side. He is dissatisfied with the land and wealth he has been given by Richard and Morton has promised him bigger gains if he joins us.'

There was a raised mumble as the people gathered began to realise what this could mean for Harry Buckingham was a duke of the royal blood and many would follow him.

I lowered my head at this revelation, my suspicions of Buckingham were proved right, and he would betray family and friends to further his ambitions. I thought on. I had known through whispers from within the Sanctuary that Margaret Beaufort, the Countess of Richmond, had already received Dickon's wrath when he found out from his spies the activities the lady was getting into behind his back.

He was going to attain the lady for treason, for sending writings, tokens and messages to her son, Henry, The Earl of Richmond, stirring him to invade the realm; but in consideration of the services which her husband, Lord Stanley, had rendered the king, he forbore to attain the Countess.

But the act declared her lands to be forfeited, degraded her from all titles of dignity, and settled her property on her husband for life, with remainder to the crown.

As the conversation began to surge around me, my mother signalled a hush with her thin pale hands and continued. 'Buckingham has agreed to lead a revolt against Richard and overthrow him. Already the citizens of London, Kent, Hampshire, Sussex, Dorset, Somerset, Wiltshire, Berkshire and many other southern counties were in agreement to overthrow the king.'

A smile came over my mother's face as she continued. 'There is one thing that Margaret asks; she wishes to bind the undertaking with a promise of matrimony between her son and my eldest daughter Bessy.'

My mother's eyes found mine and a softness came over her face as she went on. 'I am now sworn to oppose Richard and I hereby pledge my daughter, the Lady Bessy, to be betrothed in marriage to Henry Tudor.'

I could not believe my ears. My mother had not consulted in me at all, it had come as a total surprise to me and I tried hard to hide my indignations. I felt my body rock from side to side as I struggled to regain my composure. My mind was in turmoil... who was this Henry Tudor? What was his claim to the throne?

I knew that through his mother, he traced his descent from John of Gaunt's extra marital liaison with Catherine Swynford. On his father's side Henry was the grandson of an obscure Welsh gentleman, Owen Tudor, who found his way into the bed of Henry V's widow, Queen Catherine.

Keeping my thoughts to myself and remaining silent, I smiled a wry smile at the gathering whose eyes were now all upon me.

'Bessy,' my mother gushed holding her arms wide. 'Come give your mother a kiss to show those here present that you give you whole hearted support to our plan.'

Calmly I went forward and kissed my mother respectfully on the cheek, although inside my stomach was churning and a feeling of sickness gripped me.

******

For days I thought about my fate; to be married to someone I did not know, did not love. I always knew that I would be married for political reasons, for it had forever been the way of royal princesses to be bandied about like parcel goods with no thought of their feelings, but Henry Tudor, I concluded, was not a suitable candidate and anyway I was now sure in my heart that I loved my Uncle Dickon.

I knew that my mother had only agreed to this betrothal in the hope that it would spur Tudor on to invade, defeat Dickon and declare himself king and that I would become his wife and she, once again, would be a major player in the court.

I sighed and thought back to a happier time. In the past my noble father had rejected kings and princes as not good enough for his royal daughter and now I was to be married to this Welsh upstart. My father would never have dreamed of such a union.

My mind went back to the day when my father announced my betrothed to the Dauphin...I remembered the joy and the celebrations that were held at the court in anticipation of it...I thought on...that betrothal was broken; perhaps with the unravelling of time this one would be also, for firstly Buckingham had to defeat Dickon.

My dislike for the arrogant Harry Buckingham had now grown into hatred, he had been one of Dickons trusted friends; he had even carried Dickons train at his coronation.

I had heard all about how he tries to up stage the royal magnificence; his badge of the flaming wheel is flaunted everywhere.

I knew however that Dickon was grateful for his support and had given him wide powers in Wales and in the western counties. I now knew how he repaid Dickon for all his gifts and honours, by listening to Bishop Morton's lies and committing treason and rebellion!

*The old wily bishop, whilst a prisoner at Buckingham's
castle had probably fed his ego with hollow promises.*

*Giving a sigh of dismay, I continued thinking.
Although, most of the south supported Buckingham
Dickon could rely on the north and most of all he could
rely of me, for I had no intention of marrying this upstart
Tudor, but for now I would keep my feelings to myself,
as I feared everyone.*

*There were so many spies who were acting as
couriers for Margaret, relaying messages from
Sanctuary to her son, who had spent the last fourteen
years in exile in Brittany.*

*Margaret Beaufort, a lady who had only months
before carried Queen Anne's train was now a most
dangerous enemy to an unsuspecting Dickon.*

*Staying quiet and remaining almost invisible in
the shadows of the Abbey over the next few weeks I
listened keenly to those about me and I had learnt that
the uprising was set for St Luke's Day, the eighteenth
day of October.*

*Sure enough on that very day, I heard the news
from my elated mother that Buckingham had raised his
standard in Wales. To reinforce this move, Richmond
was to land upon the Welsh coast with an army of
foreign forces paid for by monies raise by Margaret
Beaufort.*

*My mother was in an exuberant mood. Making
plans for when I, her daughter, would be queen. 'We will
leave sanctuary in triumph with you as Queen of
England, my child,' she gushed.*

*I gave her a wry smile and remained silent.
Deep in my heart I wished for a different outcome. I had
heard reports from Cecily and Veronique that Henry
was thin and balding with bad teeth. Desperately I*

wanted to leave sanctuary, but not with Henry, with Dickon.

Throughout the following days I feared that their treacherous plans were going well as Dickon was still dallying in the north on progress and there was absolutely no way that I could get a message of warning to him in time. I could only pray that the right outcome would prevail.

Nigh after night I would sit alone in my room and let my mind wander, morbid images kept entering it.

Then on the morning of November fifth the euphoria that was inside the sanctuary soon dissolved and my mother's mood changed dramatically.

Cecily swept pass my open door. 'Bessy, mother calls for our company.'

Dropping the book that I was reading I followed my sister to our mother's chambers.

'My dear loyal friends,' mother began. 'I have called you here to let you know the latest position out side these four walls.'

I stood silently next to my sister as we both waited for our mother to continue. I could feel a strange feeling in the pit of my stomach as I dreaded what I was about to hear.

Taking a deep breath, my mother continued addressing us. 'The rebellion has failed. As you know the weather has been torrential rain for nigh on seven days and a harassed and low spirited Buckingham's army lost heart and melted across the Welsh boarder. Buckingham was betrayed by one of his retainers where he sought refuge. He has been caught and executed in Salisbury's market square.'

There were gasps as my mother broke down into floods of tears. I was only thankful that my prayers had been answered.

195

Henry Tudor was not a man to take chances and had immediately returned to Brittany, but I had a feeling that I had not heard the last of Henry as I knew that as long as my mother lived she would not give up her scheming ways especially now that she had a powerful ally in The Duchess of Richmond and her son.

Indeed my mother had not lost hope of a union between Tudor and me and almost immediately more secret plots were being hatched.

I too was scheming a way out of my predicament and my plans became all the more urgent when I learnt that Henry had taken an oath on Christmas Day at Reims Cathedral to make me his wife.

I breathed a sigh of relief, as thankfully, Dickon had managed to quell the rebellion without raising a sword. For the time being my prayers had been answered and Dickon had survived the assassins' plots, returned in triumph to London to hold a magnificent Christmas court.

There were, however, no festivities in sanctuary only solemn services and prayers.

My mother was looking crushed and dejected, any hope of Henry Tudor making her dreams come true had almost disappeared and the despair which she harboured and her constant laments for her brothers and sons made life in sanctuary totally unbearable for me as I was now at my wits end.

******

As the winter set in my mother's hopes of a successful rebellion was ebbing away and most of my family were becoming more and more anxious to leave the gloom of sanctuary and return to court.

It was an exceptionally cold February day and I huddled together with my sister Cecily for warmth. The *fires in our rooms were not the roaring magnificent beasts they were at Westminster. The monks and the abbot denied themselves of many of the pleasures of the flesh and a warm fire was one of them.*

Cecily began with teeth chattering. 'Mother must make her peace with Uncle Dickon or we will all die in the terrible place.'

I looked at my sister and smiled, 'I believe you may be right. We must go and speak with her right away and try and make her see sense.'

Wrapped in feather filled quilts the two of us made our way along the draughty corridors to our mother's room. We found her sitting close to the fire hearth deep in thought. Approaching her with caution, for we could never tell in what mood our mother was in, we both sat close.

Taking a deep breath I began to speak in soft tones, 'mother, we come to beg you to make peace with Uncle Dickon.'

Cecily added to the heart felt request. 'Please... we do not care if we are no longer royal Princesses... we just want to leave this dreadful place.'

I noticed that our mother was looking much calmer of late, as if resolved to her fate.

An emotionless face turned towards us. 'I have this very day, received a letter from your uncle. He swears that nothing evil has become of my two young sons and he promises that he will do no harm to any of us. He even talks about promoting Thomas.'

I looked hopefully at Cecily, could our mother be thinking the unthinkable?

Our mother took a long breath, 'I have made a decision. If Richard is willing to swear in font of Parliament what he has promised me here in writing,

197

then we will return to court. I have told the Arch Bishop to forward my sentiments to Gloucester'

Cecily and I hugged and kissed our forlorn mother. We were both elated. Reassuringly I smiled at her. I spoke with a joyous heart. 'I am sure that uncle Dickon will do that, for he wants nothing more than to be a good king.'

My mother looked at me now; she saw a radiant and confident girl and sighed.

I took her hand in mine and squeezed it as I spoke, 'I am sure that he desperately wants to make peace with his family…don't worry…everything is going to be alright.'

Later that day, once again I sought to make contact with my uncle although I had not received a reply to my previous correspondence.

Thoughts of what may have occurred went through my mind; maybe he did not receive my letter, or perhaps what he wanted to say in reply was of too delicate a nature to put into writing. Whatever the reason, I knew that the time had come to let my uncle know the exact belief of all those in sanctuary.

Later that night, by the light of a small candle, I set about putting my feelings into words.

I reiterated my mother's fears and that only if he swore our safe conduct in Parliament would my mother ever consider returning to court. I added that I personally was desperate to leave sanctuary and trusted him implicitly with my future.

I dispatched the letter in the usual way and waited, once again, for a reply. Several days passed and once again no word from my uncle reached me. Then at last, on the evening of the first day of March, the news that I had been praying for reached sanctuary.

Dickon had gather Parliament together and made a most remarkable statement...I, Richard, by grace of God King of England, in the presence of you all, promise and swear upon these holy Evangelies of God by me personally touched, that if the daughters of Dame Elizabeth Grey, later calling herself Queen of England, that is to wit Elizabeth, Cecily, Anne, Catherine and Bridget, will come unto me out of sanctuary of Westminster and be guided, and ruled, and demeaned after me, then I shall see that they shall be surety of their lives, and also do not suffer any manner of hurt by any manner person or persons...I shall put them in honest places of good name and fame...and I shall marry such of them as now marriageable to gentlemen born, and give everyone of them in marriage lands and tenements to the yearly value of two hundred marks for the terms of their lives...and moreover I promise to them that if any surmise of evil report be made to me of them, by any persons, that then I shall not give thereunto faith nor credence, nor therefore put them to any manner of punishment...In witness whereof to this writing of my Oath and promise aforesaid, in your said presence made I have set my sign manual the first day of March 1484, the first year of my reign.

To my delight, after ten months in sanctuary, my mother had finally agreed to leave the inner sanctum of the Abbey.

It was a beautiful spring morning when I, and the rest of those who had been cloistered there for nearly a year, earnestly thanked the monks for their kindness. Each of us in turn embraced The Abbot, John Eastney, and stepped into the weak sunshine.

I gulped in a deep breath of fresh air and looked around. There was no ceremony, no cries from well wishers. I then realised that I was no longer a princess of the realm but a mere gentlewoman.

Gone were the privileges and precious jewels and I now had to wear the clothing of a simple woman.

It was, however, good to be out in the world again, to feel the gentle breezes blowing softly on my face, to hear and see once again the sights so long been denied to me.

But most of all I was now able to focus on what my future held. I was too young and vibrant to be kept shut away. Moreover I was determined not to dwell on the past but to look forward to the hope and expectations of the future. Now I would return to my uncle's court a very confident, beautiful and sensual nineteen-year-old woman.

******

Richard was delighted with the outcome and insisted that they all stay at Westminster, but haughty Elizabeth Woodville was not about to stay at court and petitioned the king to be released from court attendance and be granted a separated residence. Both points were granted although, because of her past plots and schemes, she was to be under the guard of John Nesfield.

Richard had his spies, who would keep him well informed of the Dowager Queen's involvements in any further plots for his downfall.

He did however think that the lady had suffered enough for her past crimes and hoped desperately that she had learnt something form the last nine months inside the Abbey.

Richard thought on...he realised that now he had a huge responsibility for his brother's daughters and decided that they would all be put into the household of

Queen Anne. From there the girls must now rely on themselves for whatever they might accomplish there.

Richard's thoughts then turned to the challenged that the new campaigning season would bring. He knew that there were still treasonable plots to enthrone Henry Tudor and on the twentieth day of March, with the advice of those advisors who were closest to him, Richard decided to move the entire court to the middle of the country, for he felt better positioned to answer an attack from any direction from this stronghold. He established his military headquarters behind the mighty battlements of Nottingham Castle.

He did not intend, however to become a prisoner of fear...playing a waiting game...when and where Henry Tudor would invade his realm, and so in the spring of that year King Richard once again went on progress.

Everywhere the court travelled they were welcomed with gusto by the people. One place that was overjoyed in the king's visit was the cloisters of Cambridge University.

During the week spent in Cambridge the royal couple made generous endowments to King's and Queen's Colleges. Both these colleges were been begun by King Henry VI and his Queen.

Everywhere the new king and queen went the crowds cheered, Richard had saved them from more civil war and they were grateful to him for it.

The people began to love their new royal family as they began to realise that Richard was going to be a good just king.

******

I became Queen Anne's Chief Lady of the Wardrobe. I took great pleasure in my newfound role and performed my duties with enthusiasm, as Anne possessed some fine clothes made from the most expensive of cloth, silks and rich velvets and they were of the most up to date fashion brought over from the European courts.

My royal duties included supervising the laying out of the queen's garments and the overseeing of Anne's tailors who worked endlessly on presenting her with fine dresses. My duties did not, however, bring me into contact with my uncle, as he always seemed so busy with affairs of state.

I had seen little of him since I came out of sanctuary but I was well aware of his constant worry that Henry Tudor was planning to invade and challenge him for his crown.

As each day passed I began to know Queen Anne more and more and I soon recognize her to be a very kind and thoughtful person who cared much for others. She was soft spoken and her demure stature gave rise to her nickname,' 'The Gentle Little Queen.'

I spent weeks at Anne's side advising her and helping her to wear the right garments for each day's events.

My duties included making ready the queen's wardrobe for travelling. The progress was slow with villagers lining the streets of every town and hamlet that the royal party passed through.

Great swathes of guilt about my feelings for Dickon began to play on my mind and I was unable to meet Anne's gaze when serving her.

My amorous feelings that I had for Dickon began to trouble me and I made enormous efforts to change them.

A future husband for me now was in Dickon's hands and I only hoped that one would be chosen for me soon.

The evenings at the Nottingham court were very subdued from those to be had in London and together us ladies read aloud and played quiet games of chess or backgammon.

Anne's small court of ladies was known to me, for among those who attended it was my fifteen-year-old sister Cecily.

Then only three weeks after the court had moved to Nottingham it was shaken with the arrival of some dreadful news. Dickon's nine-year-old son, little Ned, had died at Middleham Castle. Everyone at court shed many tears and my aunt and uncle were inconsolable.

To my surprise, the very next day on receiving the terrible news, a summons was made for me to go to my uncle's private chambers.

On my arrival I could feel the immense grief. Anne was sitting motionless and weeping openly, Dickon looked white and drawn.

I curtseyed; Dickon touched my hair as I rose. Composing himself he turned to me. 'We would like you to accompany us to Middleham...we would like you to be with the queen constantly...she suffers terribly from the feeling of guilt...that she was not with our son when he died...she will need continuous support which I know you can give her.'

Lowering my eyes I answered him. 'I am deeply sorry for your lost...I will do my up most to comfort the queen in her time of pain.'

Dickon looked at his wife and nodded and waved his hand. I could see that they were in no mood to talk and so I made a deep curtsey and left their presence.

Although the occasion was very sad, I was, nevertheless, excited at the prospect of travelling to Middleham. I had heard lots of stories of how Dickon

*favoured it of all his residences and I was curious to see
the castle for myself.*

*After a furious twelve hours of preparations, the
very next day we left. It was a long and hazardous
journey with an overwhelming feeling of sadness.*

*The litter I shared with the queen was made as
comfortable it could be in the circumstances. The roads
on which we travelled were in a dreadful condition due
to the heavy spring rains and every bump of the wheels
and every grind of the wagons were felt by the travellers
within the wagons.*

*I stayed close to the queen throughout. Anne
always the quiet, private individual spoke very little and
I was not expected to speak unless spoken to. The little
queen was wallowing in sadness and I thought is better
to leave her to her feelings.*

*Looking at Anne's small and insignificant
demeanour I found if very hard to believe that she had
been married to a prince as well as a king and the king
being Dickon.*

*With only the sound of the wheel turning and the
occasional shout from one of the men who rode
alongside the caravan I was alone with my thoughts and
there were hours in which to think about my life, where I
had been and where I was going. What was to become
of me? Dickon had promised to find me a husband, but
none had been proposed.*

*Dickon rode, ahead of the caravan escort, and
when the party rested for the night I was dismissed from
Anne's side and so, once again, I saw very little of my
uncle and did not speak to him once.*

******

*It was a fine morning when we finally reached
Middleham. The castle was set high on a mound above*

the rolling, climbing, Yorkshire countryside, which was breathtakingly beautiful, one of the most pleasant spots in the whole of England.

Grey clad houses and the freshly mowed fields surrounded it and the people of the village had come to pay their respects to their lord who was now their king.

Everyone looked sincerely moved at the death of his son. Old ladies wept openly and men shook their heads in disbelief and shock. The boy had always been sickly, but so had the father in his youth; once the boy ceased to grow his strength would return.

But the boy was now dead, no more wishful thinking and his parents plunged into further grief and despair. No prayers or words of comfort could soothe or ease their sorrow. I watched as their anguish bordered on madness.

The funeral which was held in St Nicolas's Chapel at the little church at nearby Sheriff Hutton was a terribly sad one. The entire surroundings were draped in black mourning cloth and as well as the king and queen the attendances were dressed in black from head to toe.

Colourful garments and frivolities were banned for the foreseeable future.

I stayed close to Anne who was overcome with grief and was near to collapse throughout the service. I heard through the servants that Anne blamed herself for her son's death.

Days and weeks passed and the bereavement went on and on. Everyone waited for the sorrow to exhaust itself.

Dickon became a changed man; all the meaning was taken from him being king when his only legitimate son died. His energy had drained and he had visibly aged.

Anne had become thin and pale and I could not help but notice Anne's wracked cough and choking breathing whenever I was attending her in her private chamber.

It was the middle of June; over two months had passed since the little Prince had been so cruelly taken from his loving parents. Dickon and Anne had shut themselves away, alone with their terrible grief and I had seen little of either one of them. Each morning I would go to the queen who would almost immediately dismiss me.

While it was a very distressing time, I could understand only too well why Dickon loved Middleham so much. As well as being in a most idyllic setting it was a most up to date of castles. Although not as big as some, it boasted the most modern and innovative architecture and up to date facilities, including sanitation in every bedroom.

I would spend my days walking in the castle grounds or reading in my favourite part of the castle gardens. The view from the ramparts was wonderful, looking out towards the gently rolling hills and valleys, looking down upon a small river backed by high moors.

I would sit alone beside a small fishpond and watch the golden carp swim in and out of the water lilies.

Loneliness began to grip me...I had always been surrounded by my large family and since most of them were now at Westminster I had no one to talk to who I felt close. There were servants and ladies of the court, but I missed my intimate talks with my sisters.

June turned into July and the surrounding trees were now shedding their pearl white blossoms.

A messenger approached me. I received a summoned that my uncle wanted to speak to me.

Following the page I was, to my surprise, shown into his Dickon's private chamber and all the people within were dismissed. I swallowed hard and lowered my head. It was the first time in many years, in fact since I was a woman grown; that I had been alone with Dickon and my heart raced and thudded inside my chest. I realised then that I had not lost any of my feelings for him, if anything they had become stronger.

Dickon motioned me to rise from the deep curtsey I had made. He began to speak. 'I have been meaning to speak with you for some time.'

He gesture me to sit and he took a seat opposite me and wrung his hands. Dickon's voice was soft, almost a whisper as he continued. 'I believe that I owe you my thanks...'

My heart and head were racing and I exhaled deeply as I gathered my thoughts, as I did not know in what respect he was thanking me.

Looking up at me, Dickon smiled, it was the first time I had seen him do so in many months and it lifted my heart and instinctively I smiled too.

Seeing that I looked a little puzzled, he enlightened me further... 'helping to persuade your mother to see reason...to come out of the sanctuary.'

I noticed that he began to become very awkward as he spoke to me, biting his lower lip and pulling at his ring on his little finger. I was well aware that he had an uneasy manner when talking to people, even more so in becoming king, but he had all ways spoken to me with ease, in a light jovial manner, and I did not like the change that had come over him. I could feel the stresses that he had been through since becoming king and I now realised that the young, carefree Dickon was gone forever.

Swallowing hard I took in a deep breath, as Dickon's blue piercing eyes focused on me I gave an answer. 'I thought that I had nothing to fear from you and I made my feeling felt.'

There was an awkward silence and I saw that Dickon looked unsettled as he once more began to twist and turn the stone studded ring on his little finger. I gathered my courage; I just had to know the answer to this next question, as it would influence the way I would feel about him. Looking directly at him I posed it. 'My brothers, what has happened to my brothers?'

He rose and began to pace the room as he spoke. 'I could not reply to your letters as I was advised by those few people who were privy to my intentions not to reveal my plans to anyone. You do understand that the whereabouts of your brothers would lead to those who wish my downfall to have an alternative banner to rally round.'

He turned to face me and I knew by the look in his eyes that he was telling me the truth. 'I cannot at this moment tell you where your brothers are I can only give you my word that they are safe and hope that you continue your trust in me.'

I nodded and once again our eyes met. His gaze gave my whole body a warm glow, for now I knew that my brothers were indeed safe.

My voice intensified. 'I do trust you…I have constantly had faith in you doing right for both your family and your country.'

I stopped myself from revealing too much of my true feelings. I thought it wise not to mention the episode with Lord Hastings, although I had my suspicions that Norfolk might have already guess my identity in writing the letter.

Dickon came towards me and took my hand. My emotions began to surge. 'Dearest Bessy...' there was a moment's pause as he held me at arms length and studied the girl who was now a beautiful woman. 'The queen tells me that you are very tentative to her needs.' Dickon had changed the subject and I was thankful for it.

My voice was soft as I spoke, 'I feel deeply for her.' I lowered my head, 'and of course you also must feel the lost of your son extremely hard to bear.'

He nodded and I realised that the tragic events that had taken place over the past several months had affected him even more than I first realised.

He moved closer to me. Could he hear my beating heart? 'I would like to be alone now,' he smiled and gently kissed me on the cheek.

******

For the next few months at Middleham Richard gradually began to piece his life back together. But for Queen Anne the death of her only child played heavily upon her, all meaning of life was gone and her own fragile health began to decline rapidly.

At the beginning of August Bessy had learned that the doctors who had been treating her had pronounced her too weak to engage in much strenuous activity and she had been advised not to share Richard's bed, for fear that the malady was catching.

Bessy too had been released from her service and the queen was now being looked after by a series of doctors and healing women.

Anne's mother, whose lands had been attained years ago by Edward, had gone to live with her youngest daughter soon after she married Richard.

The lady treated Middleham as her home and was very rarely from it and Anne's mother now took over the complete tending of her daughter and she was always on hand to give her the lotions and potions to help ease her distress and her pain. Anne's mother was now in control of the day to day running of Middleham and all in the household were under her orders.

It was no doubt a relief to Richard that he had his mother in law there for he could be confident that she would run his favourite castle well when he was not there for she had been the wife of its previous owner almost fifteen years before.

He also could take comfort that she would have her daughter's best interests at heart and would supervise closely the people in her attendance.

Although the circumstances at the court at Middleham were extremely sad the summer spent there amongst its walls were a wonderful experience to Bessy. For the first time in her life she felt a freedom never experienced before. She could do as she pleased, as she had been alleviated of her duties and now not being of royal blood did not have to be escorted wherever she went.

She loved to walk alone along the very top of the castle and look out over the rolling hills and grassy dales. There she would spend hour upon hour watching the villagers go about their daily work.

She also liked to walk everyday in the lovely gardens that made up the wonderful ambience of the courtyard. They were planted with raised beds of lilies and daises and small trees had been strategically placed.

All about were wonderfully carved sundials and stone statues of beasts posturing on the tops of gaily painted poles.

But she wished to see more of Richard, as she had not spoken to him since the conversation about the fate of her brothers and she could not help but feel that he was avoiding her…but why?

She was puzzled...had she done something to offend him? Was he worried about telling her something he should not? She concluded that he was indeed a very private person, one who found it impossible to share his worries and problems with anyone.

******

It was a beautiful Sunday afternoon, the sun was shining bright and there was a little breeze blowing from the south to take the edge off the heat. I had just come from midday prayers and was walking in the beautiful gardens at Middleham.

The gardens always seemed to have an atmosphere of calm and peacefulness and I was taking one of my favourite routes amongst the winding paths when I spied Dickon sitting alone in a private corner of the rose garden on a stone bench.

He looked forlorn and in deep thought. Should I approach him? After a moments hesitation I decided to pass rather close to where he was sitting in the hope that he would see me. My plan worked and he signalled to me, with a beckoning wave, to sit with him.

'My Lord,' I said, on sitting rather close to him.

Dickon did look troubled. I noticed that deep creases had appeared on his forehead as he turned to look at me. 'I need someone to talk to Bessy, are you willing to listen to an old man speak of his worries?'

I was indignant in my reply. 'Your Majesty is not old. Why he is still very much in the prime of his life and he still looks a fine figure of a man.'

I was surprised at my sudden outburst and I blushed bright red when I had finished.

Thankfully Dickon paid no attention to my outburst and glanced down and sighed. 'I have a wife that is dying and no son.'

I remained silent; I wanted desperately to put my arm around his shoulder in an effort to comfort him.

He began to talk openly. 'I must name my heir very soon or Tudor will get even more traitors rallying to his cause. The peace that I struck up with the Bretons is fragile. They could change their coat at any time and be allied with my enemies.

It is Duke Francis of Brittany who protects Tudor and his supporters. He is asking me for one thousand archers in return for the arrest and the keeping in custody of Tudor.'

I spoke up with venom in my voice. 'Henry Tudor…My mother and her conspirators would have me marry the man.'

Raising his head Dickon looked at me squarely and with equal amount of venom fired back. 'That will never happen as long as I am the king.'

Shyly I smiled as Dickon reached for my hand. Clutching it to his breast he leant forward and kissed me gently on the cheek. I could feel myself blush a deep red and my face becoming hotter and hotter.

Dickon's eyes were fixed upon me as he spoke and I lost all sense of time or place. For a brief moment I thought that Dickon had feelings for me that were far beyond that of his niece, but instantly his gaze left me as he continued to speak. 'Thank you for listening so tentatively to my worries. Now you must leave me as I need to do some serious thinking that only I can do alone.'

I nodded and rose to my feet. 'I will take my leave then Sir,' I answered.

'I look forward to another meeting soon,' he called, as I turned to go back to my rooms.

During the following months the poor queen's health worsened, her lungs were wracked with coughing and everyone knew that her death was inevitable.

Dickon made the painful decision to leave her in the hands of her mother and doctors, as the troubles of being king mounted.

In late August Dickon made plans to leave Middleham and to travel back south, as he had been informed that there were more plots afoot in London.

To my joy I was amongst the people chosen to go back to London with him.

My thoughts were muddled. Why had he instructed me to be one of those to accompanying him back to the capital I wondered? Was it because I had been no use to Anne for several months?

After much pondering, I concluded that the reason was that he wanted to keep my whereabouts close, for he was well aware of the new plots involving a marriage between Henry Tudor and myself.

A realisation then suddenly came upon me. Or could it be that he was becoming attracted to me in a way that I could only hope and pray for and he did not want to be parted from me? I pushed all thoughts to the back of my mind and made ready for the long journey back to the capital.

******

Back at Westminster the atmosphere was very tense in contrast to the wonderful, relaxed ambience at Middleham.

Richard could not touch the hearts of the southern people even though his government was most efficient and effective than any that had gone before. Amongst other things he had abolished the practice of benevolences, a tax given to the king without the consent of parliament in the form of a gift, and he had the bones of Henry VI transferred from Chertsey and interred at St George's Chapel Windsor.

He soon realised that there were agents of Richmond's everywhere who were undermining his efforts. Sir William Collingboure nailed a sordid rhyme to the door of St Paul's, it read, The Rat, the Cat, the Lovell our dog Rule all England under the Hog. He was referring to Richard and his three most loyal and trusted friends and ministers.

The Cat was referring to Sir William Catesby who came from Northamptonshire, studied law and became a legal advisor, steward and councillor to various nobles including Hastings, Buckingham and King Edward. The Rat referred Sir Richard Ratcliffe who came from a noble family from the Lake District and became a companion of Richard's as early as 1461.

Finally Lovell the Dog referred to Sir Francis Lovell who was Richard's oldest and dearest friend, the two had first known one another as boys in the service of Warwick.

Later that same month Collingbourne, along with several others was executed for plotting to murder the king.

The weeks passed and there were no more intimate meetings with Bessy. Richard was busy as he and his advisers tried to make final peace with Scotland.

The long summer days were now coming at an end and dusk was now lengthening the late afternoon shadows.

Richard had shut himself away with only a few trusted servants. Northern men he had known all his life and had proved their loyalty to him.

He had learnt that Henry Tudor had been warned of his imminent arrest and escaped to the new King of France, King Charles, just in time.

Charles was no friend of the English King and therefore Henry Tudor began to convince Charles that he would be a better prospect on the English throne.

By the middle of September Richard had returned to Nottingham, to a more strategic position. Whilst there, more disturbing news was to reach Richard. John de Vere's, the Earl of Oxford had escaped imprisonment in Hammes Castle and had joined Tudor's exiles. Oxford had placed men, money and materials at Henry's disposal and he was one of he best and most tried of the English commanders.

This was a bitter blow to Richard who knew that he would have to defeat Henry on the battlefield if he wanted to make his crown secure.

Richard spent only six weeks in Nottingham before, once more, returning to London.

******

I had rejoined my sisters at Westminster and waited to see if Dickon would summon me to him.

'I need to know what is happening.' I began to vent my feelings one evening whilst my sister Cecily and I were alone. 'I cannot bear to think that I could be promised to a victorious Henry without me even knowing about it.'

My sister's voice was rather casual as she continued to stitch her embroidery, 'you would know.'

I shrugged, 'I would not be so sure. Our mother is forever making plans and she does not take our feelings into consideration.' With conviction, I pressed the matter of our mother further. 'I do agree with you Ce, our mother needs to be stopped working her poison...what are we to do?'

Cecily stopped her needlework and looked seriously at me. 'Mother has not recovered from our father's death and she has never stopped since that day scheming to regain her position of Queen of England.'

Deeply I frowned. 'I will never marry Henry Tudor for I love another.' Biting my lip hard, I had stopped myself before I went any further. I now felt uncomfortable that I had let this information slip out and said no more on the subject, but I could tell that Cecily had focused on my voux pas and a wry smile came over my sister's face and a twinkle appeared in her eye.

There was a momentary pause. Cecily's eyes met mine. Since my return to London, I knew that Cecily could tell that there was a difference in me; how I spoke about my stay at Middleham with a distinct wistfulness.

Putting her needlework to one side, Cecily tone lightened, 'who is your love? Did you meet him whilst at Middleham? Perhaps you would be able to marry him?'

Without thinking, my reply was instant, 'that is impossible, for the man I love is already married.' Shaking my head I rebuked Cecily. 'I do not wish to speak of such matters!'

There was a deathly silence and Cecily knew that she had spoken out of turn

My tone lightened, 'I am sorry Ce, I have been under a lot of strain lately, as we all have. I should not have snapped at you like that.'

Cecily approached me. 'I have always loved and admired you, you know that you can confide in me...who ever he is...I will not tell a living soul...who is it that has you heart?'

216

My voice was almost a whisper as I tried to answer. 'I am ashamed to tell you Ce...I need to be alone.'

'As you wish,' Cecily obliged without further questioning as she could see that I was becoming deeply distress by the situation, my lips had begun to quiver as I tried desperately to hold back my tears.

Once alone my emotions changed and a wave of fury and frustration came over me. Why had Dickon not got in touch with me in all theses weeks? I felt sure that there was something between us at Middleham. He was charming towards me and there appeared to be a passion in his eyes when he spoke to me.

All that night and the next day I thought about it. Was the time right to let my true feelings be known to him?

Again I would put my thoughts on paper and once again use John Howard as a go between. But there had to be a delicacy to my dispatch. It took me three days to compose it, each time I put words onto paper I would regret my choice of phrase and begin all over again.

I wanted to put into words my feelings and fears. Above all else I wanted to let Dickon know that he could always rely on my support. That he could always turn to me for comfort and that I long to ease his troubled mind.

I reminded him about the times when I had trusted and believed in him when the rest of her family did not. How I persuaded my mother to come out of sanctuary and finally how I loved my time at Middleham and that I also had a deep love and respect for him.

Sealing my letter and tying it tight I knew that I myself would have to deliver it to Norfolk.

For a long time now I had not the services of any court messenger. John Howard, I felt sure would

217

deliver my messenger to the king. He will be here at Westminster in a few days time. I would find him and give him the letter myself. Closing my eyes I thought on. I know that Howard is privy to Dickon's whereabouts. He could give it to him the next time the councillors met.

******

Nervously I waited not wanting to be recognised. I could not face the endless questioning of my mother if I was spotted amongst the corridors of the Palace.

I stepped cautiously out of the shadows as I saw Howard approach. His pace was swift as he walked and talked to two of his retinue. He was in deep discussion and he almost collided with me as I hindered his path.

In haste I spoke to him. 'My Lord, I hope you do not mind my obtrusion and my boldness but I must get a letter to the king.'

Norfolk fell back at the sight of me. He was courteous as he still held all of the late king's children in high esteem.

There was concern in his voice, 'why, my lady, do you lurk these corridors alone?'

Loosing any sense of embarrassment I lowered my voice and spoke to him, 'I am now but a noble woman who needs your help.'

Norfolk raised his eyebrows as he studied the girl before him. Momentarily he lost his stony faced expression and a wide grin appeared across his face. Had it dawned on him who was using master Gilles, who the secret message sender was?

I held out my sealed parchment and Norfolk swiftly took it from me and placed it in his belt. Without another word he strode off and continued to talk to his cohorts as if nothing had interfered with his train of conversation.

218

As I saw the small party turn the corridor with my important message, I realised that it was now too late to change my mind. I thought on, in just over twenty four hour's time Dickon would know exactly how I felt about him.

I swallowed hard, had I done the right thing or would Dickon think me a foolish child?

With haste I hurried back to my room and waited the outcome.

It was only one week later that I received a reply from Dickon. As soon as Master Seaton, one of the king's personal messengers, entered my chamber with news of a letter, I knew it was from Dickon.

'My lady, the king wishes me to give him a reply,' he announced on handing me a rolled scroll with a very noticeable king's seal.

With trembling hands I opened the fastening. It was not the letter of amour I had wished for but an invitation to his private apartments for a small celebration. It was to be held on the second day of October, Dickon's thirty second birthday and he would be most honoured if I attend. He then went on to stipulate that I came alone.

I closed my eyes and began to breath. Then I breathed again and again, trying to regain my composure. 'Tell the king that I would be most honoured.'

After putting the treasured scroll into my purse, I then took it out and read it once more before concealing it in a secret box, which I kept hidden under my bed; I let out a muffled squeal. With a mixture of excitement and uneasiness I began thinking of the evening.

He had included me amongst his small intimate number of friends and I felt flattered that he should think of me so.

219

It would be my chance to really get to know him, for I knew him to be a very a different person away from the formalities of the court. I hoped that he could forget, just for one evening, all his troubles and woes and to be his old self.

I knew the day to be the thirtieth day of September, only two days before my special evening and my mind was in turmoil. With my nerves all of a jingle with excitement, I took three deep breaths to try and calmed myself. Now my mind went to the most important decision…what I should wear.

My wardrobe was not as it was when I was a Royal Princess. But I had one special dress in mind, one that had been made for me only two years before, when I was still the daughter of a king. It was of the finest green tissue cloth with gold and I only hoped that it still fitted.

It was the night before Dickon's birthday and Cecily joined me in a game of chess. She did not want to be alone on such a night, especially as the weather was foul and the wind was making weird and frightening noises.

My sister could not help notice my elated mood. 'You seem very jubilant,' Cecily remarked whilst moving her bishop. I tried hard to conceal my excitement for the very next evening I would be in the king's company.

Thoughts quickly crossed my mind whether or not to let her in on my secret. I was almost at bursting point and needed desperately to share my news with someone.

Taking a deep breath I faced Cecily. 'I am to attend The king's birthday feast celebrations tomorrow. I believe that only a handful of people have been lucky enough to get an invitation.'

Cecily's tone was one of ridicule. 'The room will probably be full of old fuddy duddies like Catesby and Ratcliff.'

Giving Cecily a quizzical look, my tone became serious. 'They are not fuddy duddies they are intelligent and accomplished men. More importantly Dickon has seen fit to make me one of his trusted friends and I am forever thankful.'

Scratching her head, Cecily heaved a sigh. 'You are too serious for one so young. You should hold company with people of your own age.'

I was incensed as I continued the conversation. 'Uncle Dickon and his friends are in their early thirties and I am almost twenty.'

Cecily's laugh was cynical. 'They will talk of nothing but politics and government and you are not interested in those topics at all.'

My eyes widened as I tried to control my feelings. 'You do not understand...I have...' my voice trailed off as I realised that I was about to give my sister too much information.

Cecily squinted her eyes and I began to wonder if it had just dawned on her what I was trying to say. My sister shook her head; 'Bessy you mean our uncle is your secret love?'

I turned the brightest red and I felt my face become hot, but did not answer my sister's probing question, but I could feel that Cecily took my refusal to answer her as a signal of my guilt.

Cecily's tone was stern. 'You must stop these thoughts right away as nothing but pain and trouble will come from them.'

There was a long silence; I frowned and rose to my feet. I did not want to let Cecily into any more of my heart felt feelings in fact I was now regretting what I had already let slip. I needed time to gather my thoughts. I was not going to let Cecily's negative opinion spoil my mood. I had to change the subject before Cecily started asking awkward questions.

I lightened my tone as I continued to speak. 'You don't understand I go for celebrations, nothing more…now Ce, I thought that I would wear my green dress. I think that I have not grown too much in the last eighteen months.

Looking at my sister I could see that there were tears beginning to well up in Cecily's eyes. In almost a whisper Cecily spoke. 'I cannot believe that father has only been gone a year and a half. So much has changed in our lives since then…if he were still here we would not be in the predicament we find ourselves.'

Holding back a tear myself I replied to her. 'Yes I know but please do not upset yourself everything is going to be alright you wait and see. The hour is late and I intend to retire right now before we both break down in tears thinking about our father.'

Cecily hugged me and retired to her room, which was the very next apartment along the corridor.

Alone in my inner chamber my thoughts were wild. That night I was too excited to sleep. Over and over again in my mind I pictured myself at Dickon's party, talking and dancing with him and looking incredibly beautiful.

******

Bright and early the next morning I called for Veronique. Although I was no longer a princess, Veronique who had no duties to attend, had come to help me and I was thankful for her.

Veronique squealed with delight and clapped her hands. 'My lady can only be compared to a precious gem, a fine diamond, brilliantly reflecting her many facets and she can rely on me to make her as lovely as can be. Any man who will be in your company tonight will not fail to fall under your exquisite charms.'

I took a very excited hand and gushed. 'I thought the green dress with the gold silk trim would be a good choice.'

I hoped that Veronique did not guess whom I wanted to be most overwhelmed by my beauty.

Veronique continued with excited breath. 'It certainly would be a fine choice and for you hair?'

Putting my finger to my face and raising my eyes upwards, a slight crease came upon my forehead as I deliberated. 'Uhh...I want my hair to be free with just a few jewels about it on a fine golden band.'

The clothes were made ready and I was bathed in warm scented water. With Veronique's help the day was spent brushing and teasing my locks in a neat style, plucking my eyebrows, whitening my face and painting my cheeks and lips a fiery red.

Then it was time for Veronique to help me to dress. The undergarments and the dress needed a lot of fastening to reveal my tiny waist: clasp, buttons, ties and buckles were all part of the outfit. Finally I was ready and looked admiringly at myself in the looking glass that Veronique was holding at a distance. Although the image was a little cloudy I liked what I saw reflecting back.

Veronique gave me a kiss on the cheek and reassured me that I was the most beautiful woman in Christendom.

It was almost seven; very nervously I stood trembling. Veronique could see that an uneasy girl stood before her and tried to put my mind at rest.

223

'You will have a wonderful evening. Now take three deep breaths and try to stop worrying.'

I nodded and obeyed. Veronique kissed me again and smiled. 'It is time you made your way to The king's apartments.'

A surge of uneasiness entered my body. 'I am so anxious; will you come with me some of the way?'

Veronique agreed and the two of us set off. I tried to keep a benign look on my face as I strode through the broad corridors and up along the winding stone staircase, to the king's rooms.

'I cannot come any further,' Veronique whispered.

I nodded and took in a deep breath. I was now on my own and rounded the corner to be met by an arched wooden doorway. Outside were stationed two armed men standing guard over the royal apartments. Silently one stepped aside and the other opened the door for me and I walked in.

Inside I waited in an outer chamber. My heart was beating hard as I peered around. This was a room I knew all too well, for the whole suit of rooms had been my father's apartments when he had been king not yet two years before.

A lot had happened since then, most of it tragic but tonight I intended to enjoy myself, as I had never done before.

I stood and marvelled at the hand painted walls and ceiling, for these room were famous throughout Europe for being most exquisitely decorated.

'My lady,' a squire of the household was in my presence. 'I will escort you to His Majesty.'

I nodded and followed him through several outer rooms that were all familiar to me. He led me to what I knew to be the inner chamber. As he opened the door I saw not King Richard but Dickon standing alone beside a magnificent spread of food and wine.

I curtseyed low and Dickon took my hand and kissed it. I met his eyes; there was about him a quality which no other man could ever have for me. He seemed relaxed and began to talk feely. 'I am so happy that you consented to join me tonight.'

I rose and looked at him, 'am I the first person to arrive?'

A slight smile appeared at the corner of his mouth as he spoke, 'I have a confession...you are the only person I have asked here tonight.'

He motioned me to sit beside him. 'I have dismissed all the servants. I thought it would be nice to serve ourselves because I do not want anyone else to hear what I have to say to you tonight.'

Looking around I noticed that we were indeed alone. A few candles flickered, splashing rings of light on the walls. 'Come and sit by the fire and sup with me tonight.'

I sat quietly and listen patiently; he desperately needed someone to hear him. He had become such a lonely, sad figure of recent months. He told me of his doubts and suspicions and of his hopes for the future.

As we ate and drank, taking long draughts of wine, Dickon empty his soul out to me. 'I have decided to make my sister Elizabeth's boy my heir. Yes, I have already made the boy Earl of Lincoln and I believe he is the best choice.'

My mind quickly went to my cousin John. John de la Pole was only a year older than me. His mother, Elizabeth, was Dickons older sister and Dickon had always been close to his aunt and his cousin.

My father had a fondness for his sister Elizabeth and her young son. I found John to be nice enough and agreed with his choice.

I continued eating and sat with my eyes transfixed on him as he continued to unburden himself with his troubles. 'I have tried to extradite Tudor from Brittany, but he and his supporters have fled to France.' He paused and I could see the workings of his mind. 'I intend to open talks with Charles as soon as he is fully recovered from his illness. I propose to offer him help in his wars in exchange for Tudor.' Dickon breathed deeply and nodded as if confirming what he had just said.

I continued to listen and watch him in total contentment as he continued to tell me of his plans.

With his eyes fixed his upon me he went on. 'I feel that you are the only person in the whole world that I can talk so freely with. Anne was very supportive but now she is too sick to even listen to my woes. The death of our dear son affected her so badly she never really recovered from his lost. The doctors believe that she may have caught his malady as she was forever close to him and she only has a few months left in this world.'

I sipped my wine and picked at the array of food on my platter and my eyes thanked him silently. 'I am pleased that you deem me fit to confide in me your inner thoughts.' Lowering my eyes I stuttered… 'to take the role of you wife.'

Dickon bowed his head as his thoughts turned to his ailing wife. 'Anne knows that I have taken you into my trust; it was her who encouraged me to do so. She got to know and love you when you her Lady of the Wardrobe.'

Pouring himself another draught of wine he came and sat close to me. 'Let us not think too much on

226

our troubles for tonight I intend to relax and enjoy myself, something I have been unable to do these past months.'

As the evening went on he became a different person to the serious man of the past three years. The young carefree Dickon had briefly returned and he began to laugh and make light of his situation. Talking with me had somehow lightened his troubles, for a trouble shared is a trouble halved.

A charming smile momentarily came over his face and his eyes began to probe me expectantly and his voice intensified. 'You are a fine, sweet girl, dear Bessy.'

He stroked my cheek lightly and I could feel the words spinning in my head as he fixed me once more with his gaze.

The hour was late and the castle was becoming very quiet, everyone was retiring for the night. I was beginning to feel a little dizzy; I had drunk too much wine. Hesitantly I began. 'I believe that I should return to my own rooms as the hour is late.'

'You do not have to leave...I would like you to stay a little longer.'

Staring deeply into his eyes I recognized his sincerity. I could feel my heart beating hard in my chest as I answered him. 'The hour is almost midnight, what will the court think if they believe that I have spent the night alone with you?'

His eyes seemed to glitter with passion. He was so close to me now that I could hear his breath exhale. 'I do not care what they think. I am the King and I can do as I please. Right now I only care about one thing.'

He stared at me; 'you are the most beautiful creature that I have ever seen. With your auburn hair and big hazel eyes, your high cheekbones and sensuous mouth you have become unbearably attractive to me these past few months.'

I thought on...I was so beautiful, so appealing to him at this moment that he had forgotten who my father was. I was now almost twenty years old and my curved body told him that I was now every bit a desirable woman.

A wry smile came over his face, 'I have to think of the future...a future that I believe could be with yo.'

I returned his stares, I felt as though I was in a dream. He was now looking deep into my soul. Almost swooning I whispered, 'I love you...I have always loved you ever since I was a child. Nothing can change the way that I feel about you.'

Our eyes locked and held. There was no need for me to tell him what I wanted as it was written all over my face. He smiled again, took the glass out of my hand and exhaled, 'that is all I needed to know.'

Almost at once he kissed me passionately. His tongue was in my mouth and I responded wildly. He could feel my heart beating madly beneath my clothes. Skilled love maker as he was my response must have surprised him. My hand came upon him and began to caress his body.

'Bessy, Bessy,' he moaned you will soon be mine.'

I closed my eyes; I could not believe that this was really happening. The touch of his hands made my whole body quiver with delight. I did not resist him and he continued to hold me close.

With his strong arms about me he swept me into his bedchamber. I saw the canopy of the king's four poster bed and the drapes hanging around it. Slumping down upon it, I had become totally disengage in the reality of the moment as the ecstasy engulfed me. All I

228

knew was that my life's long dream of being intimate with Dickon was coming true.

I could taste his hot kisses and feel his muscular body about me. The talking had stopped, as bit by bit our clothes were removed and my body became known to him.

His hands and lips began to explore me totally and I too kissed, stroked and caressed him. I then knew that he was ready for me. The pain on entry soon gave way to pleasure as our lovemaking reached a climax.

Looking deep into my eyes Dickon wiped the sweat drenched hair from my face and exhaled deeply, 'you have lovely eyes; you are the most beautiful woman in the entire kingdom. When this Tudor impostor is dealt with you will be my queen.'

The dream like quality of those magic moments now left me as I felt a horror take grip of my thoughts. A lump came to my throat, 'what we have done is wrong...I am your niece.'

Dickon put his finger on my lips. ' Shhh... your father was only my half brother...I intend to get dispensation from the pope...I know that the Holy Father would grant a dispensation for he regularly authorizes marriages between uncles and nieces on the continent... I intend to marry you.'

He kissed me gently and I became relaxed with the idea.

An uncertain look then crossed his face. 'I think it may be wise for the moment to be discrete about our union. Firstly I need to talk to my ministers and inform them of my intentions.'

I did not answer, for I had complete trust in what ever he was going to do. I had never felt as comfortable as I did now in Dickon's bed.

I could only marvel at the series of events that had brought me to my present predicament. Dickon had declared his love for me and now my wildest dream, to become Dickon's Queen, was about to come true. Letting out a long satisfying sigh I soon drifted off into a deep sleep.

I was awoken early by Dickons's soft kiss. 'It is time you were gone my love,' he whispered. 'I will send word of my outcome with the meeting of myself and my ministers as soon as I can.'

I did not argue and wrapped myself in a fine blue bedspread lined with fur, my beautiful hair in disorder about my shoulders. With clothes clutched in my arms, I gave him a final kiss as I left the king's chamber.

The guards on the door were asleep and snored deeply.

Silently I ran through the dimly lit deserted corridors hoping and praying that I was not seen by anyone, as I could not face being stopped and question about my whereabouts.

An overwhelming excitement gripped me as I relived a much dreamed of fantasy of wandering through the Palace corridors fresh from my lovers arms. Out of breath I finally reached my room. I had never acted so swiftly.

The dawn cock crowed on my entering and I was brought back to reality by the surprised sight of Cecily sitting on the end of my unruffled bed, wide-awake, and full of probing questions.

'Have you been all night with the king?' Looking at my dishevelled state her voice quickened. 'What have you been doing? Will you not tell your sister the night's happenings?

Taking in a quick intake of breath I sighed and sat next to Cecily. I wondered what I should say to her. I could not carry on with this deceit any longer and anyway by the way I looked to her she already knew the story of last night. I needed to tell someone what had happened and decided to confess all.

My voice was a strained whisper, 'you must not breathe a word of this to anyone.'

Cecily nodded with conviction and swore.

I settled beside my excited sister and told her in detail what the evening held. I admitted my thoughts and feelings that I had had for years and went on to describe every moment of my evening's liaison with Dickon.

Ce listened intently, her words were rushed. 'I had guessed that you had a crush on our uncle but I never dreamt that the situation had escalated into this!'

Over the next two weeks I spent several illicit nights with Dickon...our union was always wonderful and I hated the fact that I had to steal away in the middle of the night to keep our liaisons secret.

****

For the next six weeks Dickon was away from his London court. I had learnt that he had gone north to escort Anne back to Westminster, probably to die from the dreadful wasting sickness that she had been long suffering.

While he was gone I mulled over and over in my mind what he had said; that he intended to marry me and make me Queen of England.

Although I was happy, happier than I had been in my entire life, there was a tremendous sensation of guilt inside me that would not go away. I could not help but

231

feel dreadfully sorry for Anne. The little queen had been good to me, always kind, and now ...

For months, since coming from the sanctuary, I had seen nothing of my mother. Then one afternoon, without warning she called at my chamber, she was escorted by a page that she readily dismissed, smiling and trying to give the impression of concern, she gently laid her hand on my arm and sat down beside me.

Her voice was calm and relaxed as she began to speak, 'my dear Bessy, I hear that the king has a fondness for you.'

My body visibly jolted, a tingling surge went shooting through me. Quickly I suspected that my sister had broken her promise and told our mother of my secret. On second thoughts maybe an over nosy servant had gone to her in search of some favour or reward for such information. Whatever the circumstance my mother now knew my plight.

I studied the face staring back at me and swallow hard, 'they are but rumours... idle gossip.'

Taking in a quick intake of breath my mother went on. 'I have it on good authority that the king has had knowledge of you. I have a right to know the truth, have you been intimate with him?'

I blushed deeply and lowered my head; I did not want my facial expressions to betray me. With my eyes cast down I answered, 'If my mother is right, what would she have me do?'

Leaning forward and in softer tones, as if to make sure that no one could hear what she was about to say to her eldest daughter, she went on. 'Why, I am here to help and advise you. I am in total support of you of course.'

I began to wring my hands in silence and thought on. Why was my mother all smiles? I could only guess *at what she knew. Did she know of Dickon's plans to marry me?*

My mother's voice was now venomous. 'You must only hope that Queen Anne's end is very near and that the lords accept you as Richard's new consort.'

I slumped down and a small tear trickled down my face and I buried my head in my hands as I began to sob without restraint.

My mother tried to soothe me, 'why do you cry so? This should be a happy day for you could be queen in a matter of months.'

Without hesitation, through glassy eyes, I blurted out my fear... 'I believe... that I could be with child... for I have not had a monthly flux since October.'

My mother fell silent while she took in the enormity of what had been said. Finally she broke her silence, 'we must keep this fact a secret. Does anyone else know?'

I looked at my mother through what were now reddened eyes. Trying to compose my self I began to breathe in long strangled gasps, 'no...no one else knows.'

I could almost hear my mother's mind working. 'We must put pressure on Richard to marry you at once before it is too obvious that there is a child.'

My mother stood tall and puffed out her chest. A grin came over her face that I was all too familiar with, a look she always had when she had a scheme brewing in her head, 'do not worry my dear daughter; everything is going to be just fine.'

We hugged and I felt much needed relief; the stress upon me had become unbearable. At last my secret had been shared and now my mother knew the condition that had been tearing at me all this time, my mother knew my predicament.

233

I hopped that she would now stop making wedding plans for me to marry Henry Tudor. I sighed, had I done the right thing in telling my Mother?

From that moment on my mother was very much back into my life. She persuaded me to move into her apartments, for she needed at all times to keep a very watchful eye on me for my situation needed much thought and advice that only a mother could give.

From now on I would do nothing without my mother's knowledge and consent. In this new role I saw a light come back into my mother's eyes that I had not seen for years. My mother was now in her element for she realised that she could be only months away from being mother of the queen. It had been what she had been working towards since my father so tragically died.

******

The Mayor and the aldermen gave Richard a hearty welcome when he and his court returned to London at the end of November and as expected, Anne and her household were with him.

Anne made a sorry full sight and the court could not help but think death would be a blessed relief for her.

The sight of the dying queen brought many pangs of remorse for Bessy and she was beginning to regret what she had done.

There was however, no doubt that she was with child as she began feeling faint and nauseous.

It was then that she realised it was too late to turn back; she had committed herself to Richard. But had he regretted his liaison with her? She had had no word from him since his declared love for her and she was beginning to wonder if he had regretted the whole affair.

He seemed to be taking good care of Anne as if he did not want her to die and for them to be together.

Every night at dinner Richard had his sick wife made comfortable a little distance from him and Bessy could do nothing but watch and bite her tongue.

There was the exchange of fleeting looks between her and Richard and both of them acted as if nothing had happened between them.

At night Bessy said nothing to her mother as she shut herself away in her small private chamber within Elizabeth's rooms. She would think for hours, mulling over and over Richard's words of passion in her mind.

Then her thoughts would turn to the negative. Did he know of the baby? Had her mother somehow got word to him and he was now sorry for what he had done.

She wondered if he had confided their union to any of his trusted councillors and what their reaction had been. She thought on and decided that all she could do now was to wait and see what would become of her. Her fate, she concluded, was now in Gods hands.

Richard had recently called a Parliament and as well as dealing with other issues of state he publically declared Henry Tudor and all his adherents' traitors.

Richard had been several days in Westminster and still Bessy had received no word from him. She had to be content with watching him from a distance.

With laden eyelids she would close her eyes although her sleep was disturbed and restless.

******

It was a dark December night and I was huddled around the fireside of my mother's apartments with my sisters when a messenger arrived at my mother's rooms. After bowing low he handed my mother a scroll sealed with the familiar motif of Queen Anne.

'A letter for the Lady Bessy,' he announced.

'I will see that she gets it,' Elizabeth said on taking receipt of it.

My mother approached me. 'Bessy you have a message; I believe it is from the queen.'

Looking at the tampered seal, I knew that my mother had already read the message, as she had now taken complete control of my life.

Before I had finished reading my mother was in full animation as she took my hands as I began to speak. 'She wishes for me to go to her at once as she has something urgent to tell me.'

My mother's voice was rushed. 'Come Bessy do not dally go to her at once. You must refute any wrong doing with the king...do you understand?'

I nodded with assurance and obeyed my mother, as it was impossible now not to.

Almost immediately I headed for the queen's private apartment. I met several people outside the inner rooms. Talk stopped as I approached and all eyes turned to look at me. My jaw tightened, as I had inner thoughts of what these courtiers knew of my exploits.

My tone was restrained. 'I have come on the queen's command.'

An older man approached me. 'You must not get near to her Majesty as what she has is very contagious, it is believed that she caught the malady from her poor son. Only her doctor and her mother go so near.'

I nodded, 'I understand.'

On entering the inner chamber I was shocked at Anne's appearance, she was no more than a skeleton propped up in her bed with many pillows.

Her mother sat on a small chair at her bedside and held her bone thin hand. I curtseyed and kept my eyes lowered, finding it difficult to look at Anne, I kept my head bowed as I spoke. 'You send for me Madame?'

Anne whispered her reply. 'Please rise…thank you for coming so promptly.' A choking cough interrupted her. I could feel her tremendous pain in her every word she spoke.

After composing herself and breathing heavily Anne continued to speak. 'I wanted to tell you that I know about you and Richard. He has told me everything.'

Lifting my head I saw the pain in Anne's face as she struggled to speak. 'I want him to be happy when I am dead… I want him to have more sons… all the Woodville women are fertile and have many strong children.'

I knew Anne to be right in her assumptions. My mother had given birth to thirteen children and my grandmother, sixteen. I wondered if I should divulge my news of a baby, but I remembered my mother's words and decided to heed them.

Hardly able to comprehend the queen's sentiments I spoke in puzzlement. 'Your Grace does not feel jealous or betrayed?'

Anne laboured her reply. 'Richard is still a young man…he has been living these past months as if I am already dead…he has done his mourning…he tells me that he still loves me and I accept what he says as true.'

Anne began to cough violently and her mother helped her to overcome the agony by squeezing her hand.

Feebly Anne looked at me with weary eyes. She did not need to speak anymore. She did not have the strength or the will to carry on a conversation that was obviously very painful for her.

My voice cracked with heart felt sorrow as I finally addressed the queen. 'Your Grace is truly a godly woman and I thank her for this meeting.'

Anne's mother nodded and waved her hand. I curtseyed and left the room.

On the way back to my mother's apartment's I saw Lord Norfolk walking swiftly towards me. He was in deep conversation with two companions and he was startled when I addressed him. 'My lord, would you give this letter to the king. I know that you have easier access to him than I, for he spends days and nights pondering the threat of invasion with you and his ministers.'

Without redress from Norfolk I reached into the purse that hung round my skirt on a fine leather belt and produced a letter rolled, sealed and tied with a pale blue ribbon.

I had written it several days ago and was waiting for the right moment for it to be delivered. In it I had put into words my feeling, especially my love for Dickon that he is my only joy maker in this world and my hopes that I am in his heart and thoughts as he is in mine.

I puts into writing my hopes of becoming his wife when his poor wife finally leaves the pain and suffering of this world.

Norfolk bowed low, took the scroll, and without a word to me hurried about his business.

****

The following day, my mother woke me very early. Spinning wildly like a top my mother focused her gaze on her daughter. She had a grin on her face and I wondered what had happened to cause this.

Breathing deeply to calm her emotions my mother spoke.' My child you have a message from the king.'

238

As I read it I could tell that my mother already knew its contents by the broken seal and the beaming smile that was eminent on her face.

'You will go of course,' my mother said before I had even finished reading.

I gave a deep sigh as I focused on my mother's beaming smile. 'Mother, it is not right. All my life I have been fighting my feelings towards Dickon because he is my uncle. I believe that I should go away and have the baby and never tell Dickon what has been done!'

My mother's words were firm. 'Hush now, do not talk like that. I know many an uncle and niece union that the Pontiff has seen fit to give dispensation. Richard writes he is determined to make you his queen when poor Anne is finally put out of her agonies.'

My mother's voice grew edgy. 'You must tell him the news of the baby. He will not deny you then, for the whole country knows that a legitimate son is what Richard desires above all else.'

It was at that moment that I realised what a dreadful schemer my mother was and if not for her meddling the country would not be in the precarious position it was in.

With raised tones I answered her. 'I will go but not for any reason that you give. I go because I love Dickon.' An agitation fell across my face as I realised what I was about to do.

Relentlessly my mother continued to coax me. 'That's a good girl and do not forget that your mother supports Richard in his bid for the throne against Henry Tudor.'

I could not believe how persistent my mother was once she had an idea in her mind. Only a few months ago she was pledge to destroy Richard and to marry me off to Henry Tudor and now she was willing to

239

accept Richard as her son in law. My mother's only thought was to regain her former power and if it meant through her eldest daughter so be it.

I took Dickon's letter somewhere private and re read it. In it he declares his undying love for me and his hopes of our marriage soon. Finally he told me to come to his bedchamber at midnight. There would be a guard on the door but he had strict instructions to let me in. Pressing the letter to my breast, I waited for the midnight bell.

The fires burned bright at Westminster as winter chills crept into the rooms and hallways. Dressed in a sheer satin robe, underneath my cloak, I sat alone with my mother and talked of my expectations as my mother smiled broadly and brushed my long lush hair free. It was thick and wavy and flowed down below my waist.

My mother instructed me while she worked. 'You must wear this cloak in case there are still people in the hallways.' She paused for thought and continued. 'But I think not, tonight at dinner there was much wine consumed.'

With the chime of the bell, the hour of midnight had arrived and with the mass extinguishments of the burning torches, darkness had fallen over the castle.

Within minutes my eyes had become accustomed to the light. Wrapping my fur cloak tightly around me I made a shadowy path towards the king's apartments. I could not help but remember Jane Shore all those years ago doing the same thing only it was as the lover of my father.

On my arrival I gave the guard at the door a nod and he gave me access to the king's private apartments. Just inside the doorway Dickon was waiting, alone.

I flung myself to him and was soon enveloped into his strong muscular arms and he covered me with kisses. *'My love...my love!'* Dickon repeated again and again. *'How I have missed you. You have been always in my thoughts.'*

He told me that he adored me and that life had not been worth living until I revealed my love for him.

Our passions soon were high and we were intimate. I was not as nervous as the first times we were together and I took much more pleasure in our union.

As young as I was I could give passion for passion. I was now an active partner in our fore play, running my hands over his hard strong chest and down to his stomach, still taunt and rippling.

His hands exploring my whole body stroking and caressing making me writhed in sexual gratification.

As we laid silently in the after glow of our lovemaking, I memorized by his presence and our love, propped myself up on one arm and looked at him. Although he had visible aged he was still the most desirable man I had ever seen.

A sudden chill filled me as I realised what I had to say. *'I have something important to tell you.'*

Dickon eased himself upwards and put his hand behind his head and spread his elbow ready to take in what I was about to tell him. With my eyes focused on his I told him. *'I am with child.'*

There was a pause that seem to me to last forever. Then a huge smile came over Dickon's face. *'That is the most wonderful news! Are you absolutely sure?'*

I nodded violently and Dickon found my mouth and kissed me lovingly. Cradled in his arms, I gave a deep sigh of relief, as my news seemed to be welcome by him.

Dickon sat up, a thought had occurred to him. *'When is the baby expected?'*

241

'It is early days, the babe is due to enter this world sometime in July.'

Dickon stroked my hair and held my lovely face between his palms. 'For now we must keep quiet about our joy, as our union, by many, is not yet seen as one in the eyes of God.' He paused to gather his thoughts. 'That will all change when I speak with the council and the clergy when...when Anne leaves us.'

I nodded, I trusted him totally. He kissed my face as if to reassure me, but I could not help but worry and wondered if all would turn out as well as he predicted.

******

The Christmas festivities had started and Dickon spent much time with his court. The festivities were lavish with the Palace decked out in its finest splendour.

Everyone knew that Anne had not long left in this world and that it would be her last Christmas.

Dickon tried hard to give the impression of a loyal husband and very few people knew of his secret love and his unborn child.

I kept at a respectable distance during the court celebrations, which were most magnificent.

Then on the very eve of epiphany I received a present inside a huge trunk decorated with Christmas berries. It stood still in the middle of my mother's room, apparently unhampered with, my mother had been busy elsewhere this Christmas tide and her furtive mind was, for the moment, elsewhere.

With great excitement I opened it, and inside was the most exquisite dress I had ever seen. There was a letter with it and as I retrieved it from the bottom of the box, I fully hoped and expected the gift to be from Dickon.

242

My eyes opened wide and my jaw dropped when I realised that the dress was not from Dickon, but from Anne. Hesitantly I opened the queen's seal on the scroll and began to read. The words were heart felt and brought tears to my eyes.

In it Anne spoke of her love for her husband and that he had always treated her with loyalty and that it was she who had encouraged their union, as she knew that I would be able to have many children as she realised that the county needed Richard's heirs to prosper and to be at peace.

I finished her letter…I want you to wear this dress tonight as a sign to all that you are going to be the next Queen of England and what a magnificent queen you will be. Do not divulge to anyone who sent you the dress, as many at court would never understand my motives…Queen Anne.

Although the correspondence had brought me a heavy heart I took comfort in the fact that Anne did not feel any malice towards me.

Swiftly I held the dress to my body. I could not help but marvel at it. It was a pale blue silk with pearls and other precious jewels sewn into it. The neckline was daring, it was fashioned on the new French design.

I was confused by Queen Anne's motives as I, being but now a noble woman had no right in wearing such fine attire as the Queen of England.

That evening I took extra care to get ready and when I entered the Great Hall with my sister Cecily everyone stopped talking and gasped at me. At first I thought that they were amazed at my stunning appearance but I soon began to realize that was not what had strictly caused their stunned silence. Queen Anne sitting upon the raised dais was wearing the exact same dress as me.

Cecily whispered. 'Her majesty is wearing the same dress as you.' Then she added...'you look so much better in it than her.'

All eyes were on a bewildered me as I made my way to my place at table. I felt uncomfortable to be in the gaze of all in attendance. I swallowed hard and sat for a moment with my eyes cast down. I was puzzled. What was the reason for this action went rushing through my mind. What was the meaning of this? Had Anne forced the situation? Everyone would now realise that the rumours that had been circulating were indeed true.

I could do nothing but hold myself tall and smile confidently at the audience that I had gained. Although my legs felt like rubber and my palms were sweating, I held my head high, and found my position at the top table.

I looked at the queen who was hiding her pain with weak smiles and wondered why she had done such a thing.

Everyone present thought they knew the meaning behind such an act and now the members of the court whispered and asks questions amongst themselves about the significant of my attire.

Dickon's voice was jubilant and he cried out. 'This is to be a feast of gladness and celebration.'

A fanfare of trumpet signalled for the feats to begin. As the assembly ate and drank, singers, jesters, jugglers and musicians came to entertain the king.

The evening was, in spite of everything, a very merry one, there was dancing and present giving. I gave Richard and Anne, a small gift and received many.

To my great relief my mother did not attend; she was holding her own Christmas court somewhere else in the Palace.

244

As the evening wore on Sir Ralph approached Cecily. She had been promised to him in marriage and she was clearly glowing with happiness.

After kissing my sister's hand he turned to me. 'Why Bessy you look like the queen in waiting,' he laughed. 'How did you know what the queen was going to wear?'

I stayed quiet and shrugged my shoulders, as I began to understand Anne's motives. Was this part of her plan to get the court to accept me as their next queen?

There was much drinking and the festivities went on well into the night. Anne had retired early and I wondered if I should approach Dickon, for he took his duties as king very seriously and was generally rather circumspect in public; Dickon was a changed man when he was with his court, quiet, serious and ceremonial. He came across, as cold and impassionate. Most who knew him, knew him to be a man of immense restraint. He never over drank or ate, he was discrete and deep thinking, the complete opposite to my father.

Watching him from a distance, I smiled to myself when I thought of the un ceremonial Dickon, his sense of fun and his attractive smile. It was as if there were two men inside a single body.

As the courtyard bell struck twelve midnight I had had given up all hope of getting near to Dickon when he appeared beside me. He took my hand and raised it to his lips and keeping eye contact he spoke, 'would you like to dance with me?'

Without a word and in full view of the court I held his hand. I curtseyed and Dickon gave me a discrete wink as we waited for the musicians to play.

The hall hushed and all eyes fell upon us. After the first few shaky steps the rest of the court joined in the dancing and I began to relax.

The rest of the evening was wonderful! Dickon never left my side. We danced and chatted and laughed in full view of the entire court. We were both aware that all were watching our every move.

The atmosphere was thick with the smells and sounds of the royal court at play and I drunk it all in with gusto.

Gentlemen raised their eyebrows and ladies began to whisper behind their gloved hands. However, I didn't care; I was happy, happier than I had ever been before for now Dickon had decided to show me off as his next wife and queen.

It was the early hours of the morning when, totally exuberant, I finally returned to my room. It was difficult for me to clear my thoughts, as my head was volatile with love. I was floating on air and did not feel tired at all, every moment I spent thinking about my life ahead with Dickon.

I was relieved that the secret of our love was now out into the open. Everyone must have guessed that there was a love between us they only had to gaze into our faces to see it.

The next day I was summoned to my mother and my life came back to the reality of what was happening. 'Bessy,' my mother began. 'The whole court is talking about the incident with the dresses.'

I stood emotionless. 'What do they say?'

My mother's tone was menacing. 'They say that Richard cannot wait for his wife to die and that he is intending to make you his queen as soon as she does.'

Defiantly I fired back. 'Well that is the truth!'

My mother fixed a silencing glare and continued. 'Everyone believes that it was Richard who instigated the matter with the identical dresses. He wanted to let the court know his intention and to gage their reaction.'

I wanted desperately to tell my mother that it was the queen's idea to wear the dresses, but Anne had ask me not to divulge this information to anyone and I intended to honour her wishes.

My tone continued to be bold. 'Well what else does the court say?'

My mother sat down and shook her head. 'The people love Queen Anne and they believe that you have caused her much distress. They say that Richard has already approached the Pope for dispensation for your marriage to go ahead. There could be one obstacle...the people of England will not allow what happens readily on the continent to happen here...a man marrying his niece...they will not tolerate it. '

I was glad that the whole affair was now in the open and took a deep breath. 'Dickon says that I am not his true niece, father was not his true brother.'

My mother grimaced and puffed out her cheeks 'The people do not want to know what Richard has to say. They believe that he has murdered his nephews and now intends to marry his niece.'

I took a stride towards her. 'You know that is not true. Dickon has sworn that the boys are safe somewhere in England. You yourself received confirmation that they were alive. This was as part of your agreements to come out of sanctuary. We all know that if their whereabouts were known there are many who would use those innocent boys to plunge England once again into civil war. It is Dickon's enemies who spread such wicked lies!'

'It does not matter what you or I think.' My mother was becoming visibly irate. 'The matter is a delicate one, one which we must precede with caution. You will do as you are ordered. It may not now be wise to go ahead with this marriage to Richard.'

Although I knew my mother to be right I also knew what alternative my mother had in store and whispered in insolence. 'I would not marry a man I did not love and there is the babe that grows inside me. Soon it will be plain for all to see.'

My mother stood up and came towards me; I could feel that emotions were running high. 'We will see, but that pleasure of love is denied to most women in your position.'

My mother then left me to mull over what had been said.

Alone, with only the faint snoring of one of the courts wolfhounds as company, I began to reflect on the happenings of the night before. They were indeed bold actions on both Dickson's part and on mine.

Had we done the right thing in letting the court see us together as a couple? Did Dickon gage the moment right or had he doomed us both to a future of lies and deceit?

Throughout that evening my thoughts were far away. Cecily had joined me and we two whiled away the hours playing chess. Cecily tried to cheer me but without success. She had never seen me in such a miserable state. There was little conversation as I hovered close to tears.

Cecily felt uneasy, should she broach the subject of their uncle? Seeing me in such despair, she felt better of it.

As the evening wore on Cecily sighed and seeing that she was not getting any responses from me, began to put the chess pieces back into the boxes. She took me by the hand and looked into my reddened eyes, 'don't worry Bessy, everything will be alright.'

Bursting into tears I sobbed, 'I am expecting a baby.'

Quickly I bit my lip; I had revealed the secret that both Dickon and my mother had told me to keep.

Cecily was dumbstruck as she grasped the true implications of the situation. Never would she have believed things would come to this.

I gathered all my faculties and strength and carried on. 'I am afraid... I have this nagging feeling inside that keeps telling me that things are going to go bad, terribly bad.'

My sister studied the pale face staring back at her and tried to give me a positive thought. 'You must stop distressing yourself. Richard is King. He can do as he wishes. You have nothing to fear.'

There was urgency in my voice. 'There are rumours that Henry Tudor intends to invade and...' my voice trailed off.

Cecily forced a nervous smile and came closer to me. Putting her arms about me tried to avert my fears. 'Richard is an experienced soldier he will not let anyone take his kingdom from him.' With those words Cecily hugged and kissed me.

Looking towards the heavens I could only hope and pray that she was right.

******

Anxiously I waited, keeping myself shut away in my mother's rooms, not knowing how the powerful men that surrounded Dickon were planning out my future. Solitude engulfed me as the days passed and there was no word from Dickon . I felt that I had been abandoned and a sense of panic began to take over my thoughts.

By the end of February, my pregnancy was beginning to show, although I was slender and had done a good job of hiding my condition with discreet panels being cleverly inserted in the back of my dresses, it was clear to everyone who came into contact with me that my belly was swollen and rumours began to circulate that the king intended to marry his niece and that I was indeed pregnant with his child.

At court and throughout London the mood of the people became very hostile towards me and I began to realise how popular Queen Anne was. Throughout the country, especially in the north, the little queen had been adored. During her lifetime she had endeared the people to accept and love Dickon as one of them.

In the eyes of the nation, I had become the evil wicked woman who was helping the queen to her grave. With tormented and guilty thoughts I was constantly experiencing anguish and together with the uncertainty of my plight my hurt became insufferable.

I continued to stay hidden in my mother's apartments, afraid to be seen, for this time in my young life I was truly hated by many of the nobles and most of the citizens.

Then on the sixteenth day of March there was a total eclipse of the sun for almost an hour. During this time it was announced that Queen Anne, most beloved wife of our sovereign King Richard III, had died. She was twenty-seven years old.

I knew Dickon's grief to be genuine, as he truly had loved Anne. She was born at Warwick castle in 1456 and when she was only three years old a young seven year old Dickon had been sent to Warwick to learn the skills needed to be a duke of the realm.

They were indeed childhood friends and Anne had known Dickon all of her life and Dickon was known to be very fond of Anne. It was even rumoured that they were childhood sweethearts.

He arranged a magnificent funeral service and had her buried in Westminster Abbey with grand pomp and ceremony. The people of London lined the streets and mourned their beloved queen.

More and more I would agonize over my position, I could not sleep or eat, overwhelmed by an unexpected emptiness. I spent hours at a time alone, lying in a darkened room shedding tears of despair, frantic to know what would become of my situation as everyday the political landscape changed.

Unknown to me at the time there was a crisis developing. Dickon's trusted councillors, Lovell, Catesby and Radcliff were warning him of the perils of marrying me.

******

Catesby lent forward and pressed his trembling hands against the table. 'It has been announced, as commanded, that you intended to marry the Lady Bessy. I must be honest with you my lord I have never seen the people so shocked by what they heard.'

Radcliff took over. The people of the south may eventually be persuaded to go along with your plans but the people of York will never allow or countenance such an insult to Lord Warwick's daughter. They loved the late queen immeasurably and for your Grace to marry so soon after her passing and to his niece…' his voice trailed off as Richard rose defiantly to his feet, his mind was in turmoil as he turned to Francis, the boyhood friend he loved more that any man,

Richard's reply was passionate, 'I must marry Bessy...I must...I love her.'

Francis then spoke to him with sincerity. 'You need to wait Dickon for the immediate fury to subside then...'

Richard paced about the room, too overwrought to sit. His tone was anxious. 'I will marry Bessy... but not now...you are right it is too soon...the people need time to grieve and to forget...I will go to speak with her later. I am sure that she will understand the delicacy of the present situation.'

Francis forced a smile and hugged Richard as he knew the decision he had come to was a very hard one for him to make.

The very next day Richard gathered the magnates and dignitaries in the hall of St John's at Clerkenwell. There was an audible hubbub as they waited to be addressed.

With his hands trembling and looking visibly nervous Richard then stood before them fiddling with his ring on his little finger. Biting his lip Richard began to speak to them.

He had to play the game of pretence because he desperately needed their support now, more than he had ever had, as news had reached him that the country was about to be invaded any day.

Richard's voice deepened with deliberation and he puffed out his chest and gathered his thoughts. 'There has been treachery amongst some of the nobles,' he announced. He went on, 'wicked lies and vicious rumours have been circulated to discredit me and my rule. Why these vipers want my downfall.'

Swaying visibly with his words he went on. 'I never intended to marry my niece in fact the thought had never crossed my mind. I come here today to address you with the truth.'

Trying to keep a calm exterior as his insides were churning with the untruth's he was telling, Richard continued. 'I assure the council that I intend to send The Lady Bessy to my castle at Sheriff Hutton, to keep her away from her scheming mother who I lay the blame for the nasty rumours that are circulating the country.

Swallowing hard Richard thought on, for in truth Bessy was going to Sheriff Hutton to await the birth of their child and hoping to return to court when Richard triumphed over Henry Tudor.

Richard's voice steadied as he continued. 'The country is under the threat of invasion from Henry Tudor, Earl of Richmond,' he told them. 'And what is more I have learnt that he intends to make his play for the kingship sometime soon and that he has employed more than two thousand French mercenaries to help him do so.'

There was a slight rumbling amongst the gathering as their king continued. 'I intend to raise and army to defeat this usurper who dares to invade our shores. I call upon the dukes and noblemen to make ready their retinues to fight for my cause as your true King of England!'

The people cheered, as every one of them did not want this unknown usurper to replace their Plantagenet King and Richard took heart that soon he would be in the arms of the woman he loved most in the whole world.

With Bessy safely installed in his northern stronghold Richard busied himself in preparation for Tudor's attack. His spies told him that Henry had obtained several ships and was making provisions and preparations for his landing.

All the waiting had made Richard visibly nervous. He paced his chamber continuously, slept very little and began to suspect all of plotting his downfall.

He only hoped and prayed that the day of battle would come soon and that when he was victorious the populace and the nobles would change their minds about his choice of bride. They would be euphoric and in that euphoria would accept Bessy and their baby as his heir and there would be a new beginning for England.

******

When I finally came to him he took me in his arms and told me that I was more beautiful than ever he remembered.

After dismissing each and every one of his servants, Dickon and I were totally alone in an anti chamber. Taking my hand, he led me beyond the splendidly carved oak door into his inner sanctum. He was calm as he spoke to me. 'Dearest,' he began. 'I think it better if we waited to marry. I know that there is the problem of the pregnancy...'

Spontaneously and in great distress, I flung myself on both knees before him; my face had turned a whiter shade of pale and my eyes darted about his face. Emotionally charged I spoke to him. 'I love you! I want to be with you! The baby grows everyday and soon all will know that I carry the king's child!'

Heaving great sobs, tears began to stream down my cheeks and Dickon pressed his lips tight against my forehead before he spoke. 'I want to be with you, but we must wait my love, until the time is right for us to declare our love for one another. You must go to my castle at Sheriff Hutton and when I am triumphant I will send directly for you'.

Dickon reiterated his thoughts to me once more. 'My most faithful servants will tend to your every need. Have our baby and when the time is right I will bring you and our child to London.'

I looked at him and swallowed hard and dried my eyes. Holding wearily onto his hands, I rose and resignedly moved towards the door, as I reached it Dickon clutched me close to him kissing and hugging me.

Totally exhausted by the turn of events I had no more words to give him. If only I could remain here in his arms, for the entire world to know that we are lovers.

With new urgency he spoke to me. 'Now travel tomorrow with twenty of my most loyal members of the household. Only a handful of people know the true reason for your confinement, and I will contact you soon.

I have let it be know that you are in my castle at Sheriff Hutton to keep you away from any more wicked lies and plots.'

Gently touching my stomach, Dickon continued. 'The babe inside you is a boy. I feel rejuvenated by the fact that our son will soon be in the world. You will have the best attention and when he is delivered I promise that I will come to you.'

Taking another deep swallow, I nodded my agreement. Although the thought of my departure upset me, as I could visualise all kinds of dangers ahead, I knew that I had to stay positive for Dickon's sake.

I turned and looked at him one last time, my long white fingers caressed his cheek and then I left him.

The following day I made ready to travel north and prepare for the arrival of my baby, as any lowly woman would have done.

The castle at Sheriff Hutton was warm and welcoming. Set high in the Yorkshire countryside, it was one of Dickon's strongholds with four tall towers and an impenetrable gatehouse.

Away from plots and intrigue of the London court, it made sense for me to come here and no one would think it out of place for me to do so.

In the relative calm and humble setting, I was planning for the child that Dickon and me had set so many hopes on.

It was a boy; I knew from the very first moments that a son was kicking inside me. I had no doubts that soon a prince would be born.

To my delight, I had been informed that Dickon had his brother George's children, my cousins, Edward and Margaret, living there. They had been there since moving from Middleham in the early days of Anne's illness as Sheriff Hutton, remote and foreboding was considered a more secure place to keep the royal children.

The April weather was especially mild that year and I would often sit in the company of my cousins in the small secure courtyard. To my pleasure there was also a lovely little garden within the castle walls. The centre piece of the garden was a large white marble figure of Neptune with fish and from each fishes mouth water spouted into a lily filled fish pond. I would often share a small seat by a laurel tree with Margaret.

Margaret was now a very mature eleven years old and her brother was nine. He, however, I had noticed was very backward for his age. He was dull witted and his speech was ill formed. The reason for this was a certain cloudiness of mind and he always had a nurse in attendance.

At first the two did not know me to be their cousin, as I had never met Edward of Warwick and had only met Margaret when she was no more than a baby. But there was no mistaking their blond Plantagenet looks and their fine noble bearing.

'Why are you here?' Margaret asked one day whilst sitting herself next to me on the ornamental garden seat.

I was startled; I had not met anyone before who was so direct in their questioning. I decided to be just as blunt, for in just over a month I would be delivered my first child. 'I come to have a baby.'

Margaret did not flinch at this news and continued her questioning. 'Will you be sent away with your baby like our cousins Eddy and Dickie?'

At the mention of these names I could feel my pulse quicken as I realised that the girl was speaking of my brothers.

With necessity in my voice I set about questioning a very knowledgeable Margaret. Without stopping for breath I bombarded, my now bewildered cousin, with probing questions. 'What do you know about the Princes? When were they here? Where are they now?'

Margaret sighed and began to fidget in her seat as she began to try and answer. She did not realise the meaning of the questioning or the importance of her answers. 'They came to stay at the Castle for a few weeks last summer before they were sent away...it was a long time ago now...I think Eddy said that they were to go to another one of Uncle Richard's strongholds near Wales?'

Looking unto the heavens I made the sign of the cross and let out a long breath of air. Although I had never doubted Dickon it was a relief to acknowledge that

257

what he had told me was indeed the truth; my brothers were definitely safe somewhere in Wales.

The weeks spent in the company of my cousins were pleasant enough. I would read to them and tell them stories of monsters and giants. Little Ned enjoyed my renditions and would squeal with excitement every time I would begin a new tale.

It was mid June when I received a much awaited letter from Dickon. It began with his desire to be with me and his total love and commitment to our union. He then went on to explain that he had moved his court once more to Nottingham because he had it on good authority that Tudor was about to invade. His spies had reported that a fleet was being fitted out at Harfleur and the only problem remaining was what part of the country Henry would land. Dickon felt that Nottingham was a good base as it was centrally placed in the realm and this would enable him to strike swiftly and with ease in any direction.

He had left a body of councillors in charge of London and trusted the Mayor and other dignitaries with its defence. He went on to tell me he had with him several fine nobles, but he had his suspicions about the loyalty of some.

Placing the letter next to my heart I thought on Dickon's words. Could the Stanley brothers be relied on? Sir Thomas Stanley had once before given Dickon cause for distrust two years previously when Hastings lost his head. He was married to Henry Tudor's mother and Dickon had proof that she was still aiding and abetting her son in Brittany.

Sir William Stanley, Thomas's brother, Dickon also had his doubts about. A sixth sense told him that the Duke of Northumberland also could not be trusted.

My mind continued racing with dark thoughts. These men wanted Dickon's downfall as he had alienated them when he was Duke of Gloucester and their overlord. They also believed that they could gain so much more if Henry was their king.

Dickon had impressed on me how much he needed the support of these lords as they commanded thousands of men and could control the outcome of the battle. I knew that he was hopeful in the thought that the Stanleys always backed the winning side and at the moment that looked like his.

I lifted the letter once again to my eyes to re read the last heartfelt sentiment. He finished his letter with his love for me and for me to be positive and to pray for a positive outcome.

Clutching the letter once more close to my chest I sighed. How I desperately missed him, every part of me longed to be with him.

I would pray several times every day in the tiny chapel that God would grant Dickon a victory and that the nobles would relent and that we would be married.

******

I was growing tired of the secret life I was now living. I longed for the day when Dickon would deem it safe for me to be brought forth, to declare his love openly, and for my unborn child to be acknowledged.

The days grew long and many hours were now being spent walking in the garden, talking or playing quiet games with my cousins. There was no news of my mother or of any my sisters and I could only hope that all was well with them.

It was the second day of July, the sun slanted through the leaves of the great oak tree and the castle walls seemed to shimmer in the intense light.

Shaded by a canopy, I breathed a deep breath and sipped a refreshing drink of herbs.

My cousins were much too boisterous for me now as I was tired easily as the baby now grew to full size inside me.

My eyes squinted and I raised my hands to my forehead. A hazy figure, all alone and caring a huge bag was coming into focus. My face lit up as I recognised it was Veronique coming towards me.

Images and thoughts flooded my mind of a time when I was a royal Princess and had many ladies in waiting at my beck and call. None was more attentive to my every need than Veronique and I was overwhelmed to see her. She was all alone and I wondered how she had made her way here.

Her steps were fast and paced as she neared me.

Standing to greet my friend with renewed energy my tone was urgent. 'Is it really you? Thank God you are here. I feel much better in the knowledge that you are now by my side. How did you get here?' My questions were coming thick and fast.

Taking my hand and sitting me down Veronique studied her friend. I shook my head in disbelief and let my friend chatter on, conveying important words I needed to hear.

'The king sends me as he knows that you and I have grown close over the years and he believes that my presence will lighten your worries. The escort left me at the castle gate as the king instructed them.

His Grace has confided in me the nature of your stay at Sheriff Hutton and asks that I come and comfort you. You do indeed look pale and weary. Do not worry my lady all will be well. Now come we must be optimistic for the sake of the unborn babe.'

There was an all knowing look in Veronique's eyes and I guessed that she had been told the whole story.

Veronique was the most positive person that I had ever known and everyday she would try and convince me that Dickon would defeat Henry and that I would soon be queen.

Veronique stayed close to me throughout my confinement in the darkened room adorned with religious artefacts and the virginal blue cloths, sleeping on a truckle bed next to me.

It was on the eighteenth day of July that the pains started and the birthing chamber was made ready. Two midwives, from the local village were in attendance. As far as they knew it was a noble woman from York who was there to give birth and no one questioned that story.

'Sweet Jesus!' I cried, trying to choke back the pain.

Veronique held my hand tightly and I squeezed it to the rhythm of my contractions. 'I am afraid,' I gasped.

'You are in good hands,' Veronique reassured me. 'You are a strong healthy girl you will make nothing of this.'

Panting, I stayed silent and waited for the next spasm of pain. I was well aware of the high death rate of infants and also that of mothers.

Dickon's daughter Catherine, who had married William Herbert, Earl of Huntingdon in the spring of the previous year, had died giving birth to a stillborn son and I was fearful that might be my fate too.

The pains were now unbearable and continuous. Locked in my own world of effort I was dimly aware of the other people shuffling about me. In the muffled din I could hear words of encouragement.

I gave one final push and then, relief, the pain was gone and in its place I heard the sound of a baby's cry. Tears of joy ran down my cheeks as I realised that the baby and I were alive.

'You have a fine son!' Mistress Wheatley exclaimed, smiling down at me.

Heaving a huge sigh I whispered, 'can I see him?'

The baby was already wrapped in his swaddling sheet as I gazed onto the tiny face. 'I will call him Richard for his father.'

Mistress Wheatley took the babe and placed him in his crib by my bedside, as I had demanded beforehand. I would go against tradition and keep the baby with me although a wet nurse from the local village was employed to feed the babe.

Mistress Wheatley's voice was firm, 'now you must try and get some rest, it has been a long delivery, you must be totally exhausted.'

'Ti's done,' Veronique whispered as she gazed upon the small bundle. 'You have given Richard the son he has dreamed of.'

I nodded in agreement. I had done it; I had given the king an heir of his body, surely he will come to me as soon as he hears of the boy's birth. With that final thought exhaustion finally got the better of me and almost at once I drifted off to sleep full of contentment.

Over the next few days many prayers were said in the tiny chapel thanking God for the safe delivery of the infant and the quick recovery of his mother. I also thanked God for answering my prayers and giving me the healthy son I so much wanted.

Every day I would hold my baby and look in wonderment at him. He was sturdy with a strong cry and he had a look of his father about him. He was the most wonderful thing that had happened to me but I could not understand why Dickon had not made haste to see his newborn son.

******

Wistfully I gazed at Veronique. 'Why does Dickon not come? I have been assured that a secret message had been sent telling him that he has a fine healthy son.'

Veronique stopped what she was doing and putting her hand about my waist, led me to a private corner and sat me down. 'It is a very difficult time for Richard,' she began. 'He has sworn the handful of people who know of little Dickon's birth to secrecy. He is probably doing his utmost to keep the barons on his side and therefore keep hold of his throne. As we speak he musters a large army, he will defeat this impostor and then you will be queen. Then together you will announce that there is already a Prince.'

I did not look convinced and Veronique continued to assure me of a positive outcome. 'The king has many, many more men than Henry… he will be victorious!'

I gave a weak smile and a faint nod, my friend had cheered me and I began to take heart that I could look to a happy future.

But although I knew that Veronique was right, I was tired of waiting; I had been at Sheriff Hutton over three months now. With hope I asked. 'Has Henry set sailed yet? He has lingered all summer surely he can linger no longer?'

Veronique's tone was serious. 'I know not but I do know that many of Dickons's supporters could desert him if they think that you have given birth to his son.'

263

My tone was adamant. 'I don't see why, as least now they have a Prince that will continue the Plantagenet line, a line that can be traced as far back as Henry the Second.'

Veronique shook her head. 'You do not understand, many still feel that Dickon would have committed a sin to have been intimate with his niece, and although you were betrothed to Dickon and you are not true uncle and niece, the child has been born out of wedlock.'

My whole being was laced with terror and tears began to well up in my eyes. 'All this waiting and not knowing is what I cannot bear. I know that little Dickon would be accepted as the king's heir if he could only defeat The Tudor.'

Veronique put her arms about me, 'you must have patients. Everything will be all right you'll see.'

My thoughts were fraught as I realised that the stakes were high, for the winner there would be thrones and life and for the loser there could be only death.

Dickon, I thought, was doing the only thing he could. I trusted that he would get word to me when the time was right.

Weariness settled over Sheriff Hutton throughout the rest of July and as the days of July heated into August, I was becoming more and more worried.

It was now almost four weeks since baby Dickens birth and the isolation and uncertainties were beginning to play on my mind. My sleep was interrupted by dreams of death and all its horrors. Fearful, I would wake in a cold sweat gripped in fear and anxiety.

It was early afternoon when Veronique came into my room. Her round face had a smile on it as she gave me a rolled scroll. I knew by the seal that it was the letter I had been waiting for; at last, I had received news from Dickon.

With trembling hands I began to read it. Keeping Dickon's intimate words of love and longing to myself, I relayed the rest of the message to Veronique.

I spoke aloud. 'Dickon speaks of the future with me and his son as soon as he has dealt with the impostor who would take his kingdom.' I looked at Veronique there was a gaze of concentration on her face, taking in every word uttered as I continued. 'Henry hoisted sail on the first day of August and landed, backed by a fair wind, at Milford Haven in Wales, after fourteen years in exile. Henry has marched towards Shrewsbury and Richard intendeds to meet the upstart near Leicester.'

There was a silence as I looked heavenwards. My tone was almost a whisper as I finally spoke. 'The time has almost come Veronique.'

I put the letter in my purse and slumped onto my bed. Within days I would know my fate.

✶✶✶✶✶✶

The dawn light was just appearing when I was gently shaken. At first I thought it was one of my very vivid dreams, but on opening my eyes I focused them on Veronique. 'My lady must come quickly,' she whispered.

Bewildered I did as I was told and within moments I was in the presence of several men. They bowed when I approached and one stepped forward. I recognised him as John of Norfolk and there was another man with him who I recognised to be Francis, Lord Lovell.

Stony faced, Norfolk's tone was urgent. 'The king has commanded me to bring you and his son to him, for he wishes to see you both before he leaves Leicester to do battle.'

I was shaken; I had not expected such a visit, silence gripped me as I continued to listen.

Lovell stepped closer. 'His Majesty has had terrible visions and dreams. He wants to see his loved ones in case'...his voice trailed off.

Their words brought the realisation that the battle was to be very soon and a terrible feeling of dread came into the pit of my stomach. Finding my voice I spoke in feeble tones. 'Does the king fear for the battle?'

Lovell continued. 'His Grace has had bad omens and believes that there are those among us that are treacherous.'

I was feeling terror boiling inside me, I wanted to shout and scream that Dickon had to win the battle or my life would not be worth living, but instead I signalled to my ladies to prepare for the journey. I knew that I could not deny Dickon this request and gave the order to make the baby ready.

A litter was quickly prepared for me, a wagon fifteen feet long painted red with gold gilt bearing the Royal Insignia on both sides.

The baby, Veronique, and myself together with the wet nurse were soon made comfortable for the trip, the inside of the litter was even more luxurious than the outer with large soft cushioned seats and padded walls.

It was before dawn when the party departed the grounds of Sheriff Hutton, the time of day when the grey mist begins to evaporate from the dew sodden grass and the birds in the trees begin to wake and sing their chorus of song.

'The roads are treacherous and the riding will be hard. I have men to keep the wagon wheels from becoming stuck in the mud. I only hope that I can make your journey as comfortable as possible in the

circumstances.' Norfolk announced whilst closing the wagon's heavy curtains as protection against the hot August sun.

I nodded and with a shout the wagon wheels began to turn. We travelled all of that day and into the night.

I could not sleep. The journey from Sheriff Hutton to Leicester Castle was over one hundred miles. Everyone inside the litter sat in silence in the half shaded light.

All I could hear was the endless creaking of the wagon wheels. Veronique sat silently praying and handling her rosary. I too silently prayed, I asked God to deliver Dickon a resounding victory and to forgive me for my sins. That it was not Dickons fault, I had been the instigator and if anyone needed to be punished it was I, not Dickon or our son.

The journey from Sheriff Hutton to Leicester was made in urgency, with only short stops for rest and much needed nourishment and fresh horses, as there was a desperate need to reach Leicester at quickly as possible.

Just as the light was fading on the second day Leicester Castle came into view. A more pleasing sight I had never seen, for I was totally exhausted. In the circumstances we had covered the ground in record time.

Dickon was waiting in the courtyard dressed in full armour. He welcomed me sweetly, but not overly emotional, as he instructed John of Norfolk to take my party and me to our quarters.

His manner did not surprise me, as Dickon was generally circumspect in public; it was unusual for him to be more demonstrative than handholding or a discreet kiss. I could see that Dickon was very much preoccupied with the imminent battle.

267

When at last alone Dickon put his arm gently around me, I saw a faint light of pleasure come into his eyes.

As I carried our son to the appointed rooms, he spoke in muted tones. 'Bessy, it pleases me greatly that you are here with our son. He is strong and will make a fine Plantagenet Prince.'

Cheerful I gazed at him and looked down upon the sleeping babe in my arms. Touching the baby's fine brown hair Dickon smiled kindly at the sleeping infant. 'I am contented now that you are here. I can now go and face my enemy with renewed strength.'

My tone was enquiring as I spoke to him. 'My being here, does this mean that the nobles know of our love?'

Dickon took in a deep breath. 'I am going to assemble them tomorrow. Inform them that you and I are pledged and show them that I have an heir. I only hope that my speech will make the boy a rallying point for my armies against the Welsh impostor and his foreign army of mercenaries.'

Dickon forced a weak smile and held me close to his chest. His determination to marry me had never been so fierce. 'You must not worry sweet Bessy. After the fight I am sure that the nobles will not stand in our way and I expect to receive permission for dispensation from The Pontiff any day now. I am confident that he will permit our marriage, for he often does authorize such unions and then we will reign together as husband and wife.'

That night I shared Dickon's bed. I propped myself up on to the pillow and studied his face. Moving closer I whispered, 'I was thinking of the pleasure you give me and how much I love you, a love that cannot be broken through distance or even death.'

Dickon gave a nervous smile. His countenance was serious and repeatedly he took deep breaths; his thoughts were thick and muddy. 'You must flee the country with our son if I am defeated at the battle.'

I forced the picture from my mind; I refused to think morbid thoughts for Dickon will be victorious. 'You must not think such a thing...your army is twice as many as Tudor's...you will be triumphant...I know not what I would do without you?'

Slumping downwards, Dickon looked toward the heavens as he spoke. 'I have terrible dreams that I will never see you again and I cannot bear the thought of it.'

I could see beads of sweat beginning to form on his brow and I knew that he had many doubts. 'You must believe,' I softly whispered.

After a few moments thought he spoke again. 'I have always tried to do the right thing in the eyes of God. I did not want my brother George to die... I did not even want the old King Henry to die... I even had his body removed from its place at Chertsey and reburied at Westminster...I have shown compassion and justice to all my people, from the lowly peasants to the mighty Lords. When Jane Shore's solicitor, Thomas Lydnom, came to me requesting her release from Newgate Prison did I not free her and give my blessing to their marriage?

Above all, I have asked myself time and time again why Edward could not have lived long enough for his son to come to man's estate. It was the council and finally the people of London that persuaded me to become their king.'

I tried to sooth his mind; I gently stroked his brow with my fingertips. 'The people love you Dickon...although you have only reigned for just over two years you have been a great King.'

269

Dickon could tell from my tone that I had much admiration for him and that my belief in him was unswerving.

Then a curious smile came across his features as he continued to pour out his inmost feelings. 'I wonder why men want power. If they could see me now, bowed down with work and worry, fears of plots and anguish over the plight of the nation... I never wanted power.'

My heart was breaking by his words of despair; I needed desperately to lift his spirits. 'You have been handed a sacred trust, a duty. Don't you worry God will see you through, you are the true rightful king.'

Dickon nodded and exhausted by the day's events closed his eyes.

All through the night his sleep was uneasy and on two occasions awoke in fits of shouts and curses. I tried my best to sooth him. Our sleep was little that night.

The next morning Dickon was up with the crow of the cock and preparing to leave Leicester. He took mass alone in the tiny castle chapel, before returning to his still sleeping love.

I got up and ran to him; I wanted to spend the last few precious minutes alone with him. Deep down inside I had a feeling that they may be my last and I flung my self around his neck and kissed him tenderly. Dickon did not respond to my kisses and held me at arms length. His mind was elsewhere.

The Castle was full of the shout and noises of men making ready to go to do battle and my heart began to race inside me.

His voice was determined. 'We march today, for I have news that Tudor is advancing from Fenny Drayton and is camped to the south of the little market town of Bosworth.'

I threw myself to him and kissed his lips. This time he did respond and I felt his wet kisses upon me. With my heart pounding I let him go. 'Come back soon, my love.'

Dickon smiled and nodded, turned and without looking back, left me.

He rode to the White Boar Inn. There he met with the Duke of Norfolk, Francis Lovell, as well as the Duke of Northumberland.

The next day, after a few hours of discussion and tactics, the king's army rode out to meet their adversary on the twenty first day of August. The two armies were to engage on the plain known as Redemoor on the very next day.

******

Old Dick looked at Sir Thomas; his eyes were glistening from the dampness of his tears.

Composing himself he went on with his rendition of what really happened that day sixty years ago. 'Richard, did on the eve on the battle, recognise me as his son to all the nobles that were present.

He called a meeting in his marquee only hours before the fighting. He told them that if he were to be victorious he intended to marry the Lady Bessy and that I would benefit as to my blood.'

Dick bowed his head and swallowed hard. 'But it was not to be, Richard was mercilessly killed during the battle.'

Narrowing his eyes he continued, with renewed vigour. 'Right from the start there were bad omens. When Richard rode hurriedly out of Leicester his spur scraped the bridge over the River Stour. An old crone approached. My lord, she is reported to have said. There are bad omens in you scraping the bridge.

271

As darkness fell tents were erected on the hill at Ambien. Richard wandered the camp unable to sleep. He sat with the men who were huddled in groups around fires talking quietly and preparing weapons, the men greeted him cheerfully and respectfully, they were glad to be fighting under him, the Tudor had no chance!

On the morning of the battle no breakfast had been prepared and there was no chaplain in attendance. This made the men very edgy.

More disturbing was a note found nailed to Norkork's tent. It read, 'Jack of Norfolk don't be bold, Dickon your master is bought and sold'.

On reading this Richard's feelings of insecurity were proved right, there were those inside the camp who were untrue, but it was too late now to do anything about this state of affairs as the battle was only hours away.'

Dick paused to gather his thoughts and then continued what was becoming a very difficult rendition. 'At first, however, the battle seemed to be going the king's way even though it was a great blow to Richard when his good friend Norfolk, was killed by the Earl of Oxford.

Richard then gave the order for Northumberland and his men to bring up the rear guard. But Henry Percy had no intention risking his neck in a feud that had taken the life of his father and grandfather. He took his cue from the Stanley's whose armies had not moved.

Richard now knew that Northumberland and The Stanleys were not going to commit to the battle.

Just at that moment Richard, at the top of the hill, spotted the Red Dragon banner of Henry's. Henry, who had no experience of war, was being kept away from the main battle with about fifty of his French mercenaries as protection.

Then, in a moment of great courage, together with his household knights, Richard charged down the northwestern slope of Ambien Hill and thundered out across the plain towards Henry. Richard knew that if he could kill Henry he could win the battle with one blow saving many lives.'

Dick looked forlorn as he continued remembered that day. 'He almost made it… he killed Henry's standard-bearer and another one of Henry's protectors… he almost reached the usurper. It was at this moment that his fears of treason came true, for he was betrayed by Thomas Stanley and his three thousand men, who came to the aid of his stepson Henry.

Richard fought bravely until his horse was killed under him; he put his shield before him and continued to fight on foot. In the fury of the fighting, Francis Lovell offered him another horse to make his escape but Richard refused to desert the battlefield and his men. He would die King of England this day! Outnumbered, he was mercilessly cut to pieces.'

Sir Thomas could see that the old man was becoming more and more upset at the revelations and stopped him to regain his composure.

After a few thoughtful long minutes Dick again began his account.

'Very early the next day a man came riding into Leicester shouting that the king had lost. The reign of the Plantagenets' was over.'

Dick's eyes were piercing with emotion as he continued. 'Every time the crown changed hands there had been wholesale murder among all the noble boys and men related to the dead king and Henry Tudor would be no exception.

I was whisked away, by those still loyal to the dead king, from the north and taken south. There, in great secrecy, I was given to a schoolmaster and his wife to bring up as their own son. I was only six weeks old when I was given over to a couple who were truly loyal and trustworthy and I treated my adopted parents as if they were my true ones.

From time to time a gentleman came who paid for my food and schooling and asked many questions to discover if I was being well cared for.'

The old man sighed and his tone became agitated as he retraced the heartbreaking life of his mother. 'Henry Tudor was furious when he found out, from informants inside Sheriff Hutton, that my mother had given birth to Richard's son.

After ordering a search for anyone who knew of my mother's whereabouts he shouted orders at Lord Stanley to find The Lady Bessy and take her to see Richard's naked and bleeding corpse that was being displayed at Leicester, before being hurriedly buried, without ceremony, at The Abbey of The Grey Friars Monastery nearby.'

******

Closing my eyes in complete horror, I instinctively buried my head in my hands when I first gazed upon Dickon's lifeless corpse hanging by its roped hands and covered in caked blood and mud.

Stanley forced me to look, pulling my hands from my eyes and lifting my head, until my view was of that which he wanted.

'Look! Look at the lifeless body!' Stanley shouted, savagely holding my wrist so tightly that I felt that I was going too loose consciousness.

Screaming wildly and quivering in horror I begged to be excused from this nightmare, my voice was shrill with terror as I spoke. 'Please my Lord I cannot look, do not force me!'

Stanley did not take notice of my pleas. 'It is the king's orders. He wants you and everyone else to know that your beloved Richard is dead and that he, Henry Tudor, is now King of England.'

Stanley's tone was wild. 'Richard was a fool, for he should have done away with the plotters and schemers even though the instigators were women. If he had taken a tougher line with the rebel gentry Henry would not have had the number of men who joined him at Bosworth. Richard was always too chivalrous for his own good.'

He went on to give an example. 'The king's mother, the Lady Margaret, who was the biggest traitor and she enveloped many with her giving promises of lands and wealth to all who aided her son when he became king.'

Sobbing uncontrollably, I was taken from the Abbey and made ready for my trip to London. My beloved had been brutally murdered and my son was now in a far away place not known to me and I would probably never see him again.

I cried until I had run out of tears. Although I was alive my heart was now dead. At that moment, life seemed at an end.

With the exhaustion of my grief, my motionless body was preened and dressed in finery. Henry wanted above all else to keep my secret life from the populace, to conceal my time with Dickon and to suppress rumours of a son that was fruit of that union.

Henry pacified my young cousins who had been taken from Sheriff Hutton and were to accompany me on the journey to London.

I had decided not to discuss my situation with them. Young Ned was of infant mind and although Margaret was mature for her age, I did not want her to be privy to things she could never understand.

Veronique had been dismissed and one who was Henry's choice sat with me.

The journey was a slow procession with people at every town and village coming to get a glimpse of the royal party. I did not wave and acknowledge their greetings, I was still and silent and every now and then irrepressible tears would flow down my face.

Henry was devastated at the realisation that I was not as he was led to believe. I had not been waiting and praying for him to come to England and make a bid for the kingship. My scheming mother had lied in order for him to make a public announcement of his betrothal in the Cathedral at Rennes on the Christmas past.

In front of nobles and clergy he had promised to marry me and unite the houses of Lancaster and York. Only now he knew the truth. I had deeply loved the dead king and Henry soon realised that I would never give my heart to him.

He began to have second thoughts about marrying me; he even considered a marriage with the older sister of Sir Walter Herbert and also with the heiress, Anne of Brittany.

On the thirtieth day of October Henry was crowned, but still delayed announcing his intention of marrying me.

There were numerous claimants to the English throne; most were more legitimate than Henry's and so he immediately set about imprisoning and executing all those Yorkist royals and nobles that had been captured.

He dated his kingship to the day before the battle making those who fought for their true king traitors and liable not only to be put to death but for their lands and castles to be confiscated and given to the crown.

He imprisoned the infantile Edward of Warwick in the Tower for no other reason than he was a threat to his new position.

When news reached me of my young cousin's plight I complained bitterly to all who would listen, but Henry kept the boy under his watchful eye safe under lock and key inside the capital's stronghold.

******

Margaret Beaufort entered Henry's private chamber. She was the mother who had worked so hard for him to become king and knew every secret of her son's heart. She had given birth to Henry at only fourteen years of age after a marriage to King Henry VI half brother Edmund Tudor.

Edmund had died of plague three months before the baby was born and left Margaret a very young, rich widow.

After a second marriage to Henry Stafford, where she once again became a widow, she married a third time to Thomas Stanley.

She did not have any more children and as time went by she became ever more devoted to her exiled son, Henry. He became the only meaning for her existence and she had worked tirelessly for his eventual return to England in triumph.

Dismissing the servants, she began to speak to her beloved son. Her tone was direct and assured. 'My son you need to marry Bessy of York, for the people, especially those of the north expect it of you.'

Henry bit his lip and although his mother was the only person in the world who knew his innermost thoughts he weighed his words carefully. 'Mother, the woman is opposed and has made her feelings well known to me. Her every thought is taken by her dead love and her missing child.'

Margaret went near to her son and looked up into his pale grey eyes, although she was diminutive and he was almost six feet tall, Henry respected and almost feared his mother.

Raising herself up she went on, her tone was soft but firm. 'It is our only chance for everlasting peace for it will unite the fighting fractions.' She paused and she could see Henry's mind working. With caution she continued. 'In time she will forget what has past. She is a charming girl who I am sure will do her duty, royal women marry whom they are told too and love does not enter into the equation.' I have married three times and each time politics not love came into the decision making. As for the affair with Richard and their child, I am sure we can erase it from history.'

Silently Henry nodded, for he knew that his mother was right, she was the only person he would take advice from, he had not come this far not to consolidate his position.

******

Henry had given Elizabeth Woodville all of her titles back and in the second week of December she hurried along the draughty, dark corridors of Westminster to Bessy's rooms.

Out of breath she dismissed the servants, as she did not want any in earshot of what she was about to say. She knew how they listen and then would talk amongst themselves in the kitchens or hallways.

Bessy's apartments were lavish, with sumptuous wall hangings and the costliest of furnishings. But

Elizabeth could see that her daughter was miserable, for she knew that her thoughts were far away in the past, where she was reliving time and time again happier moments when Richard was king. Elizabeth did not dwell on the past, she was realistic and practical and desperately wanted Bessy to realise that she had to pay homage to Henry if she wanted to become his queen.

Elizabeth's tone was light as she began to speak to her daughter. 'I have it on good advice that Henry has finally decided to make you his wife. Parliament itself, on behalf of the people, petitioned him to carry out his promise.'

Bessy did not answer and continued to stare at her reflection in the silver edged looking glass and continued brushing her long auburn coloured hair. She knew that any protest would be futile; she had long ago understood that she would have to accept her fate.

Elizabeth Woodville's manner became menacing as she went and sat next to Bessy. 'You should think yourself lucky that Henry has committed himself in a marriage to you…after all he knows about…' her voice trailed off.

Bessy was scathed by these words and took in a deep breath of air, 'lucky! lucky!'

Elizabeth could see the venom well up in Bessy's eyes as she responded to her.

Bessy could not understand how Elizabeth Woodville could accept Henry with such good cheer after all she knew about her daughter's situation.

Slumping back into her chair and exhaling deeply Elizabeth Woodville continued to cohere her daughter. 'My dearest daughter I do what I must and so must you. Henry is a man who will not let any obstacle stand in his way.'

With indignity and without another word she upped and left Bessy to think over what she had said.

Bessy could not fight her destiny. Was her life now to be buffeted from one situation to another? Never to be consulted of her wishes, they would do with her now what suited them best?

So on a misty morning on the eighteenth day of January 1486 the marriage took place at Westminster. The people celebrated the event with dancing, songs and banquets throughout London.

But for Bessy being queen was the beginning of a life of misery with someone she could never ever love or care for as in her eyes Henry had been the destroyer of all her dreams.

Almost immediately after the wedding she found her new husband to be cold and uncaring, with a scheming personality who lived his life in a web of secrecy, for Henry confided in no one.

His appearance was that of a scholar, with a balding head and bad teeth. He was tall and had acquired a stoop. Realising at once that he was devious and acquisitive, with an unrevealing gaze; she felt abhorrence deep within her.

She remained numb to all her lamentation and she had no choice but to surrendered herself into the rough hands of Henry.

She cringed at Henry's feeble attempts to woo her and was inwardly repelled by his advances. Throughout she did not take part in any of their lovemaking, feeling like a lifeless corpse as Henry aroused himself about her. She felt repulsed by his intimacy and as each new day began she wished herself dead so she could once again be with her beloved Richard.

Then one day she found herself to have symptoms that she dreaded, sickness in the mornings and a light dizziness of the head. She knew that she was pregnant.

This child would be born a royal Prince and her confinement would be made a public declaration. The rooms would be made darken and warm and she would be churched in a ceremony for the whole court to attend.

This was in complete contrast to her firstborn who was now living with a secret identity and she knew not where he was.

******

Sir Thomas made a gesture for Dick to stop his tale, for as darkness began to fall he needed his servants to return momentarily to light the room that they were in. He could hear and indeed smell that the lanterns were being lit all around the great house and he knew that anyone overhearing the old man's reminisces could report what they had heard to the authorities and then his lordship would find himself in serious trouble.

Sir Thomas knew the importance of complete secrecy. The political atmosphere was volatile; it was now a new age where the Plantagenet past seemed a long, long time ago.

There was a renaissance sweeping Europe but in England an ageing Henry VIII kept a vice like hold on all his subjects. Over his thirty five year reign, he had become a tyrant and had executed many Plantagenet and Yorkist sympathisers.

By the glow of a hundred candles smothering the newly refurbished hall, Dick looked at the earl and lifted his empty glass. Sir Thomas poured out two more draughts of wine and looked expectantly at Dick for him to continue. Sir Thomas could not believe that there were even more remarkable revelations.

'Almost two years had past since the merciless killing of King Richard and many of the Yorkist supporters were now on the continent far away from Henry's court.

Henry was shrewd and had many spies for he knew that there were those ill bent on his downfall and most of the plots were uncovered.

There had been many attempts on Henry's life and he now surrounded himself with a newly formed body guard, The Yeoman Warders.

There was a slight pause as Dick weighed carefully what he was about to say. 'Francis Lovell, one of the few Yorkist nobles to survive Bosworth and Richard's nephew, the twenty three year old, John de la Pole, Earl of Lincoln, had backed a pretender called Lambert Simnel as their supporters needed a viable candidate to rally around.'

The young Earl of Lincoln gathered those still loyal to his dead uncle; passion could be heard in his voice. 'Many will flock to our banner as the Tudor is hated by many whose power he has stripped by his new laws of liveries.'

No longer could mighty subjects keep and maintain large armies of men...only the king could now, by the new laws, do that.

Francis backed his friend's viewpoint and addressed the crowd. 'Yes John is right when Henry banned liveries he made many of the nobles weak and in servitude to him. He is masterful at making new laws that weaken his subjects' powers but strengthen his.'

John took over and laid out his plan to those gathered. 'We intend to oust this Henry Tudor by any means possible. We need to gather support for this man

Simnel by spreading about that Simnel is indeed a lost Plantagenet Prince.' John lowered his head and Francis knew that his emotions were getting the better of him.

Francis continued. 'We who had been close to Richard know that the real Princes were safe somewhere in England or maybe Wales at the time of Bosworth. It is considered that Henry could now have them in prison somewhere in the west. When we are triumphant we would then free the Princes, the true Yorkist claimants.'

Dick closed his eyes as he recounted what happened to the last of his father's faithful supporters. 'They had gathered an army and clashed with the king's men on the sixteenth day of June at, The Battle of Stoke.'

Then Dick squeezed tight his eyes as if to stop the flow of tears he was now feeling well up within him. A lump came to his throat as he struggled to speak. 'It was here that all the remaining gentry loyal to Richard, all who knew of his secret amour and his child, met their end.

Now Henry could breath a sigh of relief and to begin to feel safe in the knowledge that the episode with the Princess of York and the dead king would now pale into history.'

Dick sighed and went on. 'The episode was a complete victory for Henry as it was proved that Simnel was in fact the son of an Oxfordshire pastry cook. To favour with the people, Henry pardoned the boy, who he believe to be an innocent partaker in the events, and took him into service as a kitchen scullion and years later he became Master of the King's Falconry.'

******

Henry was angry as he sat with me in the privy garden. 'It is rumoured that your mother was involved

*with the baker's son. She was privy to his plans. Your
mother is a source of irritation to me. Ever since my
plan to marry her to the King of Scotland had failed she
is forever meddling in affairs that do not concern her. I
have thought long about it, she will have to be removed
from court. I intend to send her to Bermonsey Abbey.'*

*I did not answer him; I would not put it past my
mother to be involved in such a scheme. My silence
prompted Henry to further explanation. 'She will have
her own apartments and apart from the seclusion from
the court she will live a comfortable life.' There was a
short pause where Henry fired himself, 'It is a nunnery
or The Tower!' He fumed.*

*I swallowed hard and nodded. I could see no
way to defend my meddlesome mother. In any case I had
long ago learnt how to hide my true feelings.*

*It was within a few days that Henry's orders
were enacted. Without ceremony or even a last audience
with any of her family, my mother was taken to
Bermondsey Abbey with only a personal maid as
company. She was no longer permitted to travel around
the country or communicate with whom she liked.*

*My thoughts were ones of sorrow as I
remembered how magnificent my mother was at the
Plantagenet Court and how now she had become so
pitiful.*

*Inside Bermonsey Abbey my mother reflected
upon her life. Had it come to this, once the queen of a
much love king and the mother of the Queen of England
to be locked away from society in a cocoon of people
vetted by Henry?*

*She had twice suffered the sanctuary, but there
she was in charge of her own fate, she was in power of
her own little world and the people who came and went*

left her informed about the goings on in the outside world.

There was none of this now. She never again would see her grandchildren and rarely any of her daughters came to visit, as Henry did not want her to become informed of the outside world. My mother knew that it was not our will, as she was very close to her daughters ...it was Henry's. He had made a decision that it was almost thought dangerous to visit her as she could so easily get involved into more treason.

It was true my mother lived well inside the Abbey, but she felt pangs of frustration when she heard that I was to have a wondrous coronation and she was not permitted to attend. It was monstrous that the mother of the queen would not be at her own daughter's coronation... If only my father had lived...if only Dickon had been victorious.

My mother thought that when Dickon took the crown he was being unreasonable holding her sons captive and declaring that he was the true legitimate king. Now she knew that what he had said was true; she had married my father whilst he and Eleanor Butler were betrothed. Now on reflection she should have supported Dickon and then maybe these Tudors would not have had such a hold on her.

My mother had been locked up inside Bermonsey for almost three years and word had reached me that she was unwell and may not recover from her ailment.

I arrived at the nunnery, Henry did not know of my intended visit to my sick mother. Leaving my ladies and personal guard at the chamber door I entered my mother's modest room. 'Dear mother,' I whispered as I knelt beside her bed. I had never seen my mother look so sickly.

Slowly my mother opened her eyes, at first she must have though that she was dreaming. Putting her hand out to touch me, she gave a small cry of joy, 'Bessy,' she wheezed. 'I am so glad to see you.'

Tears began to fill my eyes and I instantly forgave my mother for all her misguided deeds in the past. She had suffered greatly for them and I knew that now my mother's life was almost at an end.

Struggling with every word she spoke in laboured breaths she went on. 'How are your sisters?'

My heart sank to see her this way but I smiled a weak smile as I answered her. 'They are well and send their love.'

Wearily closing her eyes my mother nodded as if this news was all she needed to send her happily to the grave.

Trying to raise her head she dismissed the tending lady who was seated on a stool beside her bedside.

Once the lady had left us she beckoned me near to her mouth, as her voice was now barely a whisper. 'Dickon was telling the truth, your brother's were alive at the time of Bosworth...I received a letter from your brother Edward only two days before the battle. I was afraid of what Henry would do if I let it be known publicly...it was the last time I ever heard from either of my dear little boys.' Still battling to speak she went on, 'Henry and his mother lied to me...when I found out I was locked away.'

I wanted to question my mother about her revelation but I could see that the lady was in no fit state to carry on. Kissing my mother gently on the cheek, I left her to dream away her last earthly moments.

On the eighth day of June she passed into God's hands and four days later she was given a simple burial paid for by her only remaining son Thomas.

I did not attend as Henry and his mother had express that I should not.

My sisters and my half brother Thomas dressed entirely in black and weeping openly attended the mass and the internment of our mother next to our father in St George's Chapel, Windsor.

******

Dick let out a long sigh and fixed his gaze unto the heavens. Lowering his head his eyes set firmly on Sir Thomas. His voice was lowered as he continued. 'The next episode of my story, if anyone outside this room was to overhear would mean my immediate arrest for treason. Do you absolutely swear on the Holy Bible that my disclosures will be safe with you?'

Sir Thomas was in too deep and had a curiosity that had to be satisfied and so nodded his head.

'Henry was not as lenient as he had been with Simnel when three years later another young man was claiming to be one of the Plantagenct Princes.

Although most of the family and friends of Richard were now dead there were still those who knew that the Tudor had no right at all to the English throne. These lords and nobles had fled to Melees, to the court of Richard's sister. Here they were to plot the downfall of the Tudor usurper.

In the winter of 1490, a young man, who's named turned out to be Perkin Warbeck, was claiming to be my mother's younger brother, Richard of York. He had been taken to Margaret by a courtier who had known Richard well and was sure that this man Warbeck was indeed the lost Prince.

Perkin had recounted to Margaret that he could remember when he was eight or nine years old being taken to Tournai by a group of men and placed in the care of a leading merchant and taking the name Warbeck.

When he was seventeen Perkin worked as a merchant and in the course of his job he had come into contact with Sir Edward Brampton.

Brampton was one of Richard's allies and was convinced by the young man's story and without delay took him to The Duchess Margaret.

Margaret now had no doubt that one of her lost nephews had been found. His resemblance to her brother Edward was uncanny and he retold stories of his youth only her family would have known.

Since the death of her husband Margaret had become very powerful and she found a new determination to help Perkin capture the English throne.'

Sir Thomas looked about him to make double sure that they were indeed alone for he knew that anyone even mentioning the name Warbeck could be arrested for treason. What Dick was about to say could rock the the Tudor dynasty to its foundations?

Dick sipped his wine and closed his eyes. 'No one would ever believe how evil Henry was. He spent his whole life denigrating Richard when it was he who was the monster of history.

What I am about to tell you will answer many unanswered questions about the wicked nature of his son, and why he feels so uneasy as king and at all costs wanted a male heir to succeed him.'

Taking a deep breath and letting out a long slow sigh, Dick continued. Sir Thomas sat in silence mesmerised by the story that was emanating from this old man.

Dick's memory was detailed as he spoke. 'Perkin raised an army with the monies given to him by Margaret. She was convinced that he was young Richard come back to claim the English crown, which was, many thought, rightfully his. These included the Irish who had already crowned him King of England in Dublin Cathedral. The Scottish King James VI had given him a cousin, the lovely Katherine Gordon, to marry.

Perkin landed at Land's End in Cornwall with a small band of men in 1497. At first he took heart from the warmth of the reception he received. Henry had been taxing the people beyond the point of endurance and many flocked to his banner. But men are fickle and he did not regain his lands as his support fizzled out and his little army of supporters were unable to make a stand against the king's troops. Henry's new laws had disempowered the new nobility. The king now had more and more control over the armies and the land.

By this time Henry was an absolute monarch and had made a special crown for himself known as, The Crown Imperial. This fabulous multi jewelled crown sent a message to all that saw it... Henry was the supreme monarch.

A lonely and disillusioned Perkin was captured by Henry and imprisoned in The Tower in the next cell to my mother's infantile cousin Edward of Warwick, who had been held there since 1485.'

Dick stopped and looked at Sir Thomas with watery eyes. 'For almost twelve years my mother had endured living with Henry, and although her time spent with a man she despised had been one of total misery what happened next, totally broke my mother's will to live.'

******

My eyes were pleading as I sat in the solar with my husband. 'Why can I not see this man Perkin?'

Any reference to Warbeck made Henry uneasy. Henry lowered his head and I instinctively knew that he was hiding something from me. 'It is not a good idea for you to be seen with him. It can only give credence to his claims.'

'But I will know for sure if the man is indeed my brother.' I paused to gage Henry's reaction. He was tentative to my words and I continued with venom in my tone. 'I will never speak to you again if you deny me this one request.'

Pausing again, I stepped closer to Henry. His countenance was even more sly and weasely than usual. I took courage as I spoke, 'I have these last twelve years done your will without question or complaint and now you refuse me this one wish that I am asking you...I must see for myself if this man is or is not my brother.'

Looking deeply into my eyes Henry roughly took hold of both my hands and forcibly led me to the nearby chair. Dismissing all who were in waiting, Henry poured me and himself some wine. Henry's tone was deliberate and cold. 'I know that the man inside The Tower is an impostor and not your brother.'

I interrupted, 'how...how can you be so certain?'

Henry turned from me, 'your brother is dead!'

My tone was defiant, 'that's not true...Dickon swore to me that both my brothers were safe at the time of Bosworth and I believed him. I will never believe what you and your cronies, the likes of Bishop Morton, say about Dickon. You know what you say is untrue. It is you who is the ugly hunch back!'

Henry was reeled by this outburst and was fast losing his temper with me. His faced darkened with rage and his voice became raised. 'I know that both your brother's are dead because...' he stopped abruptly... and then turned from me sharply.

Then it hit me like a bolt of lightening. I was stopped in my tracks by thoughts that were now moment by moment becoming clear to me. He knew that they were dead because... he had killed them!

It then began to dawn on me... a clear picture of Henry began to develop in my mind... it was the only way that Henry could become king and have me as his legitimate queen... for, as my mother inferred, the Princes were alive two days before Bosworth... kept away from view at a remote castle in Wales... they were the rightful heirs.

I thought on. Was that what Henry was doing in the five months from Bosworth to their marriage trying to remove the stain of illegitimacy from his future bride's name but feared to take a step which would clear the two Princes of the same stigma?

If they were still alive... the two boys would then become a greater danger to him than they could ever have been to Dickon, for he had already cleared the hurdle of winning the consent of the people who mattered for his accent to the throne.

Henry could have acknowledged that they were alive and claimed that they were illegitimate... but that would have meant that I too was illegitimate and unable to become his queen and the struggle between York and Lancaster would once more take hold. I had fathomed it all; he need not say another word.

Henry's back was turned from me, in an admission of guilt, as he now realised that I knew all which he wished above all to keep form me.

I felt a compulsion like no other; to run from the man I now hated more than any other living creature.

Without his permission I fled from his presence. For two days I continued to mull it over and over again in my mind. That is why Stillingworth and others had been arrested; they had known the truth behind Dickon's actions.

Henry wanted to destroy all evidence of any pre nuptials. He had every copy of the Titulus Regaina, the act that declared my brothers and I illegitimate destroyed. If Dickon had ordered the murder why had Henry not brought the culprits to trial?

Most of England was pointing the finger at Sir James Tyrell and several others who were thought to have been acting on Dickon's orders, I now knew that they were Henry's men and that was the reason that Tyrell and several of the said accomplices had not been brought to justice. Strangely they had received land and other rewards.

I took a deep breath and concluded that my husband had somehow done away with my brothers a few weeks after he had become king and from that day on he had been putting the blame onto Dickon.

It may also have answered another burning question that was concerning me...my mother. This once influential figure was greatly distress when Henry ordered her to withdraw into the Abbey of Bermondsey. She did not want to retire from public life, but Henry was adamant.

Although there were handsome apartments at Bermondsey, the rules laid down for her amounted almost to imprisonment. She spent the remaining years of her life unable to talk to anyone of importance and I had not been allowed to see her for over five years before she died.

Had my mother threatened to reveal what she knew about her sons? That she had proof that they were safe when Dickon was king? I could only guess.

Soon after Henry's physical admission to me of his guilt he had Perkin Warbeck and my cousin Edward executed. Warbeck, on the charge of treason, Edward on the charge of trying to escape with Warbeck and raise an army against the King.

I could not believe this as my cousin had the mindset of a seven year old boy and could never think of such a complex thing. I guessed that Henry had put the two in the same cell, no doubt to implicate my poor, innocent cousin with Warbeck. I put my cousin's death down to the same reason as most of Henry's other victims...they had more right to the throne of England than he did.

******

Dick looked at Sir Thomas who was visibly shaken by what he had heard before continuing. 'Henry never admitted his deeds to anyone except the tiny number that were his inner circle and who were probably deeply involved in the actions. Henry was secretive by nature and there were many things he kept to himself.

My mother had long ago resigned herself to her fate and her time with Henry Tudor was one of total misery. She knew that she was confined to a kind of prison that was to last her whole life. Throughout their marriage there was coldness between them that could be felt by any one in their presence.

Henry's dominating mother accompanied her almost wherever she went; indeed the two were rarely separated, for Margaret had a deep distrust of her daughter in law.'

Dick shrugged his shoulders as he empathised with the predicament his mother must have been in.

'She could not betray Henry now as she had children that she adored, for they would ultimately be involved with any further struggles for the throne. She had a son who was to become the next King of England, two beautiful daughters and an infant son who she was very close to and was actively involved in teaching him to read and write.

Although, after a time, Henry began to treat her with kindness and with some fondness she never returned his affection.'

Dick sighed. 'At only thirty seven she was tired and weary, completely worn out. Life had been so cruel to a woman whose life began with such promise and joy.'

Her grief was impounded when in 1502 she lost her eldest, beloved son Arthur, to the wasting sickness.

Henry wanted another boy to strengthen the Tudor line as only little Henry now remained.'

Dick looked at his lordship with wonton eyes. 'The following year, Bessy did not survive the birth of a baby girl named Catherine who also died a few days after her mother.'

There was a pause and Sir Thomas knew that Dick's thoughts were bringing him close to tears. Thomas stayed silent and Dick continued his lament after struggling to regain his composure.

'Queen Elizabeth was laid to rest at the newly built Lady Chapel at Westminster Abbey. The whole country mourned her passing, there was an unprecedented outpouring of public grief as the people said goodbye to the lady they had now taken to their hearts.'

Dick gave an ironic look towards his lordship. 'I can remember vividly my adoptive father taking me to the funeral of Queen Bessy. Taking our places along the procession route we waited with our candle flickering with the thousands of others who had also lined the streets to pay their respects to their beloved queen.

She had reigned without complaint with passion and dignity. Always a voice for the common man, the people had named her, The Queen of Hearts.

The funeral cortège came into sight. Bessy's sisters, Cecily, Anne, Catherine and Bridget could be seen openly weeping as they followed a stern faced Henry.

The carriage passed me, pulled by six magnificent black horses. I did not know it then that the woman inside the regally draped coffin was my mother.'

Dick paused and wrung his hands and sighed. 'I only found out my true identity six months after her funeral when my adopted father called me to his bedside on the night he was dying. I was almost eighteen years old and the only father I knew lay close to death. Of course I thought he was delirious as his story of my being was incredible.

But then he gave me something; a gold ruby ring, inside the wide gold band bore an inscription...To Bessy...My Love...Dickon. On reading it I knew that what he was telling me was not a figment of his imagination as a jewel of that magnificence he would never have been able to afford, and with the inscription there was no doubt that his story was indeed true.

With laboured breaths he told me that it was my mother's and he had been instructed at the time of his death to give it to me together with this story of my birth. I had to swear to him that I would keep it a secret. The few people who did know my true identity and whereabouts were extremely loyal to the memory of King Richard and kept the secret of my existence to their grave. This I was eternally grateful as in later life I went constantly in fear of the rope or the axe.'

Old Dick swallowed hard and continued with a voice not much louder that a whisper. 'With the death of my adoptive father I said goodbye to my ageing adoptive mother and began to wonder the countryside.

I could read and write in both English and Latin and from books I taught myself a trade and I have been able to get honest employ ever since.'

There was a reflective silence as Dick came to the end of his rendition.

'Well Sir that is the end of my story. I thank you for listening so patiently.'

His Lordship had sat for hours in wonderment at this fascinating story. Thomas rose to his feet and stretched his arms above his head and blinked his eyes. The session with Dick had been a long and arduous one and Sir Thomas called for his servants to accompany the old man back to the workman's quarters.

Thomas gave a final word as old Dick slowly got to his feet to leave. 'Well, I am indebted to you, Dick for enlightening me of your story this day.'

For weeks afterwards Sir Thomas pondered what he had been told. Could he believe what the old man had told him? The times, Thomas reflected, had been devastating for any surviving Plantagenets.

Henry Tudor did immediately go about turning King Richard into a hunch backed monster, accusing him of every heinous crime possible. He did have Perkin Warbeck executed together with Queen Elizabeth's cousin, the infantile Edward.

Sir Thomas, however, thought it wise to keep what the old man had told him in strict confidence and never to repeat it to another living soul.

As far as he knew Dick had no children and was therefore the last of the Plantagenet line.

He decided to retire his most distinguished worker and gave him a small cottage within the manor grounds to live in and instructed his steward to provide food for him every day. Dick was thus able to spend his final years reading and walking about the lanes of Eastwell, no doubt remembering the turbulent times that had changed his life.

After five years of living peacefully in his little house the old man died, just three day before Christmas 1550.

Sir Thomas held a special service for him in the little church of St Mary's at Eastwell and had him laid to in rest in a small tomb in its churchyard bearing his name, Richard Plantagenet.

Printed in Poland
by Amazon Fulfillment
Poland Sp. z o.o., Wrocław